QUILT BY ASSOCIATION

A Harriet Truman/Loose Threads Mystery

D0012444

ARLENE SACHITANO

ZUMAYA ENIGMA

AUSTIN TX

2011

QUILT BY ASSOCIATION
© 2011 by Arlene Sachitano
ISBN 978-1-936144-18-1
Cover art and design © April Martinez

"Zumaya Enigma" and the raven logo are trademarks of Zumaya Publications LLC, Austin TX. Look for us online at
http://www.zumayapublications.com/enigma.php

Library of Congress Cataloging-in-Publication Data

Sachitano, Arlene, 1951-
 Quilt by association : a Harriet Truman/loose threads mystery / Arlene Sachitano.
    p. cm.
 ISBN 978-1-936144-18-1 (trade pbk. : alk. paper) -- ISBN 978-1-936144-19-8 (electronic)
 1.   Widows--Fiction. 2.   Quiltmakers--Fiction. 3.   Quilting--Fiction. 4. Murder--Investigation--Fiction. I. Title.
 PS3619.A277Q854 2010
 813'.6--dc22
                                            2010051185

Shopping could wait for anothe_ _ _ _, _ _ _ _, _ _
needed to get on with checking up on Carla and her
preparations.

A red-and-white taxi was pulling out of the long
driveway to Aiden's house, and she had to wait as it
made the turn onto the street. It was empty except
for the driver, and Harriet assumed he or she had
taken a wrong turn on his way to pick up a passenger.

It soon became clear, however, the taxi was not
there by mistake. As she eased her car up the drive
and into the parking area, she saw that the cab had
left two passengers, one of whom now appeared to
be in a rather heated discussion—if her gestures
were any indication—with Carla.

"Neelie," she called as she got out of her car,
interrupting the two women. "What are you doing
here?"

"You know what I'm here for."

"I told you Aiden is not in town."

"That's what I've been trying to tell her," Carla
said, "but she won't listen."

She was wearing a rose-pink long-sleeved T-shirt
with stonewashed denim capri pants. Her long dark
hair hung in loose curls around her shoulders and
no longer had the stringy, greasy look it had when
Harriet first met her. The young woman had come
a long way in the last seven months.

"You're the one who won't listen." Neelie was
wearing skinny black pants and a lime-green
sweater that had a designer look to them. Probably
not Paris, Harriet guessed, but definitely not Walmart. "I get that he's out of town," she shouted.
"What you don't seem to grasp is I've got this baby."
She jounced the child on her hip for emphasis. "And
she needs her father."

ALSO BY ARLENE SACHITANO

The Harriet Truman/Loose Threads Mysteries

Quilt As Desired
Quilter's Knot
Quilt As You Go

The Harley Spring Mysteries

Chip and Die
The Widowmaker

Chapter 1

I t looks hideous," Harriet Truman stated. She pushed her chair back from the table and stood up. "Anyone else need a refill?" She held up her empty mug and looked at each of her fellow Loose Threads in turn. Several raised their cups, and Harriet took them, cradling her own in her elbow.

"I'll help," Robin McLeod said. She picked up the mugs of the two women on either side of her and joined Harriet in the small kitchen of Pins and Needles, Foggy Point, Washington's, best and only quilt store.

Harriet filled the large electric kettle and turned it on. Robin did the same with the coffeemaker then proceeded to execute a painful-looking yoga maneuver. She inhaled deeply then slowly let her breath out.

"I don't think more tea is going to help," Harriet said as she dropped fresh tea bags into the mugs. "But staring at those blocks isn't getting us anywhere."

When the drinks were ready, they returned to the women seated around a large table in the bigger of the two classrooms at the back of Pins and Needles. Having distributed the hot beverages, they returned to their own seats.

The Loose Threads quilt group had turned the interior wall of the classroom into a makeshift design wall by tacking a large flannel-lined plastic tablecloth, flannel side out, onto it. Assorted quilt blocks were arranged on the flannel, and they studied the resulting pattern as they sipped their tea.

"I'll say it if no one else will," Connie Escorcia said. She stood to emphasize her point, an effect lost thanks to her less than five feet of height. "This is a disaster. Our quilt blocks all look great by themselves, but together?" She broke into rapid-fire Spanish that even Harriet, who was fluent in seven languages, couldn't follow.

"There has to be some way to make them work," Harriet's aunt Beth insisted.

"Don't waste your time," Lauren Sawyer said as she entered from the hallway. She went to an empty place at the table and set her canvas quilting bag and stainless steel travel mug down before pulling out the chair and sitting.

"Would you like to explain?" Aunt Beth asked.

"The rival gang is meeting at the senior living center right now, and they have this same quilt on their wall, only theirs looks good," Lauren reported. "Sarah asked me to help—by that, I mean she sat at her desk and I did the work—install a software upgrade on the center computers. When I walked by the cafeteria, I noticed they had a design wall up, so I made an excuse to go in, and the Small Stitches were there working on their raffle quilt. I'm telling you, theirs looks good."

Connie collapsed into her chair. "Dios mio."

"I thought they were doing a Maggie Walker appliqué pattern," said Jenny Logan, one of the group's more mature members.

"I'm telling you, they've changed their plan," Lauren insisted. "They have twelve appliquéd blocks, each one with the face of a dog—our Rottweiler." She pointed to one of the blocks on the wall. "Only they all used the same six shades of brown and black, and they used the same background for all the blocks."

"Using the same background would have helped us," Jenny mused.

"Help me understand the rules again," Harriet said. "I thought this was a benefit, not a competition."

"It *is* a benefit—for the Foggy Point Animal Shelter," Mavis Willis replied. At seventy, she was currently the group's most senior quilter. "In the old days, the Clallum County Quilt Guild was the only quilt group in town. They provided one raffle quilt plus a stack of functional doggie quilts every year at the shelter fundraiser.

"As the Guild grew, smaller groups formed, and each year one of those groups had the task of making the raffle quilt. The shelter's needs also grew, and somewhere along the line, all the groups started making quilts for the event. One is chosen to be the raffle quilt, and the rest are sold in a silent auction. Any unsold quilts are donated to the shelter for functional use."

"So, our quilt could end up in a dog cage if it's too ugly," Harriet said.

"We would never turn in anything that was in danger of that happening," Jenny protested.

"Having your quilt chosen for the raffle is a matter of group pride," Aunt Beth explained.

"One this group takes very seriously," Connie added. "We've won every year but one since I've been retired. How long has that been?" she asked Mavis.

"Long enough," Mavis replied.

"Nothing in the rules says we can't submit more than one quilt," Robin said. An attorney by trade, she always knew the rules. "Let's set these blocks aside and see if we can come up with an idea for them later. I say we pack it in for today and meet again tomorrow to brainstorm ideas for a new quilt."

"I'll go reserve the room," Jenny said and got up from the table.

Harriet leaned back in her chair.

"I'd like to know how they ended up with our same design."

"Well, duh," Lauren said. "Don't you think dog faces are an obvious choice for an animal shelter raffle?"

"I guess." Harriet gathered her scissors, thread and pincushion and put them back in her tote bag. "I've got a quilt on the long-arm machine I have to finish. I'll see you all tomorrow."

Chapter 2

I don't suppose *you* have any ideas," Harriet asked her fluffy gray cat Fred the next morning. Fred wove in and out of her ankles then meowed. "I know—you'd make it a cat quilt."

"Who are you talking to?" Aunt Beth asked as she came into Harriet's sunny yellow kitchen. "I see you've got that purple quilt off the machine."

Beth had let herself in through the studio she'd added when she became a long-arm quilter, having owned the house for more than thirty years before giving both it and the shop to her niece earlier in the year.

"How late did you have to stay up to finish it?"

"Not all that late. Aiden canceled dinner, so I grabbed a quick snack and kept working until it was finished."

"Trouble in paradise?"

"He's leaving for Ephrata." Harriet looked at her watch. "In about two hours."

"What's he doing in eastern Washington?"

"He's not supposed to be talking about it, so you have to promise not to tell everyone," Harriet cautioned. She knew her aunt could keep a secret when she had to, so she continued. "A really bad pet hoarder situation was raided a week and a half ago. So far, they've kept it from the press, but Aiden says it's horrendous.

"It's by far the biggest animal abuse case in the history of Washington State and maybe even in the country—just awful. And it's hard on the vets who have to work on the animals, both physically and emotionally, so they rotate them in and out from animal clinics all over the state."

"I suppose Aiden has to go because he's still the newest vet in the clinic," Aunt Beth guessed.

"Actually, it's because of the research he was doing in Uganda. He also worked at a free clinic in his village, and I think he saw more extreme problems than the average vet stateside."

Harriet got Fred's prescription cat food from the refrigerator and scooped a gob into his fish-shaped ceramic dish.

"How long will he be gone?"

"He said their schedule is a work in progress. The first vets on the scene worked thirty-six hours straight and then collapsed. They're hoping he can stay a week. He thinks he'll be able to do more, but that could be his youth speaking."

"Are you ever going to let go of the fact that he's ten years younger than you?" Aunt Beth scolded. "Age isn't all about the calendar, you know."

"I'm not talking about our age difference. I'm just making a general observation about the self-perceived invincibility of youth."

"Good, because frankly, we're all getting a little tired of your constant harping about it."

"I don't harp."

Aunt Beth rolled her eyes. "You ready to head out?"

"Let me get my bag and sweater," Harriet said.

Beth followed her into the studio then out to the driveway, where they got into Beth's silver Beetle and made the short drive to Pins and Needles.

"Hi, Carla," Harriet said as she came into the quilt store. Carla Salter was the youngest member of the Loose Threads and worked part-time at Pins and Needles. She no longer needed the extra income since Aiden Jalbert had hired her as his fulltime housekeeper, but clerking at the store allowed her to get out. Her toddler Wendy enjoyed going to the drop-in day care at the Methodist church, too, so it worked well for all concerned.

"Did you guys make any progress on the dog quilt yesterday?" Carla asked. She had missed the meeting because of Wendy's well baby checkup.

"Our quilt blocks didn't go very well together, and then Lauren arrived, and she had just seen the quilt the Small Stitches were working on, and it was our idea, only better. They used coordinated fabrics instead of going scrappy, like we did. I guess they did similar dog faces, too."

"That's sort of weird," Carla said as she folded the half-yard piece of fabric she'd just cut.

"That's what I said, but Lauren pointed out there are only a few specifically dog-related images, and dog faces are probably on everybody's short list."

"I guess."

"That's why we're meeting again today. We're shelving our dog-face blocks and trying to come up with another plan. Will you be able to help us?"

"Yeah, Marjory said I could take a break for the meeting, but I'm just making half-yard cuts of the new Jo Morton fabric that came in. If no one cares, I thought I could move my cutting mat into the meeting room and keep working while we talk."

"I'm sure the Threads will applaud your industriousness," Harriet said, causing Carla's cheeks to turn a becoming shade of pink.

"Is anyone else here yet?" Jenny asked as she came through the door. She was dressed in chestnut-colored corduroy pants and an olive-green sweater, one of the first in the group to concede that summer was truly over and pull out her fall wardrobe.

"Aunt Beth is in back there somewhere," Harriet said and gestured toward the classrooms. "This is as far as I've gotten, so I don't know who else is."

"Mavis and Connie got here just before you," Carla volunteered.

"Am I late?" Sarah asked as she breezed in, late as usual.

"See you inside," Jenny said and headed for the back.

6

"The meeting hasn't started, if that's what you're asking," Harriet told Sarah.

"I hope they plan on starting soon. I have to be back to work in…" She glanced at her watch. "…fifty-two minutes."

"You better get in there, then, and get everyone organized," Harriet said.

Sarah hurried to the back of the store, brushing Harriet as she passed.

"You're bad," Carla said when she was out of earshot.

"Mavis and Connie can handle Sarah," Harriet told her.

"I thought Mavis said Sarah's parents owned the senior center where she works."

"They do. If you're thinking she can't be fired, you'd be thinking right. In fact, I'd be willing to bet money the other people working at the center are hoping our meeting runs long."

Carla smiled and gathered her rotary cutter and three bolts of fabric and headed to the meeting. Harriet followed, and was settling in her customary place at the table when Robin McLeod and DeAnn Gault entered the room.

"Anyone want coffee or tea?" Robin asked after she set her bag on the table.

"I'll take some tea," Harriet said, and after a few minutes Robin delivered a steaming mug then took her seat at the table.

"Well, ladies," Mavis began. "Did anyone have any brilliant ideas overnight?"

The Loose Threads spent the next hour brainstorming. They didn't allow any criticism of the list until it had ten designs on it. This didn't mean Lauren and Sarah didn't comment on every choice; it only meant everyone tuned them out more than usual.

"Okay," Robin said and laid her pen down. "We should be able to come up with something out of all this." As the member who always had a tablet and pen in her purse, she invariably ended up facilitating any planning functions the Loose Threads did. "Shall we discuss them one by one?"

"Why don't we see if anyone has an outright objection to anything on the list?" DeAnn suggested and looked around the table to see if anyone agreed with her.

A soft rap on the doorjamb interrupted the discussion before it got started.

"Marjory told me it would be okay to come back and talk to you," said a slender, sandy-haired man—Joseph Marston, a social worker for a local adoption agency.

"Hello, Joseph," Mavis said. "Come on in."

He did but remained standing. A large pink-and-green pastel-colored quilt was folded over his right arm.

"Here, set that down," Aunt Beth said, and took the quilt from him. Connie got up and helped her lay it on the end of the table.

"What have you got there, Joseph?" Mavis asked.

Marston cleared his throat.

"Someone donated four quilts to the agency, and I'm not sure what to do with them," he said. "They're really big, so I brought one to show you."

The agency Joseph referred to was Little Lamb Adoption Services. Harriet wouldn't have known about the place except that DeAnn was in the process of adopting a baby girl, and Marston was the social worker overseeing the process. Most of their Loose Threads meetings lately had begun with DeAnn describing the various interviews and inspections she and her family were going through. Joe was a gentle, soft-spoken man, an attribute that helped his clients keep their sanity as they negotiated a stressful undertaking.

"Let's see what we've got here," Aunt Beth said.

She unfolded the quilt, and the Loose Threads cleared their bags and cups off the table and helped spread it out. The quilt had been done in an overall pattern of large pinwheels separated by equal-sized blocks of plain fabric. Harriet estimated the blocks were ten-inch squares.

"We don't really have a use for bed quilts," Joseph offered. "Baby quilts would have been more useful."

No one said anything for a minute while they examined the quilt, turning edges over and rubbing the fabric between their fingers.

"This one's in great shape," Connie said. "Grab the other end, mi'ja," she told Harriet. "Let's fold it into quarters."

Harriet did as requested, and they re-centered the folded blanket on the table.

"Are you thinking we should cut it into quarters and rebind them?" Aunt Beth asked.

"Good idea," Jenny said. "We can remove the old binding completely so we don't have to try to match the fabric."

"We could add a four-inch border to each piece, too," Robin suggested. "That way, we'd have fresh fabric to apply the binding to. We could put batting in the border like you do with the quilt-as-you-go technique."

"I like that," Harriet said. "It would insure the quilts are crib-sized. I could stitch pinwheel designs in the borders with my machine. It looks like they did stitch-in-the-ditch for their quilting," she added, referring to the technique where quilt stitches are hidden by placing them very close to the seams in pieced quilt tops. She flipped the top layer of the folded quilt over, revealing the backing fabric.

Jenny ran her hand over the stitched fabric, tracing the patterns she found.

"Definitely stitch-in-the-ditch," she pronounced.

"How does that sound?" Beth asked Joe.

"If I understood all that, you're going to cut the quilt down into baby-sized blankets," he said. "That sounds great. When we have them, we like to send a quilt home with each child we place."

"When do you need these?" Jenny asked.

He looked embarrassed.

"Yesterday, I take it." Mavis guessed.

"Since we rely on donations, the inventory ebbs and flows," he said. "In fact, our shelves are bare at the moment. What money we have for such things is going toward pajamas and underwear—often the children are wearing rags when we pick them up, and we want them to look nice when they go to their new families."

"Say no more," Beth said. "We'll get these out right away, and then see what we can do to make sure your shelves don't go bare again."

"Thank you so much," Joseph said, and took her hands in his. "You don't know how much this will mean to our children. Shall I go get the other three quilts?"

Aunt Beth arranged for him to drop the quilts off at Pins and Needles on his way home from work that afternoon, and after he left, she went back to the Loose Threads meeting.

"I suppose you expect all of us to work on those quilts, too?" Sarah whined. "I barely have time to do all these dog blocks."

"All one of them?" Lauren shot back. "It must have killed you."

"Ladies," Connie said, standing again and giving a stern look to each woman in turn. "No one has to do anything they don't want to. If Sarah is too busy to do charity work, that's her business."

"Well, maybe I *could* sew the binding on one while I'm manning the front desk at work," Sarah conceded after a moment of silence. "But only if we're not busy."

Lauren rolled her eyes skyward but kept silent.

"We will appreciate anything you can do," Connie assured her.

"What did I miss?" Beth asked. "Did you choose a new design while I was getting Joseph squared away?"

"We waited for you," Harriet said. "So far, we have several options on the list, but that's all."

"It's hard to tell without seeing a sample," Jenny said. "We all thought the dog faces were a good idea until we saw them."

"Why don't we divide up the list and each of us make a one-block sample?" Robin suggested. "Two people could do each idea, not including DeAnn, who needs to finish getting ready for the baby."

She looked around the group and saw no objections. Even Sarah kept quiet for once.

"Shall we meet again tomorrow?" Beth asked. "If you can't get your blocks done, come anyway, and we'll see what we have."

"But try," Connie added, and looked over her black-rimmed reading glasses directly at Sarah.

"I didn't say anything," Sarah protested.

"Speaking of the new baby," Robin said. "DeAnn and I better get going. We've got some last-minute shopping to do. Put me down for any of the blocks and let me know later."

The two women got up, and Robin ushered DeAnn out ahead of her, then turned back when her friend was out the door and made the universal hand sign for *call me* while mouthing the words.

When the remaining Loose Threads heard the tinkle of the bells on the outer door, signaling that Robin had DeAnn out of the building, the discussion turned to the baby shower they were planning.

"Aiden said it was okay for us to have the shower at his house," Carla said.

Aiden's mother had been a member of the Loose Threads, and the older members of the group had attended many gatherings in the large formal dining room of her grand Victorian house. Aunt Beth had suggested his young housekeeper be the one to ask, knowing he would agree but giving Carla an out if she felt hosting the event was too much for her. She was pleased the younger woman hadn't used it.

"I ordered the cake," Mavis volunteered. "I asked Kathy to decorate it in pink and purple. I wanted it to be a little more girlish and not quite so much like it's for a newborn baby."

DeAnn's new daughter was a three-year-old toddler.

"I've got the paper plates and napkins," Harriet added.

"Sarah?" Aunt Beth asked.

"I haven't got the mints or Jordan almonds yet, but I'll have them by tomorrow afternoon, a full day ahead of the event."

"My husband put the last coat of paint on the little table and chairs," Jenny said. She'd found a gently used table and chair set at a garage sale and given her husband the task of stripping and repainting it for DeAnn.

Aunt Beth looked at Lauren.

"I already told you I've had the jogging stroller for weeks," she said, referring to the present the group had pooled their money to buy.

She used both hands to sweep her long blond hair back away from her face. The purchasing task had fallen to her, since she was

11

the best computer researcher in the group, and they wanted to be sure they were mindful of the latest safety ratings before they made their purchase.

"Okay," Aunt Beth said. "Now that we have the shower on track, we've got dog bones, dog houses, stars with dog centers, and snowball blocks."

The last one referred to a traditional hexagonal pattern made by stitching a triangle of contrasting-color fabric to all four corners of a square piece—in this case, a dog print fabric with contrasting corners.

"That doesn't come out even," Sarah pointed out.

"I have an idea I'd like to try out," Harriet said. "How about I try my idea, and if it works, I'll present it to the group?"

Aunt Beth looked around the table. "Everyone okay with that?"

No one objected, and the group quickly divided up the remaining work and said their goodbyes.

"If you don't mind, I'm going to look at fabric for a minute," Aunt Beth said. "I'd like to make a couple functional dog blankets for the shelter. I know we said any quilts that aren't purchased will be donated, but that hasn't happened in years, so they're going to need bedding."

"I noticed Marjory putting a fresh batch of fabric on the sale shelf when I went to the restroom a while ago," Harriet said. "Let's go see what we've got to work with."

✂ - —— - ✂ - —— - ✂

Aunt Beth had three bolts of cotton print fabric in various shades of blue laid out on a cutting table in the middle of the store, and Harriet was comparing first one and then the other of the two bolts she held in her arms to the grouping to see which one would work best as a backing. The first was a good match for color, but she wasn't sure how well the plaid print went with the quilt-top choices. The second fabric was white dots on a mottled beige background—a better pattern, but she wasn't sure about the color. Aunt Beth was back at the sale shelf trying to come up with a better option.

Harriet was still debating the choice when the front door of the quilt store opened, and a short, heavyset woman with white cotton-

12

candy hair came in. She walked with a sort of rolling limp that was partly because of her arthritic knee but mostly because she carried her substantial weight almost entirely in her hips.

"Harriet," Phyllis Johnson said when she reached the center of the store. "I'm glad I caught you. I have a quilt I need to have done. My niece is getting married next weekend, and I was hoping you might have space in your schedule to fit her quilt in."

Harriet had enough long-arm quilting business to keep her machine stitching for as many hours as she was willing to run it, but she purposely kept a block of time free each week for just this sort of "emergency." She did a quick mental rearrangement of her schedule.

"If you don't want anything too complicated, I could have it for you the day after tomorrow," she offered.

"That would be perfect," she said. "Am I correct in assuming you'll be at DeAnn's shower?"

"Yes, and I'd be happy to bring your quilt to you there."

"Thank you," Phyllis said. "I'm so excited for DeAnn. I know she loves her boys, but she's so happy she's finally going to have a little girl. This is the part of my job I love most. It's just a win-win when we can place a precious orphaned child with such a deserving set of parents."

Phyllis Johnson was the owner and president of Little Lamb Adoption Services. Harriet had learned from DeAnn that Phyllis had started her agency more than thirty years ago and had provided adoptions to the citizens of Foggy Point ever since. Her agency specialized in international placements.

"I know DeAnn and her husband and the boys are excited."

"My quilt is on the front cutting table—I was choosing the binding fabric, but I've decided on one. You can take it with you now, if that's convenient, or I could drop it by after work if that's better."

"Now is fine. Do you have a bag for it?"

Phyllis produced a pillowcase that matched the quilt top and put the top and backing inside then handed it to Harriet. "Do you have bulk batting available like your aunt did?"

"Yes, just tell me which one you want."

After a brief discussion of batting, Phyllis chose wool and then went to the front checkout area to pay for her binding fabric.

"Are you ready?" Harriet asked her aunt.

"I suppose." Beth had replaced the blues with greens but was still struggling with the backing.

"I don't think the dogs care what backing you use."

"I can walk back to your house if you're anxious to leave."

"I'm sorry, I didn't mean to rush you. Phyllis gave me a quilt she needs done right away. I told her I'd give it back to her at the shower."

"Have you used your emergency spot for the week?"

"No, but I was going to play with my idea for the auction quilt with that time."

"I'm about done here," Beth said with a sigh. "Neither one of these bolts is going to change color, so I'm just going to choose one and be done with it."

"I'll go look at fat quarters for my dog block idea," said Harriet, referring to the eighteen-by-twenty-two-inch quarter-yard cuts of fabric favored by quilters.

She was pawing through a basket of red-toned fat quarters set on an antique chair by the front door when a tall, slender black woman came in, a baby less than a year old perched on her left hip, its back to Harriet. The woman strode to the checkout counter, where Marjory was ringing up Aunt Beth's purchases.

"Do you know Aiden Jalbert?" she asked Marjory without waiting for her to finish with Aunt Beth. The woman's voice had a lilting accent Harriet couldn't place.

"Why do you ask?" Marjory countered.

"What business of yours is it if we do or we don't?" Aunt Beth asked.

"I need to find him, and I went to every veterinary office in town, and no one would say anything. Finally, a lady in the waiting room of the last one said to ask at the quilt store."

"We know him, but it's not going to do you much good." Beth said.

"Let me be the judge of that."

The baby started fussing, and the woman jiggled her hip and at the same time reached into her pocket and pulled out a lint-covered pacifier she shoved into the child's mouth.

"He's working out of town," Harriet said. "We don't know when he'll be back."

The woman's shoulders sagged briefly; then she squared them again.

"Can you recommend a good hotel nearby?"

Aunt Beth could have suggested The Fogg Victorian Hotel, which was located three streets over, or even The Harborside, which was, as the name implied, located at the waterfront. Instead, she gave her the name of two chain hotels out on the main highway. She sketched a simple map and wrote the names on a piece of paper provided by Marjory, and handed it to the young woman.

"If you see Aiden, tell him Neelie Obote is looking for him."

The woman turned to leave. The baby lifted her head from the woman's shoulder and smiled at Aunt Beth, her pale-blue eyes trained on the older woman.

The bells that hung on a ribbon from the front door tinkled then fell silent as Neelie and the baby left the store. No one moved.

"I think I'll go see how Carla is coming with that fabric," Marjory said when the silence had stretched to the breaking point. She handed Aunt Beth her purchase and headed for the classroom.

"Okay," Aunt Beth said. "I'll address the eight-hundred-pound gorilla that just left the room. That baby's eyes bear a passing resemblance to those of a certain veterinarian of our acquaintance."

"A *passing* resemblance?" Harriet said in a cold voice. "*Passing* resemblance?" she repeated. "Aiden has an extremely rare eye-color. It sure looked like that baby does, too."

"That doesn't mean anything," Aunt Beth said.

Harriet glared at her.

"Okay, it might mean something, but let's not jump to conclusions without hearing what he has to say about it."

"Are you ready to go?" Harriet asked.

"Let me go get my bag." Aunt Beth went to the classroom and came back a moment later with her canvas tote on her arm and her purple nylon purse slung over her shoulder.

15

Chapter 3

Do we have time to stop at the grocery store on the way back to your place?" Aunt Beth asked as she climbed into the driver's seat. "It'll save me having to backtrack."

"Sure, if you don't mind a stop at the coffee shop, too. I need some hot chocolate to settle my nerves before I start working on someone else's quilt."

"Sounds good to me. Have you tried that new place yet?"

"The Steaming Cup? No, but it's in the right direction."

Beth circled the block then headed west.

The new coffee shop was decorated in dark wood and rich jewel-toned overstuffed upholstery. One wall was covered with artwork done by local people in response to a contest challenging artists to create the best interpretation of the shop's name, using the jewel-tone color pallet. The winning piece, a mosaic of a coffee cup made from shattered coffee cups, was displayed in the front window, its creator the happy recipient of a one-year free-coffee certificate.

Harriet ordered a large cherry hot chocolate while Aunt Beth went for a smaller mocha. The shop's only other customer was a slender young man seated at a small table near the wall, his laptop plugged into the nearby socket.

"Is this okay?" Aunt Beth asked as she led Harriet to a grouping of armchairs.

"Perfect."

Harriet carefully set her cup on the table between two of the chairs. Her cell phone began buzzing and played the first few notes of the ringtone she had assigned to Aiden's calls. She dropped her purse in the chair and pulled the phone out, streaking her finger across the touchscreen to answer the call.

"Aiden," she said as she put the phone up to her ear.

"Hi. Sorry I couldn't call sooner. The cell reception is terrible out here."

"How are you?"

He replied, but she didn't hear what he said as her phone was ripped from her hand from behind. She whirled and found Neelie Obote holding the phone to her own ear, the baby on her opposite hip.

"This is Neelie Obote," she said and paused, listening. "When will you be back here?…I have to see you. It's important…No, it can't wait."

Harriet came around behind the chair arrangement and grabbed for her phone. She had it for a brief moment before Neelie pulled it from her hand then lost her grip and dropped it. The phone skittered across the tile floor before landing screen-side-up, a large crack across its face.

"I'm so sorry," Neelie said, and began bouncing the baby, who was now crying, in a futile attempt to calm the child.

"May I try?" Aunt Beth asked and held her hands out.

Neelie handed her the child, and Aunt Beth carried the baby to the art wall and began talking in a low voice. The baby quieted, listening to Beth's voice.

Harriet bent down and picked up the broken remains of her phone.

"I'm so sorry," Neelie repeated again. "I didn't mean to break it."

"So, you're not sorry you grabbed it?" Harriet said and glared at her.

"You don't understand—I have to talk to Aiden Jalbert."

17

"I get that. What I don't get is why you think that gives you the right to grab my phone and break it."

"I wasn't trying to break your phone, I just heard you say 'Aiden,' and—"

"And you couldn't just *ask* to speak to him?"

Neelie looked down. "I'm sorry," she said again in a quieter voice.

"Why don't you stop apologizing and tell us why you need to talk to Aiden so desperately you're willing to tackle my niece to do it?" Aunt Beth said. Harriet hadn't notice her return to the sitting area with the now-sleeping baby in her arms. Beth sat down and looked pointedly at the two chairs on either side of her.

Neelie came to the chairs and, after a moment's hesitation, sat down. Harriet took her own chair, picked up her hot chocolate and took a sip.

"Start talking," she said.

"I need to find him to give him his child," Neelie said.

"And we're supposed to take your word for it that this is his child?"

"You don't have to take anything. I don't know you, why should I care what you think? If you know Aiden Jalbert, then you know he will want to take care of his child."

"Why are you giving the child away?" Aunt Beth asked.

"I'm not giving her away," Neelie said. "I'm bringing her to her father."

"Why?" Aunt Beth repeated.

"It's not your business, but Kissa is not my baby. She is my sister Nabirye's child." Tears welled in Neelie's eyes. "My sister passed away two weeks ago yesterday, in the hospital in Jinja."

Harriet handed her a napkin, and the young woman dabbed at her eyes.

"Before she died, she asked me to bring Kissa to her father."

"Does Aiden know about Kissa?" Aunt Beth asked.

"I don't know. Maybe not. He left Uganda before Kissa was born."

"You didn't ask your sister?" Harriet asked.

Neelie looked at her and started crying again.

18

"She was in pain. It was difficult for her. She asked me to take the baby to Aiden, and I promised I would. That's all I know." She sagged back in her chair and wept quietly into her napkin.

Harriet looked at her aunt. Beth gave a slight shrug.

"Look," Harriet said. "If Aiden calls back..." *After I get a new phone, thank you very much.* "...you'll be the first to know. How will I get in touch with you?"

"I'm staying at the Hampton Inn on Highway One-oh-one."

Neelie took Kissa from Aunt Beth and, without another word, left the coffee shop.

The two women sat in silence for a few minutes.

"I pity that child if she ends up with that woman for a mother," Aunt Beth said.

"I didn't get that she wants any continued involvement. She talks about the baby like she's a package."

"If Aiden doesn't want her, she may have no choice."

"I think we both know Aiden better than that. If that's his baby, and it very well could be, he'll do the right thing."

"I wouldn't jump to any conclusions about the baby's parentage until we talk to him," Beth said. "Yes, she has blue eyes, but I took a good look at her while I was holding her. She doesn't really look like Aiden or any of the Jalberts. And her eyes have more blue color than his—they look lighter because of her dark skin. They are definitely blue, but I didn't see a speck of that icy-white color Aiden has."

"Why would the woman lie about something like that? And why would she come all the way from Africa if he isn't the baby's father? Aiden's been back for eight or nine months—the baby might not have even been born when he left."

"Don't you think he'd notice if his girlfriend was nine months pregnant?"

"You'd think, but he told me he traveled among three locations. Maybe he didn't see her when she was big."

"They were close enough to have a baby, but he didn't say goodbye before he left? And then he just moved on with you without a backward glance. Come on—does that sound like Aiden to you?"

"You're right. Ignoring my own insecurities, you're right. It doesn't sound like him."

Beth picked up her mocha and took a long drink.

"There's one way to find out," she said. "Call him."

Harriet held up her broken phone and laughed.

"I wish I could."

Beth started digging in her purse for her own phone. Harriet reached over and stilled her aunt's hand.

"This can wait," she said. "Aiden is dealing with a horrific situation with the dogs in Ephrata. He doesn't need this on top of everything else. Especially since he can't do anything about the situation until he gets back. Assuming there *is* something he needs to do besides telling Neelie Obote to take a flying leap."

"Let's hope that's the case."

Harriet leaned back in her chair and shut her eyes.

"At least we haven't talked about our dog blocks for…" She opened one eye and looked at a clock built into the side of a striped coffee mug on the art wall. "…one hour and twelve minutes."

Aunt Beth sipped her mocha again. "I know Lauren thinks the Small Stitches coincidentally came up with the same dog face design we did, but I'm not so sure. They might have thought of the idea of using a dog face, but how many different breeds are there? What are the odds they would accidentally choose those with the same colors we did?"

"Yeah, and Mavis told me they are some of the worst offenders when it comes to using a commercial pattern without giving the designer credit."

"She's right. I can't remember them ever doing an original design, now that I think about it."

"Jenny said she'd heard they were doing a Maggie Walker pattern—one of her golfing friends is a Small Stitch. Why would they change that once they were started?"

"They might be doing more than one, just like we are," Beth suggested. "But I agree, something is a little off about all this."

"I think we need to be careful who's around when we unveil our next batch of blocks. In fact, maybe we should meet at the studio next time."

"What if we suggest that if anyone has their blocks done, they bring them to DeAnn's shower, and we can preview them afterwards?"

"I'll call people when we get home."

"No, I'll call. You need to get busy on that quilt for Phyllis. Besides, you need to spend your spare time getting a new cell phone."

"I'd better get started, then."

Harriet stood and drained the remaining chocolate from her cup, picked up her aunt's mug and took both to the dirty dish station. Aunt Beth gathered their purses and her sweater and met her at the door.

Chapter 4

If Harriet had lived anywhere else, she probably wouldn't have bothered with a land line at home. However, the spotty cell phone reception in Foggy Point, combined with the existing phone number that had long been associated with Quilt As Desired, the long-arm quilting business, meant she'd kept the business phone and its antiquated answering machine. When she got home and listened to her messages, she was glad she hadn't gotten rid of either—Aiden had called.

"I've been trying to reach you since we got cut off," his mechanically distorted voice said from the speaker. "What happened? One minute I was talking to you, and the next I was connected to some strange woman who sounded pretty desperate to talk to whoever it was she thought she was talking to. Weird, huh?

"Well, I worked at the site all day, and now I'm headed to the clinic. We don't have good phone reception here—I had to drive out to the top of one of the bluffs to make this call. You can leave a message, and I'll get it and answer when I can."

He asked about his dog Randy, who was at home under Carla's care. Before he'd left, Harriet had promised she'd visit the strange little dog he'd brought home from Africa and had also promised she'd hug her and tell her daddy loved her at least every other day. He said goodbye and promised to call again soon.

Harriet played the message three more times, but Aiden still didn't magically explain about the baby or the woman.

The phone rang, and she grabbed it up, so quickly it slipped from her grasp, and she had to catch it in midair to avoid dropping it.

"Aiden?"

"Sorry," Mavis replied. "It's just me."

"I'm being silly. I was listening to a message on the machine from Aiden. He told me he was going back to work. What's up?"

Mavis explained she had taken one of Joseph's quilts, cut it into quarters and was in the process of sewing the new borders onto the first piece. She wanted Harriet to quilt this first one before she put borders on the other three pieces in case she needed to make any adjustments to the scheme. They agreed she would bring it over in the morning, and Harriet would put it on her machine as soon as she could work it in.

Chapter 5

M avis arrived at the studio promptly at eight the next morning, her quilt piece in a flowered cotton tote slung over her shoulder, a white paper bag with the Annie's Coffee Shop logo in her hand.

"Is that what I think it is?" Harriet asked as she stood aside so Mavis could enter.

"If you're thinking cinnamon twists, then yes, it is," Mavis said with a smile.

"You're an angel."

"No, I'm just an old gal who knows how to get her project moved to the top of the list, do you want to see what I've done while the tea water's heating?"

Harriet took the flowered bag, pulled out the quilt piece and laid it on her large cutting table. She ran her hand along the seam between the cut edge of the quilt and the new border Mavis had attached.

"This looks good," she said. "I think we should put some basting stitches between the two pieces to keep them butted against each other so they don't separate when my machine goes over them. If you have the time, you could do that while I work on Phyllis's quilt."

Harriet had put the kettle on the stove when she'd seen Mavis's car in the driveway. It whistled, and she led Mavis through the connecting door from the studio to the kitchen.

"Have you started your block for the dog quilt yet?" Mavis asked.

"No, I haven't had time. I worked on Phyllis's quilt last night."

"If you ask me, I think we gave up on the dog heads too soon."

"Some of them did look okay. I think part of the problem was we had too many styles. Jenny's appliqué block looked good."

"I know my paper-pieced version wasn't the best. I haven't done much paper piecing, so I probably shouldn't have tried it for this."

"I'll try my idea after I finish Phyllis's quilt and your border."

"Fortunately, we have a little time to fiddle with it yet. On a whole different subject, your aunt told me about the woman you met at the quilt store yesterday."

"Did she tell you about the coffee shop, too?"

"Yes, she did." Mavis pulled the cinnamon pastries out of the bag and set them on a plate while Harriet poured hot water over tea bags. "What do you make of it?" she asked when she was settled on her stool at the bar.

"I don't know what to think. I have a hard time believing Aiden would get a woman in Africa pregnant and then just turn his back on her and go on with his life back home." Harriet broke off a piece of cinnamon twist and popped it into her mouth.

"I think it's strange the baby's aunt would come all the way to Foggy Point, Washington, USA, without so much as a call to see if Aiden actually lived here." Mavis took a bite of her pastry. "Mumm, these are so good."

"Maybe she did call Aiden," Harriet suggested. "Although that's even harder to believe. If he knew he had a baby, and it was coming to live with him, he wouldn't be off in Ephrata."

"Something's going on here," Mavis said. "And I don't think it has anything to do with Aiden being a father. I'll tell you something else. I went to the store to pick up some cat food after dinner last night, and there was a young black woman with a baby in line, two people in front of me. She was arguing with the clerk about a coupon she was trying to use, and she definitely did *not* have a foreign accent, African or otherwise."

"That could just be a coincidence."

"Oh, honey. You know as well as I do Foggy Point doesn't get that many strangers on a week night, and two young black women

25

with babies of a similar age on the same day? It has to be the same person."

"I don't know what to say." Harriet took a sip of her tea. "You can bet we haven't seen the last of her."

They finished their breakfast in silence, each lost in her own thoughts for a few minutes.

"I better get on my way," Mavis said finally. "It's my day to make lunches for Meals-on-Wheels at the Methodist church."

"I've got a few more hours of stitching on Phyllis's quilt, and then I'll put your piece on the machine. I promised Aiden I'd look in on Randy, so I think I'll do that in between."

"Maybe I'll see you over there. I told Carla I'd come over when I finish at the church to help her get set up for tomorrow."

"Okay, maybe I'll see you later, then."

Chapter 6

The time went quickly, as it usually did when Harriet was guiding the big sewing machine head over a well-made quilt. Phyllis wasn't one of her more demanding customers; she usually had an idea for an image—flowers, swirls, gridlines—but she left the details up to Harriet.

She got up from her stool and stood with her feet together and her shoulders in the Mountain Pose, or at least she thought she was in the correct position. Robin, who taught yoga when she wasn't being a lawyer, was always encouraging the Loose Threads to adopt it as an antidote to long hours hunched over their sewing machines. Harriet met her halfway—she did the yoga stretches she could do from a standing position. Somehow, rolling around on the floor when she got up from her quilting machine held no appeal.

Robin continued to lobby for the additional moves, but for now, Harriet stood in Mountain Pose then went into Chest Expansion and, finally, the sideways-leaning motions of the Simple Triangle. With one last cleansing breath, she picked up her purse and went out the door.

It had rained while she'd worked on Phyllis's quilt. A large drop of water fell off a tree branch and slid down the back of her neck. She shivered and batted at it. Summer was definitely over. Soon, the hoodie she was wearing wouldn't be enough to ward off the cold, and she'd have to deal with getting a jacket that was more than just rain protection.

Shopping could wait for another day. Today, she needed to get on with checking up on Carla and her preparations.

A red-and-white taxi was pulling out of the long driveway to Aiden's house, and she had to wait as it made the turn onto the street. It was empty except for the driver, and Harriet assumed he or she had taken a wrong turn on his way to pick up a passenger.

It soon became clear, however, the taxi was not there by mistake. As she eased her car up the drive and into the parking area, she saw that the cab had left two passengers, one of whom now appeared to be in a rather heated discussion—if her gestures were any indication—with Carla.

"Neelie," she called as she got out of her car, interrupting the two women. "What are you doing here?"

"You know what I'm here for."

"I told you Aiden is not in town."

"That's what I've been trying to tell her," Carla said, "but she won't listen."

She was wearing a rose-pink long-sleeved T-shirt with stone-washed denim capri pants. Her long dark hair hung in loose curls around her shoulders and no longer had the stringy, greasy look it had when Harriet first met her. The young woman had come a long way in the last seven months.

"You're the one who won't listen." Neelie was wearing skinny black pants and a lime-green sweater that had a designer look to them. Probably not Paris, Harriet guessed, but definitely not Wal-mart. "I get that he's out of town," she shouted. "What you don't seem to grasp is I've got this baby." She jounced the child on her hip for emphasis. "And she needs her father."

"I'm not sure what you expect us to do until Aiden gets back and can sort this out," Harriet said in what she hoped was a reasonable tone.

"I'll tell you what I expect you to do," Neelie said. "I expect you to give us a place to stay. It cost me dearly to come from Africa with a baby. Of course, I did this gladly because of my precious sister, but I can't give what I don't have. I don't have money to keep Kissa in a hotel until Aiden returns."

The rain that had eased up while Harriet made her drive began to come down again in earnest.

"Let's go inside," she said and ran for the door.

Carla's eyes widened, and she looked like she was going to protest, but she kept whatever she'd been going to say to herself. She brushed past Harriet and went to the back door, holding it open for the others.

"I've got to go check on Wendy," she said, wiping the rain from her face. "She's napping."

Harriet ushered Neelie and Kissa into the kitchen; she didn't want to take her any farther into Aiden's house than she had to.

"Can I get you something to drink?" she asked. "Tea or coffee?"

"I'm fine," Neelie said. She sat down and rubbed her hand across her forehead.

"Are you okay?" Harriet asked. "I mean, besides the baby drama."

"I just need to talk to Aiden Jalbert." Neelie's chin dropped to her chest. Her hand shook as she grabbed the edge of the table for balance.

"Are you diabetic or something?" Harriet asked as she opened the refrigerator door and pulled a gallon jug of milk out so she could look behind it.

The summer before her late husband Steve died, his nephew Brad had stayed with them in Oakland for a few weeks while he attended a math seminar in Berkeley. Brad was a fragile diabetic, and after half a dozen episodes, Harriet had learned to recognize the signs of low blood sugar. She set the milk on the counter and picked up a carton of orange juice, opened the cupboard she knew held drinking glasses, selected a tumbler and filled it with the juice.

"Drink this," she said, and to her relief, Neelie drained the glass. Harriet refilled it. "How long has it been since the baby's had anything to eat?"

"A couple of hours, I think."

29

"Does she drink milk or formula?" Carla asked as she came back into the kitchen, a monitor receiver in her hand.

"Milk," Neelie said.

"Cow's milk?" Carla pressed.

"Of course. I bought two percent at the grocery store. It was all they had."

"Is that what your sister fed her?" Carla asked, the shock plain in her voice.

"Where we come from she was lucky to get that," Neelie said defensively.

"Let me fix her a bottle."

Carla held out her hand. Neelie stared at it.

"Don't you have an empty bottle in that bag?" Carla pointed at the tote slung over the other woman's shoulder.

Neelie set the baby on the floor and rooted around in the bag, finally producing a dirty bottle. Carla took it in two fingers and dropped it into the sink. She opened a cupboard and pulled out a clean bottle, nipple and ring, filled the bottle with milk then held it under hot tapwater and finally handed it to Neelie, who set it on the table and took another drink of her juice.

Kissa began to cry and reach for the bottle. Carla picked the child up and tilted her back in her left arm in one smooth move, plugging the bottle into her mouth at the same time. The baby drained it and promptly fell asleep.

Harriet was wondering who had stolen her shy friend Carla and replaced her with this mother lioness. Neelie sipped on the remains of her orange juice and didn't say anything when Carla took the sleeping baby out of the room. She returned a moment later without her.

"Wendy's portable crib is in the front parlor," she explained. "It's quiet, and that baby looks like she needs a little of that."

Neelie glared at her, but before either woman could say anything, the back doorbell buzzed. Harriet opened it and let Mavis in.

Mavis made a show of taking off her plastic rain bonnet and shaking the drops off in the sink.

"How is everyone doing this fine afternoon?" She took off her coat and hung it on the back of the chair opposite Neelie. Harriet could tell the older woman had sensed the tension in the room. "Carla, honey, could you make me a nice cup of tea?"

Carla turned from the group, banging the kettle onto the stove.

"You must be Neelie," Mavis said, and held her hand out to the young woman. "Welcome to Foggy Point."

Neelie took it and smiled.

"I guess you don't get too many Africans in your town," she said in her lilting English.

"That's a fact," Mavis said. "I'm so sorry you're here under such sad circumstances."

"Yes, it is a terrible thing that happened to my sister."

"It's hard to lose someone close to you. You *were* close?"

"When we were younger, we were like twins. After we grew up, I moved to the city, and my sister stayed in our village, so we didn't see each other as often as we wished."

"Well, that makes it more difficult, I'm sure," Mavis said.

"It has been very hard. And also the baby…"

"Beth told me you've brought your sister's baby to Aiden." Mavis looked her in the eye. "Why is that?"

Neelie sat back in her chair. "I should think that would be obvious. My sister Nabirye told me to bring the baby to her father, and she gave me his name and address."

"So, this was a plan you two had, just in case?" Harriet asked.

Mavis glared at her.

"My sister was very ill. When it became clear she could not live, she asked me to take baby Kissa to her father. There was no plan. It was her wish in death, so I had to do what she asked, though I spent all the money I had paying for the doctor to try to save my sister, an effort that failed."

"If you spent all your money on the doctor, how did you get here?" Harriet persisted, in spite of the murderous look Mavis was giving her.

"My sister's church gave me a ticket and a small amount of money, which unfortunately is now gone," Neelie snapped. "Things are very expensive in America."

"Let me call Pastor Hafer at our Methodist church and see if there are any emergency funds for this sort of thing. I'm sure he can help us sort this out."

"She can stay here," Carla said.

Mavis and Harriet both whirled to face the younger woman.

"That baby looks exhausted," Carla went on, "and they have all kinds of baby stuff in the nursery here for when Avanell's grandchildren came to visit. Besides, they're already here."

"I'm not sure that's a good idea," Harriet said.

"I can ask Aiden when he calls."

"No!"

Harriet knew her response was a little too loud. Carla's cheeks burned.

"What I mean is, I was hoping we could save all this..." She waved toward Neelie. "...until Aiden is back. He's dealing with a very stressful situation at work, and he can't do anything about this until he comes home anyway."

"They could stay with me at my place," Mavis offered.

"It's kind of you to offer," Harriet said, "but I think Carla's right. This place has a full nursery setup and lots of room."

Mavis raised her left eyebrow as she turned and looked at Harriet. Harriet gave her a slight nod.

"Well, honey, if you think it's the right thing to do..."

"I'll show you to your room," Carla told Neelie as she set Mavis's tea on the table. "You look like *you* could use some rest."

Neelie got to her feet. She wobbled a little, then followed Carla out of the kitchen.

"Okay, why are you so agreeable about this stranger staying with our Carla? And what's wrong with that girl?"

"We need more information, and what better way to get more information than by having Neelie and the baby where we can keep track of them. Besides, from Carla's behavior, I'm guessing she doesn't think Neelie is taking care of the baby properly."

"I was getting that feeling myself. Neelie looks like she's not doing a very good job of taking care of herself, let alone a baby."

"She *was* looking pretty shaky before you got here. I asked her if she's diabetic, and she didn't answer, but she did perk up after I gave her some orange juice, so she either was starving or she *is* diabetic."

"Something about her story just isn't ringing true," Mavis said. "And by the way, she *is* the one I saw arguing with the checker—minus the accent."

"I wish Aiden was here. He could clear this up in a minute."

"No sense dwelling on that. If he's not going to be home for a week or so, we'll just have to deal with it ourselves."

"Do you think Carla will be safe here with that woman under her roof?"

"It's a little late to be worrying about that now, isn't it? Besides, our meek little friend seems to turn into a tiger when a baby is involved."

"I wonder what Terry's up to these days," Harriet said, referring to Terry Jansen, Carla's new Navy-investigator boyfriend.

"I asked Carla at our last meeting, and after much blushing and stammering, she told me he is still very present. I wonder if maybe we should put a bug in his ear about the current situation."

"Too bad I lost my contacts when my phone got crunched. I had his number."

"Fortunately, when he was questioning us all about what happened last month, he gave me his number, too. Being the hip yet old-fashioned grandmother that I am..." Mavis smiled. "...I not only put it in my cell phone, I also wrote it in my address book at home, just in case I lost my phone or something."

"Well, aren't you the smart one."

"I'll call him about Carla's situation when I get home. Maybe you could give Lauren a jingle and see if she can she can find anything out about Carla's new house guest."

"Sure. I haven't had a good dressing down by Lauren in, oh, I don't know, three days, maybe."

Mavis smiled. "I'd say you're due, then."

Carla came back into the kitchen, ending the conversation. She was still holding the receiver to Wendy's monitor.

"Did I just make a big mistake?" she asked Mavis as she collapsed into a chair. Her cheeks turned pink.

"No, honey," Mavis said and patted her hand. "You were speaking from your heart."

"She's been starving that baby. Did you see how thin her little legs are?"

"It sounded like she's only had the baby for a few days," Mavis said. "And they did come from Africa."

"But she's not in Africa now, and she's still not feeding the baby right."

"Now, honey," Mavis soothed. "She isn't a mother herself. This is her sister's child. She might not know how to take proper care of a baby."

"Well, I *do* know how to take care of a baby, and as long as she's here, she's getting three squares."

"I'm sure she'll appreciate that," Harriet said. "As long as they're going to be here, try to find out what you can about them. Keep it friendly—don't make her suspicious, or we won't get anything—but keep your eyes and ears open."

"I can do that." Carla's cheeks turned a darker pink.

"Not to change the subject," Mavis said, doing exactly that, "how are the shower preparations coming along?"

Carla stood up. "Come see," she said, and led the way across the hall to the formal dining room.

Mavis and Harriet spent the next twenty minutes admiring the pink streamers and balloons Carla had hung from the chandelier, checking the placement of forks, knives, spoons and napkins as well as Carla's choice of china teacups and saucers. Harriet was proud of her young friend, and knew she'd had a daunting collection of china and silver to choose from at the Jalbert house. Aiden's mother had been an avid collector of both.

"This looks great," she said.

Carla looked down at her feet. "I got a book from the library to see how to set the table."

"You did a fine job," Mavis agreed.

Carla lifted the lid of the delicate floral china sugar bowl. "I got that special turbine sugar."

"Turbinado?" Harriet said.

"Yes, and I got white cubes in case people don't like the brown kind." She lifted the lid of a cut-crystal sugar bowl.

"Seems like you're all ready," Mavis said. "It's a good thing, too, since now you're going to be playing host to Neelie and Kissa."

"I don't mind," Carla said quietly. "I know how hard it is."

"Just don't let her take advantage of you," Harriet cautioned.

"Don't you worry," Mavis said and put her arm around Carla's thin shoulders. "It's a good thing you're doing for that baby, and I don't believe for a minute you can't handle Miss Neelie."

"I need to go stitch your quilt," Harriet told Mavis. "Carla, call me if you need anything, and I do mean *anything*. I'll see you both tomorrow."

She understood why Carla was reaching out to Neelie, but she didn't like leaving her vulnerable friend with a stranger who seemed to have only a passing acquaintance with the truth.

Then she prepared to endure the abuse she was sure to get from Lauren—it would be worth it if she could find out who Neelie Obote really was and why she'd come to Foggy Point.

Chapter 7

H arriet had planned to go straight home and back to her long-arm machine, but as she started to pull out of Aiden's drive-way, she found herself turning the opposite direction, toward Lauren's place.

According to Aunt Beth, Lauren had joined the Loose Threads quilting group three years earlier. She'd been a beginner when she moved to Foggy Point and, unfortunately, had been taught by a quilter who had a very vague understanding of copyright as it applied to patterns and designs. It had taken the Loose Threads two of those three years to undo that bad early training and convince her that, if she wanted to create her own patterns, she couldn't start with someone else's copyrighted photo or drawing—rendering an image in fabric didn't erase the image owner's rights. Lauren had been convinced and was now attending classes in design and stitching at a folk art school in Angel Harbor.

In spite of her acerbic personality, and her tendency to blame Harriet for her quilting misfortunes, Lauren had high-level computer skills and, Harriet had to grudgingly admit, was good at crisis problem-solving.

Lauren lived in a large apartment over a wooden boat sale-and-repair business near the dock in Smuggler's Cove; she'd moved there the previous month. Harriet parked on the street and walked around the boat showroom to a flight of exterior stairs that led to an upstairs porch and Lauren's door. She savored the fish-tinged smell of the sea for a moment before reaching toward the wooden door.

It opened before she knocked.

"So, what do you want me to look up now?" Lauren asked without preamble. "Don't pretend this is a social call. You never come calling unless you want something. Let's have it."

"Are you busy?" Harriet asked while she tried to think up a reason for her visit other than the real one, which was, in fact, to ask her to look something up on her computer.

"I'm always busy. What do you want?"

"After the last Loose Threads meeting, Aunt Beth and I stayed to look at fabric for functional dog quilts."

"Can we move on to the part where I have to research something?" Lauren circled her hand to encourage Harriet to move along.

"I'm trying to tell you if you'd stop interrupting."

Lauren performed her standard eye-roll but kept her mouth shut.

"As I was saying, Aunt Beth and I were at the quilt store after everyone else left, and a woman with a baby came in. She claimed she's brought her sister's baby to Aiden."

"Why on earth would she do that?"

"She said her sister in Africa died and asked her to bring the baby to him."

"Oh," Lauren said in a louder voice. "So, Aiden has a kid we didn't know about, an African one, at that? How'd he explain it? I mean, the part about not telling anyone about it."

"He didn't. He's out of town, and he doesn't have cell reception."

"I suppose you want me to find the baby's birth certificate. That could be impossible, depending on whether the baby was born in a hospital or not."

"Actually, we were wondering if you could check out the sister, the one who brought the baby here. And the mother, if you can."

"We *who* were wondering?"

37

Harriet explained about Neelie showing up at Aiden's and the subsequent arrangements.

"This Neelie sounds like she's got a lot of nerve, trying to bully her way into Aiden's house while he's gone. Are you sure it's a good idea for her to be there with Carla? She's kind of a wimp. Who knows what she'll let the girl carry out of the place before he gets back."

"Well, that would be why we were hoping you could check her out. She's very pushy. And she broke my cell phone, so if you need to reach me, either call on my business line or call Aunt Beth. Carla is worried about the baby. Mavis is going to call Terry and let him know what's going on."

"Back up," Lauren said. "She broke your cell phone?"

"You don't want to know."

"It's probably a good idea about Terry. Here." Lauren handed her a small tablet and a pen. "Write the names down and anything else you can think of. I'll see what I can find out."

"Let me know as soon as you find anything."

"The usual disclaimers apply."

"I know, no promises, and your paying customers come first, etc., etc., etc…"

"Have you done your dog block yet?" Lauren asked, changing the subject.

"No, Phyllis gave me a last-minute rush job, and Mavis has the first piece of Joseph's quilt ready to go on my machine as soon as I get home."

"I'm glad Robin or whoever it was decided we need a few more days. I'm playing with a doghouse block that's showing promise. I went to the senior home again this morning to help Sarah with a software problem, and she showed me hers. And yes, in spite of all her whining, she had a block done. Anyway, she's trying to do something with dog bones. I tried not to laugh, but her bones didn't look like bones, and I'm pretty sure her result would have to have an X rating."

"Did you tell her that?"

"I laughed, and she stuffed it back into her bag. After that, she wasn't interested in anything I had to say. And I did try to be tactful."

Harriet wished she could have been a fly on the wall for that conversation.

"I like your new place," she said as she started to leave.

"You want to stay for some tea?" Lauren asked. "I'll understand if you're too busy," she added in a rush.

"I think I have a few minutes," Harriet replied. "I'd love a cup of tea." She set her purse down by Lauren's sofa and followed her into her kitchen.

Harriet hadn't planned on spending an entire hour, but Lauren was reaching out to her, and she couldn't ignore that. She was sipping her peppermint herb tea with clover honey when she realized that, in all the uproar of Neelie's arrival, she'd forgotten to check on Randy. It was unlikely she'd talk to Aiden before the shower, so she'd just add it to her ever-growing list of to-do items.

"Where have you been?" Aunt Beth asked when she finally came into her studio through the outside door.

"Having tea with Lauren."

"Don't you lie to me," Beth scolded.

"I'm not, and what are you doing here, anyway. Not that I don't love seeing you anytime, but I wasn't expecting you, was I?" She set her purse on the floor by one of the wingback chairs in the small waiting area set up near the door.

"Mavis filled me in on the doings at Aiden's house. I wanted to hear your take on it, and since you don't have a cell phone anymore, I couldn't call and ask. Anyway, I have a few tricks up my sleeve that might come in handy on Mavis's quilt piece."

"Have you been holding out on me?"

"Well, I can't tell you everything I know, now, can I? You might not need me anymore if I did that."

"You know that will never happen." Harriet put her arm around her aunt's shoulders and quickly filled her in on Neelie's arrival at Aiden's and Carla's decision to let the woman and child stay with her.

"Mavis is going to call Terry and let him know what's going on, and I stopped by Lauren's to see what she can find out about Neelie and her sister. She also told me she'd seen Sarah, and that Sarah's attempts at making a dog bone block hadn't gone too well."

"I've been fiddling with novelty print fabrics with dog images on them," Beth said. "The problem I'm running into is that none of the fabric companies make an extensive line of pet fabric that coordinates. I've collected half-yard cuts of every dog fabric on the market, and they're all over the map. I've got cartoon images, realistic dogs, pastel backgrounds, bright-colored backgrounds and everything in between. None of it goes together."

"Remember that class we took where we cut four-inch squares and mixed them all up in a garbage bag and then blindly pulled them out and sewed them into four-patch blocks? It was supposed to prove there *were* no bad combinations."

"*Supposed to* being the operative phrase there." Beth sighed. "Trust me, my combinations are terrible."

"Maybe we can water them down by alternating them with a lot of great batiks."

"Let's see what we can do with Mavis's piece first," Beth said. "I took the liberty of loading it onto the machine. I had an idea I want to show you about how to deal with the seam between the old and the new parts."

Chapter 8

Harriet woke up early on the morning of DeAnn's baby shower. She'd forgotten to put a midnight snack in Fred's food bowl the night before, and he'd punished her by head-butting her awake at six-thirty. By the time she staggered downstairs and provided a gob of the gelatinous goop Aiden had prescribed for Fred to clear up his dandruff, she was wide awake.

"Listen, you little wretch," she said to him as he circled his dish and rubbed his face on her bare leg. "This was your idea. We could still be in our warm bed."

She hadn't changed the thermostat on the furnace to fall settings yet, and consequently, the kitchen was freezing. She was in the midst of her daily internal debate over the merits of going out for a walk versus going back to bed for another half-hour when the flashing red light on her answering machine caught her eye.

Aiden, she thought with a smile and picked the phone up. She pushed the play button on the ancient machine and listened in anticipation for the sound of his voice.

"I have to give it to you," Lauren said. "Your problems are never boring."

Harriet's shoulders and spirits sagged.

"I haven't found birth or death documents for either of the adults and nothing on the baby."

"Why are you calling me, then?" Harriet wondered out loud. Fred looked up at the sound of her voice.

"I did find something interesting, though."

The phone in her hand buzzed, and Harriet startled so hard she again had to juggle the phone to avoid dropping it.

"Hello?"

"Guess what I just found?" Lauren asked.

"I was about to find out from the answering machine, but you cut yourself off."

"Guess."

"Lauren, it is not even seven o'clock yet. Could you just cut to the chase?"

"Oh, you're no fun."

Look who's talking, Harriet thought.

"I suppose going to your computer and watching a YouTube video clip is out of the question."

"Lauren, if you don't tell me something useful in the next thirty seconds, I'm hanging up."

"Fine," she grumbled. "The video clip you refuse to watch shows a woman named Nabirye Obote talking about contaminated water wells near Oraba, Uganda, which is apparently a village or town near the Sudanese border. I think she is saying that the wells were contaminated on purpose, but I'm not sure because my translation program had a hard time with her accent."

"So, she made a video at some point before she died."

"You are definitely not a morning person, are you?" Lauren said. "If she'd made a video in the *past*, I wouldn't be calling you. This video was posted yesterday."

"Yeah, but couldn't it have been made earlier and just not posted until yesterday?"

"It could have, but why post it after she died, and if you were going to post it after she died, don't you think you'd mention her death?"

"Are you sure it's the woman we're looking for?"

"Of course not, how could I know that? All I can tell you is that a woman named Nabirye Obote made a video in Uganda two days ago. Oh, and she looks to be of childbearing age. I don't know how common the name is, but with nothing else to go on, that's what I've got."

Harriet sat down on a stool at her kitchen bar, phone in hand.

"That's a lot," she admitted. "If it is our Nabirye Obote, then she's clearly not dead."

"Which makes us wonder why her baby is here with some other mother."

"What it really makes us wonder is if Nabirye has a baby at all."

"If she's doing politically dangerous work, she might have sent her baby here for safety," Lauren suggested.

"Or Neelie might be trying to take advantage of her sister's situation and find a better life for her own baby."

"Didn't you tell me yesterday the baby's eyes were blue? So, we have to believe Neelie just coincidentally had a blue-eyed baby?"

"If she did have a blue-eyed baby, and she'd seen Aiden, it might have given her the idea."

"It sounds pretty bold, if you ask me."

"My experience with Neelie is that she's definitely bold enough to try something like that."

"If she's staying at Aiden's house maybe we can grill her after the shower."

Harriet could hear the clicking of computer keys in the background.

"I just sent you the link. When you've had your coffee, take a look."

"Thanks for finding this so quickly," Harriet said.

"It's what I do," Lauren said with a long-suffering sigh. "Later," she added, and hung up without waiting for a response.

Harriet turned on her bar stool.

"This puts a different spin on things, Fred. After that bit of news, I think a walk is in order after all."

Beth had taken Mavis's quilt piece home the night before, so Harriet spent the morning auditioning fabrics for her dog quilt block. Her plan was to try to fashion a tumbling block pattern using light, medium and dark fabrics, one of which would be a dog print. If her color choices were good, three diamond-shaped pieces would be joined, creating a three-dimensional effect that would make it appear blocks were tumbling out of the quilt.

She cut two diamonds from each of the dog-print fabrics she'd collected then searched through the fabric on her storage shelves to find coordinating shades to complete each trio. It was a slow process—cutting diamonds, arranging the pieces on her flannel design wall and rejecting them when they didn't create the desired effect.

A glance at the clock told her she needed to end the process and get ready for the shower. For all her efforts, she'd found only one trio of colors that looked like they might work.

"Take a message if Aiden calls," Harriet instructed Fred after she'd showered, dressed and wrapped her shower gift. "And don't open the door for strangers."

Fred meowed his agreement, and Harriet left for the party.

Chapter 9

Was that Neelie I saw driving your car down the driveway when I came in?" Harriet asked Carla when she entered Aiden's house.

Carla set a bowl of fruit salad down on the dining room buffet.

"I sent her to the store to buy formula and diapers that fit for the baby."

"Did it occur to you she might just take the car and run?" Harriet asked.

Carla's cheeks turned a dark pink.

"She wants something, and it isn't a car," she said. "Trust me. My mom had boyfriends with that same look she has."

"Our Carla's clever enough not to let Neelie take her car without leaving a security deposit," Mavis said as she came into the dining room carrying Kissa.

"Aren't you the sly one?" Harriet said.

"Not sly enough," Carla told her. "I didn't get any new information from her."

Mavis patted Carla on the back.

"Now, honey, she's hardly settled in. You just keep your ears open. Let us do the rest."

The Loose Threads started arriving en masse, fixing plates of snacks and making tea.

"Did you tell everyone what I found?" Lauren asked as she sat down next to Harriet at the table. She had on a pink linen blouse with a Peter Pan collar, and navy blue pants. Her hair was swept back from her face with a navy blue headband. She looked younger and more vulnerable than usual.

"I haven't had a chance. Why don't you tell them?"

"I can't believe you're sitting on this gem. Where is the subject, by the way?"

"If you mean Neelie, she's at the store, and you don't need to say it, I already asked why she got to take a car. Carla's holding the baby hostage."

"Way to go, Carla," Lauren said. "Looks like our little friend is growing a spine."

Harriet shushed Lauren. Fortunately, Carla was in the kitchen and well out of earshot.

"What did you find out?" Jenny asked. Her shoulder-length silver hair was turned under in her customary page boy style, and she was wearing gray wool slacks and a pale-blue crepe blouse.

The room quieted as Lauren explained her discovery that Neelie's sister was possibly still alive. She also told them about the lack of documentation for Kissa and Neelie.

"That's all the more reason Carla shouldn't be here alone with that woman," Connie said when Lauren had finished.

"Who are you talking about?" Phyllis Johnson asked as she wedged her soft bulk into a dining room chair.

Three people started talking at once, but after only a few minutes, Phyllis was up to speed.

"Do you really think Aiden abandoned a pregnant woman in Africa?" Phyllis asked. "I've known him since he was a guppie. He used to give Avanell fits bringing home every stray dog and cat in Foggy Point. He wouldn't leave his own baby." Her chair creaked as she settled her bulk. She tugged at the two sides of her pastel piecework jacket. "Mark my words, something else is going on."

DeAnn came into the dining room, ending all talk of Neelie, Aiden and Kissa.

"This is still happening, right?" she asked Phyllis. She wore a black vest with red appliquéd flowers connected by a green vine that twined from one front panel, around the neck, down the back and onto the other front piece. Leaves in three shades of green were spaced between the flowers. The vest was very striking over the red turtleneck sweater she'd paired it with. She wore tapered black pants and ankle boots to complete the outfit. It was a definite change from her usual jeans and green polo shirt with the Foggy Point Video logo she wore most week days—her family owned the video store, and she worked there part time.

"Yes, it's all real," Phyllis said with a smile. "If everything goes as planned, this time tomorrow you're going to have a beautiful daughter."

"It's all so hard to believe," DeAnn said. "I mean, Avery was born while David was still in graduate school. And Hansford…" She paused. "Well, he was a bit of a surprise, so he got AJ's hand-me-downs, which were already secondhand."

"Well, honey, you just enjoy every minute of it," Aunt Beth said.

"No baby shower is complete without a couple of games," Mavis said. "Let's move into the parlor across the hall."

In her mind, Harriet groaned. She'd been to a few baby showers when she lived in California, and she'd clearly demonstrated that her upbringing, in the hands of nannies and at boarding schools in Europe, Asia and only sometimes America, had left her without the common cultural references most children grew up with. Her parents believed reading children's books to children stunted their potential. When her mother read to her, it was from the periodic table; her father read her Shakespeare.

"Okay, everyone," Mavis said when the women were settled on the chairs and sofas of the large dayroom. "In this one, there are small gold 'diaper' pins mixed in a bowl of rice. Your task is to pick out as many pins as you can in thirty seconds—while blindfolded."

This task proved harder than it sounded but didn't require previous knowledge of babies or culture. The next two games didn't, either, and Harriet relaxed. She knew she was among friends, but she was still sensitive about her weird upbringing.

Neelie came in the front door as the group was returning to the dining room to have cake and ice cream.

"Oh, hi, Neelie," Carla said. "Would you like to join us for some cake?"

She looked wary.

"Where is Kissa?"

"She's in the nursery with Wendy," Carla told her. "I hired a babysitter to stay with them during the shower."

"Okay, but just a small piece for me."

"Here, come sit," Aunt Beth said and brought another chair to the table, placing it between herself and Harriet. "What would you like to drink? We have punch, tea and coffee."

"Coffee is fine," Neelie said. Harriet could see the woman was uncomfortable.

"Let me introduce you," Harriet said. "Ladies, Carla's houseguest is going to join us."

She proceeded to present each Loose Thread, and they, in turn, each said a few words of welcome.

"Phyllis Johnson isn't a Loose Thread. She works for the adoption agency that is placing DeAnn's baby with her." Harriet looked around. Phyllis had disappeared. "I guess she's in the restroom."

"Welcome," Robin said. "I hope you enjoy your visit to Foggy Point."

"So, what's Oraba like?" Lauren asked.

"Excuse me?" Neelie said in her lilting English.

"I saw in a video on YouTube that your sister's working in Oraba. I was wondering what kind of place it was."

If Neelie noticed Lauren's use of the present tense in reference to her sister, she didn't show it.

"It is like all of Uganda—hot and dusty."

"Are there problems with the water there?" Harriet asked.

"I don't know," Neelie snapped. "She had her work, and I had mine. We didn't talk about it."

"What sort of work did you do?" Harriet persisted.

"I work at a bank, just like you have here. I wear a dress. I stand at a window and take people's money or give them their money."

"How about some more coffee?" Mavis said, and refilled Neelie's cup without waiting for an answer. "Pass her the milk," she told Harriet.

The conversation effectively ended, the group ate cake and chatted.

"I'm going to go check the baby," Neelie said when she was finished.

She stood and left the room. Phyllis returned to the table when she was gone.

"Are you okay?" Beth asked her.

"I'm fine. I got a phone call I had to return right away, so I stepped outside where it was quiet."

DeAnn looked at her.

"Don't worry, it was good news," Phyllis assured her. "Your little girl is on her way. This time tomorrow, she'll arrive in Seattle and, shortly after that, in Foggy Point."

DeAnn smiled and sagged back into her chair in relief.

"How about we open some presents?" Connie said and wheeled in the jogging stroller. She and Mavis had set it up and stashed it in the kitchen eating area. The Loose Threads had strapped a baby-sized teddy bear into the seat and surrounded it with smaller wrapped gifts.

"Oh, my gosh," DeAnn said. "You guys shouldn't have."

"Isn't that the point of a shower?" Sarah asked. "You shower the person with stuff."

Aunt Beth took a package from the stroller and handed it to DeAnn.

✁- - - ✁- - -✁

Almost an hour later, the last package had been unwrapped, and DeAnn was surrounded by piles of mostly pink pajamas, dresses, pants and shirts as well as more than one little-girl-sized quilt. Harriet had made two nightgowns. Since they didn't know the correct size, she and the rest of the Threads had stuck to flexible, loose-fitting garments.

A knock on the door interrupted the oooh-ing and ahh-ing.

"Am I too early?" Joseph Marston asked when Carla had let him in and escorted him to the dining room. "I found another big quilt that was donated. Mavis said to bring it by here."

"I'll take that," Mavis said and stood up. "Here—sit down and have a piece of cake."

"I don't want to interrupt," Joseph protested, but Aunt Beth had already sliced a large piece of the lemon-filled white cake and set it in front of him. Jenny brought a china cup and saucer from the sideboard and put it beside the cake.

"Coffee or tea?" she asked and, when he indicated coffee, picked up the coffee carafe and filled his cup. Carla put the sugar and cream within his reach.

"Thank you, ladies." he said. "And I hope you know these quilts you're remaking will be put to good use."

"Well, it's a very good cause," Mavis said. "And we're happy to do what little we can to help those babies get a good start in life."

Joseph looked across the room at DeAnn, who was giggling as she held up a pink tutu and leotard and showed it to Robin and Jenny.

"I've been doing this for almost twenty years now, and that…" He pointed at a smiling DeAnn. "…is something that never gets old."

"Joseph," Phyllis said from the other end of the table, "do we have a final arrival time to tell DeAnn?"

"Assuming the customs process goes smoothly," he said, and pulled out his smartphone, clicking buttons as he spoke and staring at the little screen, "they land in Seattle right around noon. Assuming thirty minutes to get through customs, give or take another thirty, depending on how full the flight is, my best guess is between two-thirty and three o'clock."

"Where do we go to pick her up?" DeAnn asked.

"Oh, don't worry, honey," Phyllis said. "At Little Lamb, we bring your bundle of joy to your home." She took the last bite of her second piece of cake then hoisted herself up. "Speaking of Little Lamb, I better get back. We don't want any of our new parents to wait any longer than they absolutely have to, to receive their new family member." She looked over at Joseph. "You take your time, Joe. I can finish up the verifications tonight."

He started to rise.

"I can finish them for you," he said with a longing glance at his cake.

"Don't be silly. You go home when you're done with these ladies. Thanks to Harriet here, I've got plenty of time to bind my
quilt before the wedding."

The expression on Joseph's face said he wasn't comfortable being sent home when the boss was going back to work, but it was
also clear he wouldn't argue in front of the assembled women.

"Let me get you some more cake," Harriet said, breaking the
awkward silence.

Phyllis gathered up her quilt, which Harriet had placed under
her chair when the shower started, then buttoned her jacket and
left.

"Oh, Harriet," she called, pausing at the front door. "Let me
write you a check."

She was holding the invoice Harriet had tucked into the quilt
bag with the finished product. Harriet waited in the foyer as she
pulled a pink plastic checkbook with a matching pen from her
purse and began writing.

Movement on the steps caught her attention, and she looked up
as Neelie retreated back upstairs.

"I hope he'll take my advice and go home," Phyllis said in a
hushed voice. "I'm not one to pry, so I don't know what's going on
with him, but he looks like a man who hasn't gotten a good night's
sleep in quite some time."

Harriet hadn't been in town long enough to know what Joseph
Marston should look like, but as she studied him from the foyer, she
had to admit the dark circles under his eyes and too-prominent hol-
low of his cheeks, combined with worn-looking gray slacks that
were a bit looser than was fashionable, suggested he wasn't at his
peak.

She returned to the dining room and got Joseph a second piece
of cake. Aunt Beth and Mavis were picking up plates and cups
from the table, while Jenny and Connie helped DeAnn pack up the
presents.

"I've got to get back to work," Sarah announced. "Congratula-
tions," she said to DeAnn. "Do we have a time to show our next
blocks?" she asked no one in particular.

51

"Since DeAnn isn't going to be doing a block in any case, what about tomorrow?" Lauren suggested.

"Actually, that's not a bad idea," Robin said. "That will help us all respect DeAnn's request to let the first couple of days with the new little one be immediate family only."

The look of relief on DeAnn's face suggested that plan worked for her.

"I'll check with Carla," Harriet said. "Anyone see which way she went?"

"She went upstairs to take a piece of cake to the babysitter," Mavis said.

"I'll see if she's available." And see how she feels about leaving Neelie here alone for that amount of time, she added silently.

Mavis followed her into the kitchen. "I know you're wondering if Carla is willing to leave home with Neelie staying here, but you don't have to worry. Terry's taking a few days off and said he would come stay here. He said Aiden bought a new sound system, and he had volunteered to hook it up and wire speakers into two other rooms as soon as he had some time off. Now he does, and it will provide a perfect excuse for him to be around the house. Since he lives on the base, and it's so far away, there's a good reason for him to stay here while he's doing it."

"I'm going to go say goodbye and see if she's free in any case," Harriet said and went up the servants stairs to the second floor. She met Carla on the landing.

"Hi, Harriet, I was just taking Haley some cake. Wendy and Kissa are napping."

"Mavis said Terry was going to come stay a couple of days."

"And it's sort of cute that you all think I don't know you asked him to come stay here until Aiden gets back. Don't worry—when Terry told me he was coming to work on Aiden's sound system, I didn't let on I knew the real reason."

"When did you get so smart?" Harriet said with a smile.

"When I started hanging out with you." Carla's cheeks turned pink, and she laughed.

Harriet laughed with her then sobered.

"Even with Terry here, you need to be careful. And keep your eyes and ears open. See if you can learn anything more about Neelie."

"I'm trying, but she doesn't give up much. She reminds me of my mother's 'friends'—they come from some vague place that doesn't have a name and they always have families they don't want to talk about and they're always one deal away from the big score."

"Has she mentioned what her one big deal is?"

"No, but you can tell she's got one."

"Well, like I said, be careful. And it may be cute that Terry is coming to protect you, but we don't know who this woman is or what her intentions are so, until we find out, let him do his job."

Carla looked at her feet.

"I'm sorry, I didn't mean to sound so harsh, but I don't want you or Wendy to get hurt."

Carla lifted her gaze to Harriet's face.

"Do you really think we're in danger?" she asked, her dark eyes serious.

"I don't know. Right now, it's just a feeling. All the same, you be careful. On a lighter note, are you available tomorrow to do our dog blocks?"

"My block is done…"

"But you don't want to leave Neelie here by herself," Harriet finished for her.

"Not until Terry is here, and I don't know when he's coming."

"What if we meet here? I mean, you'd have to be invaded by the Loose Threads again, but I can come early and help you get ready."

Carla smiled. "That's a good idea. Not the part about you coming to help get ready, the part about having the meeting here. You can come early if you want to have tea and leftover party food, but with a house this big, there's always a room ready, especially with Aiden away. I think Avanell used to have meetings in the upstairs parlor. I found a portable design wall in a carry bag in the closet."

"That's perfect. Let's go see what the others think."

Connie was standing at the kitchen sink, hand-washing the delicate teacups and saucers. Mavis was drying them, and Aunt

Beth was carefully putting them back into the kitchen china cabinet.

Harriet told them about Carla's offer to host a dog block meeting the following day.

"I suppose we're inviting *la diabla*?" Connie said.

"No, we're not inviting Neelie to join us. Carla would just feel better not leaving her here alone if she doesn't have to," Harriet explained in a hushed voice.

Connie rolled her eyes. "Dios mio," she muttered.

"I'll call Sarah, since she's already gone, and Robin, too." They all could see Robin getting into her car in the gravel parking area outside.

"If you ladies have the cleanup under control, I'm going to go find Randy and say hi to her so I don't have to lie to Aiden when I finally get to talk to him."

"This sounds like the dog ate my homework," Connie said. "I've heard that one before."

"You gave homework to first graders?" Harriet said and laughed. "No wonder they all fear you, even as adults."

"Don't change the subject," Connie said. "Go check the table and sideboard and make sure there aren't any more cups that need washed."

Harriet did as instructed and did find two more cups hidden behind a large vase of flowers on the sideboard.

"Now can I go?" she asked Connie as she handed her the dishes.

"Yes, honey, thank you."

She left through the kitchen door and circled around to the back of the house. Aiden's property had a separate kennel with its own fenced yard that had once been home to his father's hunting dogs. Randy was happy to see Harriet, since she lived in the main house when Aiden was home and lately had taken to spending her days following Wendy everywhere as Carla tended to the care and cleaning of her master's residence.

Harriet unlatched the kennel yard gate and let the little dog out. After a minute or two of joyful jumping up and down and circling Harriet's legs, she started running in large circles and figure-eights on the lawn in a pattern only she knew. Harriet moved out onto the lawn, positioning herself in the middle of the pattern. As she got closer to the house, she heard a woman's voice coming from an open window on the second floor.

"Do not come here. You have no business here." There was a pause. "No, you're the one who's going to be sorry."

Either the conversation had ended or the speaker moved away from the window. Harriet couldn't be sure. She hadn't recognized the voice. Her only two choices were Neelie or the babysitter, Haley. It hadn't sounded like the voice of a teenager, but on the other hand, it lacked Neelie's accent. She wasn't familiar enough with the second floor of Aiden's house to be able to figure out which room the window belonged to.

One more reason to be glad Terry was going to be staying with Carla, she thought as she reached down and patted Randy's head. She led the exhausted dog to the back porch.

"Is it okay if she comes in?" she asked, holding the kitchen door open with her free hand and holding Randy with the other.

Aunt Beth agreed, and she pushed the dog inside and left.

Chapter 10

Her phone was ringing as she came from her studio to the kitchen.
"Hello."

"I just missed you at my house," he said, the fatigue clear in his voice. "Carla told me your phone was broken, and to try this one."

"It is, and it's a long story that can wait until you come home." Harriet was still holding out hope Neelie would get tired of waiting for Aiden and give up on her scheme.

"You'll be happy to know it'll be sooner rather than later."

"That's great news," she said. "Were things better than you expected?"

"Unfortunately, they were worse. The team ahead of mine lost a couple of dogs. After we assessed the cases we have left, we talked to the head of the project and convinced him we're better off doing a scoop-and-run."

"A what?"

"Sorry, that's what we call it when we move the patient as quickly as possible as opposed to doing triage and emergency treatment in the field first. Most of these dogs have open sores and infections and need to get to a more sterile environment."

"How are *you* doing?" she asked.

"I'm fine. I just wish I could say the same for all these dogs. I know hoarding's a disease, but when you see how they've suffered, it makes you want to put the owner in a dirty, crowded room and see how he or she likes it."

"I'm so sorry you have to deal with that."

"Don't feel sorry for me. It's the dogs that need your sympathy."

"I'll ask the Loose Threads and see if anyone needs a pet."

"Don't get them too excited—these will be special-needs dogs. They aren't used to normal human contact. Tell them that, and if they're still interested, they can talk to me. On a more important subject, have you been staying out of trouble while I'm gone?"

"Of course," she lied. "I've just been stitching quilts and working on quilt blocks for our dog adoption benefit quilts."

"Good, I wouldn't want to have to worry about you on top of everything here. I better go—I just wanted to let you know I'll be back in a day or two. The first temperature-controlled truck is arriving tomorrow, and when we load the last one, I'll head back."

"It's so good to finally talk to you."

Whatever Aiden said was lost in the ether as the connection went abruptly dead.

"Fred, my boy, this is going to get real interesting," she said to her fuzzy companion.

After playing with Randy in Aiden's perfectly manicured yard she had resolved on her way home to clean out and winterize the modest flowerbeds passed on to her along with the house. Fortunately, Aunt Beth stopped by periodically and pulled weeds or divided plants, since Harriet had a bit of a black thumb where the outdoor plantings were concerned.

She realized she was still holding the phone. She set it back in its cradle and turned to look out the window. A light rain was falling. The tall Douglas fir trees at the head of her driveway glistened with silver drops. Saved! she thought.

Unlike the rest of the northwest, rain wasn't something that could be counted on in Foggy Point. The town sat in the "rain shadow" of the Olympic Mountains, and rainclouds had a tendency to pass right over the area without dropping their load.

She knew she should go work on her dog block but instead went to her computer and opened the email Lauren had sent her.

"Who are you?" she said as Nabirye Obote's image resolved on her screen.

She pressed the white play arrow and watched the entire clip without stopping. Nothing jumped out at her, so she watched it again and again. If Nabirye was, in fact, Neelie's sister, there wasn't a strong resemblance. There was a little similarity around the eyes, but Neelie had a narrow nose where Nabirye's was broad. Both women had full lips, but Neelie's mouth wasn't as wide. Or maybe it was just that she always seemed to have her lips pursed. Nabirye smiled easily in the video, speaking on a topic she was obviously passionate about.

"What am I missing?" Harriet said out loud. She pressed the white arrow again and, this time, forced herself not to look at the woman but at everything else in the scenes.

The action was divided into three parts. The first showed a mud hole. Animals were drinking on one side, and a child was scooping brown water into a plastic bucket on the other. There was nothing to indicate when in time it had been filmed.

The second scene was what Harriet assumed was a clean-water well. It looked like a large metal tray with a pipe, topped by a square metal box. A spout protruded from the side of the larger pipe, spilling clean liquid into a white bucket. Again, nothing that would pin it down to a particular date.

The final scene was in an office of some sort. This was the shortest. She stopped the play at the first full frame. It would have been nice if there had been something as obvious as a newspaper with the current date, or a calendar with the days marked off until today. No such luck.

Harriet printed a copy of her computer screen showing the office. She pulled it from her printer and turned the picture so the image was upside-down. She took another piece of blank paper and laid it over the picture, exposing only the first inch of the image. She searched the picture inch by inch in this manner, and when she was midway down the page she hit pay dirt.

She returned to her computer screen and hit the zoom button. Nabirye stood in front of a table. Under the table was a shipping carton. What appeared to be manufacturing data was printed on the side of the box. While it wasn't conclusive proof, whatever had been in the box had been manufactured or shipped ten days ago.

Given travel time for the package, Nabirye had been alive and appearing in a video a week ago, give or take a day. When you added the time Neelie had been in Foggy Point and the time it would have taken her to make arrangements and travel, it would seem that rumors of Nabirye's death had been greatly exaggerated.

Harriet moved to her cutting table and pulled out the sets of diamonds that were going to be her dog block. She needed to keep her hands busy while she thought about this latest revelation.

An hour passed, and she hadn't made any progress on her dog block, so she decided to put it aside for a while. The shower had provided a light lunch, but that had been hours ago, and she was starting to get hungry. Tico's Tacos could take care of that problem.

Harriet hadn't thought about it before, but she generally got an urge for enchiladas when she needed advice. Jorge Perez not only owned Foggy Point's best Mexican restaurant but was the father of Aiden's closest friend Julio, and had taken over as father figure when Aiden's own father died when he was still in grade school. Jorge was bound to have some insights for her on the subject of Neelie once she'd filled him in on what had been happening.

Chapter 11

Hey, chiquita," Jorge called from the kitchen as Harriet entered the restaurant. "You alone?"

It was early for dinner, and only two tables were occupied. A teenaged couple sat in the back corner, their heads close, whispering words meant only for each other. A larger group was clustered around two tables that had been pushed together and were laden with an assortment of nachos, quesadillas and taquitos. Probably co-workers on their way home from work, Harriet mused.

"Here we go," Jorge said a few minutes later as he set a heaping stoneware bowl of freshly made guacamole and a basket of warm tortilla chips on the table at the booth where Harriet was sitting. He slid into the seat opposite her. "Next time you have a party, you let me know, and I'll fix food that will stick to your ribs."

Harriet stared at him.

"I can make fancy food, too, you know," he said with a smile.

"How…?"

"Your aunt and Mavis picked up burritos a half-hour ago, Carla called in a takeout order for her boyfriend to pick up, and if you didn't see the blond one with the smart mouth in the parking lot, then you just missed her."

"Lauren was here?" Harriet was only surprised because, even though Foggy Point wasn't exactly a metropolis, people who lived on or near the water at Smuggler's Cove tended to frequent the cafes and pubs in their neighborhood. As a new resident of the area, she'd thought Lauren had been doing the same.

"Yeah, that's the one. She's become a bit of a regular since you had all those secret meetings in the back room. She likes my cheese nachos," he added with a grin.

Harriet dipped a chip into the guacamole and slowly ate it, savoring the smooth flavor.

"Mmmm," she said with a groan.

"Okay, I know my guacamole is good. Your theatrics are good for an old man's ego, but I've got chicken in the oven I have to tend to. What is it you want, chiquita?"

"I can't fool you, can I?" she said and laughed. "Okay, I was just wondering if you'd seen a young black woman with a baby around town."

"The same one your aunt was asking about?" Jorge grinned.

"That would be the one."

"I'll tell you what I told her and Mavis. I saw the woman, but not the baby. She came in here earlier today, met a guy for an early lunch and was out of here in less than an hour."

"What guy?"

"I don't know his name. I've seen him in here once or twice. Not with the señorita, though."

"What did he look like?"

"Skinny, pale, probably late thirties or early forties. Light-brown hair. Looks like he works indoors." Jorge paused and looked up for a moment. "That's all I can think of. He looks like a lot of guys."

"That must have been during the baby shower, when she was supposed to be out buying baby formula."

"I have to go check my pollo. If I see her—or him—again, I'll give you a call."

"Thanks, Jorge," she said and then explained about her phone and the need to call her land line.

"No problem. You want to try some of my pollo verde?"

"Sounds great," Harriet said and dug into her chips again.

A few minutes later, a young woman with long dark hair in a braid down her back, dressed in a bright pink-and-orange ruffled skirt and white embroidered peasant shirt, set down a platter heaped with chicken in a green chili sauce, red rice and pinto beans topped

61

with crumbled cotija cheese, and a generous scoop of sour cream. She also brought a plastic container that held soft hand-sized flour tortillas. She left, then returned a moment later with a frosty glass of fresh-squeezed lemonade.

Harriet pondered Neelie's lunch date as she ate. There was clearly more going on with her than the story she was telling.

"You need a box for the leftovers, chiquita?" Jorge asked when he returned to her table a half-hour later. He set a foam carry-out box next to her plate.

"This was enough for three people," she said. "It was very good, though."

"And you're going to need to feed that young man of yours."

"He's not home yet, and I don't know when he'll be back."

"As it happens, he's on his way now."

"What?"

"He called while I was fixing your plate. He tried your home phone, and when you didn't answer, he took a chance and called here. He was just leaving Ephrata. That should be a four-and-a-half-hour drive, but with a truckload of dogs it could be twice that."

"How did he sound?"

"I won't lie, chiquita," Jorge said and rubbed his large hand over his face. "He sounded bone-weary. He won't be driving the truck, so don't worry about that," he hastened to add.

"I wish there was something I could do."

"There is. Just be you. Be there for him, and don't expect anything for a while. He's a tough boy. He'll get through this. He just cares a lot for the animals."

Jorge sat with her for a few more minutes, neither of them speaking.

"I better get back to work," he finally said.

"Thanks for letting me try the chicken."

"De nada," he said. "And don't even try to pay. Just because Aiden isn't here doesn't mean the rules change."

Jorge took his job as surrogate father seriously, and steadfastly refused to take money from "family," a fact that made Harriet decidedly uncomfortable.

She walked slowly back to her car. If what she'd seen on the video was true, Neelie's sister was still alive. Could she have sent her baby to Aiden for some reason other than her health? Did she not want the child? If that were true, then who was Neelie having lunch with? If she were simply a courier for her sister, she wouldn't know anyone here—certainly not well enough to be arguing with them.

For a moment, she wished Aiden wasn't coming home. She instantly felt guilty for the thought, but she needed time to figure out what was going on.

She drove home turning things over in her mind and, hindsight being what it is, was starting to wonder if she'd done the right thing when she didn't tell Aiden everything right from the start.

Chapter 12

O h, my gosh," Harriet screamed. "I haven't been to class all term."
She wasn't sure who she was talking to, but it didn't matter. Her
algebra final was due to start in ten minutes, and as a result of having not attended a single class, she didn't know where it was held.
She had a schedule in her locker, but that location was evading her,
too.

She felt needles pierce her face. She shook her head and was
brought to consciousness by Fred's screech as she pushed him away.
He'd apparently tried to wake her from her nightmare by slapping
her in the face with the tips of his claws.

"Thank you, Fred, I needed that," she said.

She reassured herself she had passed algebra long ago, not only
in high school but in college; her "lost in high school" dreams were
an indication of her anxiety level. This one was well-deserved, she
decided.

She fed Fred then went back upstairs to shower. She was just
returning to the kitchen when she heard a knock on the outside
door of her studio, followed by the sound of the door opening.

"Hello?" called a male voice.

"Aiden?"

She hurried toward the door between the kitchen and studio; it
opened and she fell into Aiden's open arms. He put his hands on
either side of her face and kissed her, his unshaven face rasping her

skin when he finally pulled away and gazed at her with his white-blue eyes.

"I've missed you so much," he said.

He stepped to the bar and collapsed onto a stool, pulling her with him. He wrapped his arms around her waist and leaned into her.

"You look exhausted," she said.

He was dressed in his customary work clothes—surgical scrubs and washable canvas shoes. A rust-colored smear stained the left shoulder of his shirt. She didn't want to think about what it might be.

"I just need some coffee," he said. "I've got to get back to the dogs."

"You can't possibly do those dogs any good the condition you're in." Harriet pushed out of his arms. "You need to rest."

"I don't have time to rest," he argued, but then he folded his arms and, leaning on the bar, laid his head on them.

"Come on," she said and pulled on his arm. She freed one hand and tugged until he stood then led him upstairs to the guest bedroom.

"Wake me up in thirty minutes."

"Okay," she agreed, her fingers crossed behind her back.

"Promise," he said, and lay down on the bed. The fact he didn't try to talk her into joining him was an indication of how tired he was.

Harriet took a down throw from an armchair by the window and spread it over him. He'd been asleep before his head hit the pillow. She tiptoed out the door and pulled it shut behind her.

The phone started to ring just as she reached the kitchen. She grabbed it, though she imagined it would take dynamite to wake Aiden at this point.

"Hello," she whispered into the receiver from force of habit.

It was Aunt Beth, suggesting they ride together to Carla's for the Loose Threads meeting. She agreed, and wrote a note to Aiden explaining where she'd gone and that she'd left him sleeping because he needed it.

"Hey, chiquitas," Connie greeted them as they entered through the kitchen door. "Would you two like a cup of my orange spice tea?"

"Sure," Harriet said, even though spice tea wasn't her favorite. Aunt Beth agreed also, and Connie poured them each a steaming mug from a pot she'd just made.

"How are things going with your house guest?" Harriet asked when the four women were settled in the upstairs parlor. Wendy was perched on Connie's lap, playing with her earring. Carla was holding the receiver from Wendy's baby monitor, which indicated to Harriet that Kissa was asleep in the nursery.

"It's been like she's not even here," Carla said. "Probably because she mostly *hasn't* been here."

"What do you mean?" Harriet asked.

"She left a while after the shower, and I haven't seen her since. I fed the baby dinner and put her to bed when Wendy went down. Kissa woke up crying at around midnight, and I didn't figure Neelie was likely to get up, so I fixed her a bottle and rocked her back to sleep."

"And you didn't see Neelie? No light under the door or anything?"

"No, but the baby is sleeping in the old nursery. Wendy sleeps in the room that adjoins mine. but when I asked Neelie where she wanted Kissa to sleep, she said the baby kept her awake at night and she'd rather have a room to herself. I figured I was going to be the one getting up in the night, so I put her in the nursery where there's already a monitor set up."

"So, Neelie has been missing since last night?"

"We don't know that Neelie is actually *missing*, do we?" Aunt Beth pointed out. "Seems like all we know is that she isn't here."

"Dios mio!" Connie said. "I knew that girl was trouble."

"Did you tell Aiden she was here?" Harriet asked Carla.

"You said not to tell him until he was back, but I was afraid he would walk in and find them here with no warning."

"What did he say?" Connie asked.

Carla looked down, letting her hair fall around her face.

"I only told him that the sister of a friend of his in Africa had come to see him, and that I'd let her stay here until he came home."

"You didn't mention the baby?" Harriet asked.

Carla looked up, her cheeks crimson. She shook her head.

"I know you didn't want to——" she tried to explain, but Harriet interrupted her.

"That was good," she said. "He did need to know someone was staying here, but you saved the big news until he could come home and see for himself. He hasn't been here yet, right?"

"No, he called and said he was going to be at the clinic and would probably just catch a few hours sleep on the couch there. He said it would take a while to get the vet techs up to speed on the hoarding survivors, and he said he would call when he was on his way here."

"FYI, he's asleep at my house at the moment," Harriet said. "He came by to say hi, but he was asleep on his feet. I persuaded him he wasn't going to be able to help his patients until he got some rest."

The doorbell sounded, and Carla went downstairs to greet the arriving Loose Threads. Mavis and Jenny had come together, and while they were fixing their cups of tea and coffee, Sarah arrived followed shortly by Lauren. Harriet went downstairs to refill her cup as Lauren was taking her jacket off and hanging it in the coat closet in the front entry.

"Follow me," Lauren said.

"What's up?" Harriet asked.

Lauren glared at her. "Could you keep your voice down?"

Harriet sighed but followed her until they were out of earshot of the others.

"What?" Harriet, following her.

"There is a spy among us," she murmured dramatically.

"What are you talking about?" Harriet whispered.

"I was just at the senior center, giving yet another training session on their patient-tracking software. I went into their big dining room to get a bottle of water, and I saw the Small Stitches group meeting in a smaller dining room they have that opens off the main one."

"And?" Harriet prompted.

"They were facing away from me, looking at a flip chart they'd set up. They had a list of quilt block names—*our* quilt block names. And they were assigning people to make them."

"Huh," said Harriet. "That's weird. Why would anyone do that?"

"Why does anyone do half the stuff they do? What should *we* do?"

"What do you mean?"

"We can't keep letting our ideas be passed directly to the enemy."

"First of all, we don't know for sure there *is* an enemy. It still could be a coincidence."

"Once maybe, but twice? They had all our block names except your experiment."

"We better join the others. Let's see what everyone's done. We may have a new list by the end of the meeting."

By the time Lauren and Harriet got their tea and climbed the servants' stairs from the kitchen to the second floor parlor, Robin had arrived by the main stairs and was adding her block to the array already stuck to the portable design wall. The design wall was a plastic pipe framework with a large sticky flannel fabric laced to the pipes. Its light weight allowed Carla to reposition it once everyone was seated so they all had a clear view.

Mavis settled in an overstuffed chair, her feet on the matching ottoman and her tea on a heavy cherry side table.

"You better be careful, making us so comfortable," she said to Carla. "People might decide they want to meet here all the time."

Carla's cheeks turned pink.

"That would be okay," she stammered.

"We wouldn't do that to you, honey," Aunt Beth assured her and reached over to pat her hand.

"So, who wants to talk about the blocks first?" Robin asked, bringing them back to the reason they were there.

"I want to take mine back, now that I've seen Jenny's," Mavis said, referring to Jenny's intricate appliqué design. She had created the face of a Yorkshire terrier out of batik fabrics in tan, brown and grays, complete with a pink bow holding the dog's hair out of its eyes. The face was surrounded by a wreath of dog bones inter-mingled with a green ribbon.

"Yours are cute," Robin protested.

Mavis and Beth had been assigned the snowball blocks. They had fussy-cut squares with dog faces in the center of novelty print dog fabric, with Beth using realistic images of dogs and Mavis us-ing a cartoon-style print. They'd chosen contrasting corner trian-gles to form the snowball image.

"They would be easier to make, too," Jenny offered. "I won't pretend my appliqué was quick or easy. It was the only thing I could think of that wouldn't make the dog bones look goofy." She turned to Sarah. "Sorry."

Everyone couldn't help but focus on Sarah's block after Jenny's comment. Lauren had been right—Sarah's images didn't look like dog bones at all. No one wanted to say out loud what they did look like.

"I like—" Carla started to say, but she was interrupted by a loud screech from the baby monitor now sitting on the table. Carla grabbed it and turned down the volume, but not before Wendy's bottom lip started trembling as the toddler prepared for a sympathy cry.

Connie stood up and carried Wendy to the picture window at the back of the parlor. The view was of the back garden.

"Hey, chiquita," Connie called to Harriet, "Aiden's dog looks upset."

Harriet came to the window. Connie pointed at the kennel, where Randy was jumping wildly and howling like a whole wolf pack. She threw herself against the chain link walls of her enclosure.

"That's weird. I'm going to go see what's wrong with her."

She had just started to turn away from the window when some-thing at the edge of the garden caught her eye. By the base of a large rhododendron was a splash of lime green that didn't belong to the landscape.

Harriet froze.

"Chiquita, what is it?"

"I'm not sure." She pointed to the patch of green.

"Dios mio," Connie murmured and made the sign of the cross.

"I'm going down to look."

"I'll come with you," Mavis said.

"How about I go instead," Robin offered. "No offense," she added, referring to an incident during the summer when Mavis had fainted after going to investigate a suspicious situation with Harriet.

"It was very hot that day," Mavis protested.

"We know," Aunt Beth said, "but it's probably nothing, so let's not climb the stairs for no good reason."

Robin grabbed her cell phone from her bag and followed as Harriet went down the servant's stairs and out the kitchen door. They took the gravel path around the house to the large back yard.

"Randy," Harriet said in a firm voice. "Hush."

Randy stopped howling and switched to barking as Harriet and Robin crossed the large grassy area and finally arrived at the rhododendron bushes. The mature shrubs had to be ten feet tall, and were at least that wide. The leathery dark-green foliage was dense and nearly touched the ground at the bottom of each bush.

"It's Neelie," Harriet said and rushed the last few feet to the woman's side.

She was curled in a fetal position, facing toward the center of the rhododendron. The curve of her spine was all that had been visible. Harriet put a hand on her shoulder and rolled her out from under the bush and onto her back. Robin knelt beside her and felt for a pulse.

"She's alive." She started punching numbers into her cell phone. "We need an ambulance," she said when the 911 operator answered.

Harriet pulled her zip-front hoodie off and laid it over Neelie's chest.

"Are you okay?" she asked.

Obviously, Neelie *wasn't* okay, but Harriet's first aid training had kicked in, and it was what they taught you to say.

Robin shrugged out of her Lycra yoga jacket and handed it to Harriet, who added it to her own shirt on the supine woman. She took Neelie's cold, clammy hand in hers.

The fir trees beyond the formal gardens rustled in the wind, like bystanders whispering about the scene in front of them. Aunt

Beth and Lauren came around the corner of the house and strode across the grass to join Harriet and Robin. Lauren handed Harriet a worn flannel quilt.

"Carla said we could use this to cover her," she said. "It's one of hers," she added, as if she wouldn't have brought it otherwise.

"What have we got here?" Aunt Beth asked in a businesslike tone.

"She has a pulse," Harriet reported. "She's unconscious, and Robin's on the phone with nine-one-one." She heard the faint sound of sirens in the distance.

Aunt Beth dug in her pocket.

"I have a cough drop here," she said and pulled out a paper-wrapped oval. "If she's diabetic, she needs sugar."

Robin turned from her phone.

"The operator says we shouldn't try to give her anything while she's unconscious."

Aunt Beth stuffed the drop back into her pocket.

"What happened? Can you tell?"

"Not really," Harriet said. "She was curled in a ball when we found her. She doesn't have any big cuts or scrapes or anything like that—at least that I could see."

The sound of a siren got louder then stopped. The women could hear the paramedics before they saw them.

"Over here," Robin called.

Mavis was with the three jumpsuit-clad EMTs. They trotted across the grass, and the cluster of women separated so they could reach Neelie.

"We think she's diabetic," Harriet offered.

"Type one or two?" a chunky blond asked as he knelt beside the fallen woman. He looked up at Harriet and paused, recognition showing on his face. "You," he said. They'd met in the summer over another body.

"The type that requires a person to take sugar quickly," she answered, not wanting to explain why she was once again at the scene of a serious medical emergency. "We don't really know for sure."

"Here we go," the paramedic said and pulled up a metal tag that hung from a chain around her neck. "Type One."

71

The second paramedic pulled a clear bag of fluid from the large orange plastic box. He tore off the wrapper off a tubing kit and quickly attached an IV to Neelie's arm. The third paramedic, a slight, older man, set down the backboard he'd been carrying and applied a stabilization neck collar.

The blond paramedic quickly and efficiently ran his hands over Neelie's arms and legs—checking for broken bones, Harriet assumed. Finding no obvious injuries, they strapped her onto the backboard and carried her to the ambulance, where they transferred her to the padded gurney.

Chapter 13

The Loose Threads stood in a silent cluster as the ambulance drove away , once again turning on the lights and siren.

"Would someone like to tell me what's going on here?" Sarah demanded. "Why was there an unconscious woman in Avanell's bushes?"

"Don't you think if one of us knew what had happened we would have told the paramedics so they could help her?" Lauren shot back.

"We think she's diabetic," Carla offered, her cheeks turning their customary pink.

"Yeah, but why was she under the bush?"

"It seems like she had a blood sugar crisis and wasn't able to think clearly enough to come in and ask for help," Mavis said. "We don't really know, so there's no point in speculating until we have more information."

Harriet folded her arms across her chest and rubbed her hands on her upper arms.

"Can we go inside, please," she asked. "It's cold out here."

Robin was holding both Harriet's sweatshirt and her own yoga jacket. She looked at Harriet and wiggled the sweatshirt slightly. Harriet shook her head once, and Robin let it fall back against her arm.

"Does anyone want to go back up and look at our blocks?" Harriet asked.

"We might as well," Robin replied. "We're all here."

Everyone else had gone in when Harriet started up the stairs to the porch. A crunch of gravel signaled a vehicle coming up the driveway—fast. Aiden's Bronco slid to a stop, and he jumped out.

"What happened?" he shouted. "Where are Carla and Wendy?"

Harriet turned to meet him as he leaped the porch steps two at a time.

"Wendy and Carla are in the house," she said. "They're fine."

He stopped. "So, why did Angela hear on the police scanner there was a ten-forty-five-C at my address?"

"Who is Angela, and what's a ten-forty-five-C?" Harriet asked.

"Angela works in my office. She heard the police scanner calling for an ambulance pick-up for a person in serious condition." He raked the fingers of his left hand through his silky black hair.

Harriet put her hand on his back and gently patted.

"Let's go inside," she said.

"Let's stop treating me like a child and tell me what happened."

"Okay. We were having a Loose Threads meeting in your upstairs parlor, and we looked out the window, saw something under a bush, investigated and discovered an unconscious woman."

"An unconscious woman?" he demanded. "What woman?"

"Can we please go inside? It's cold out here."

He brushed past her and wrenched the door open. She followed, and as soon as she was through the door, he whirled to face her.

"What woman?" he demanded.

"She claims she's the sister of a friend of yours from Africa—Nabirye Obote."

"She was conscious when you found her?"

"No, she wasn't conscious today. She said that when she first came to town."

"So, you know her? Did she come here to see *you*?" His voice was getting louder as he paced across the kitchen.

"Can we sit down a minute?" Harriet went to the breakfast nook and sat at the table.

"Harriet, what's going on here?"

She sighed. Her decision to spare him the additional stress while he was in Ephrata didn't look like such a good one now.

"This woman came to town looking for you—" she began.

"What woman? Why was she looking for me?"

"I'm trying to tell you." She put her hands on her knees and took a deep breath, willing herself to relax. "This woman, Neelie, came into Pins and Needles. At first, she just said she was looking for you. We—Aunt Beth and I—told her you weren't here. She asked us about a hotel and left."

"Is she the one who grabbed your phone?" Aiden asked, his voice still too loud.

"The Threads are upstairs," Harriet pleaded.

"I don't care," he said, louder than before. "It's my house. Or, at least, I thought it was."

She knew it was his lack of sleep talking, but it still hurt.

"The next day," she continued, "she showed up here. She claimed the baby she had with her was her sister's and that her sister had asked her to bring the baby to you."

"Why would her sister send her baby to me?" he interrupted.

"Aiden, I don't know why any of this happened. I didn't tell you this because I thought you already had so much to deal with, and you couldn't do anything about it until you were back anyway."

"So, she came to my house with the baby…" He made a rolling motion with his hand.

"She said she didn't have any money for a hotel, so we assumed she didn't have money for formula or milk, either." Harriet paused. "Then she had some sort of episode. She's a diabetic, but she wouldn't admit it. She got sort of faint. I gave her orange juice, and she perked up. Anyway, we didn't know what to do—"

"I told her she could stay here," Carla said. Neither one had seen her come down the servant's stairs. Kissa was perched on her hip. "She was starving the baby."

She set the empty bottle in her hand on the counter. Kissa started fussing, and Carla jiggled her gently. As she turned to take a seat, Aiden got his first look at Kissa's face and her pale-blue eyes.

His reaction was palpable. His face froze then turned an angry red.

"You thought this was *my* baby?" he hissed.

"We didn't know," Harriet said in a quiet voice.

"What? You thought I got a woman in Africa pregnant and then just left?"

"We assumed you didn't know about it."

"But you *assumed* I could have."

"Aiden, we didn't know what to think. This woman showed up, said her sister died and that she'd brought you a baby at her sister's request. What were we supposed to think?"

"You let some strange woman and her baby into my house without even asking me?" he shouted as he stormed across the kitchen, stopping inches from her.

Aunt Beth and Mavis came down the servant's stairs.

"You lower your voice, young man," Aunt Beth commanded.

"And back off," Mavis added.

Aiden strode to the back door, running an angry hand through his hair.

"I've got to check on my patients," he said in a low voice. "And I want everyone out of here before I get back." He slammed the door as he went out.

The women stared after him, and then all started to speak at once.

"He's tired and stressed," Aunt Beth said.

"And I'm sure he'll see the sense of what we did when he's had time to think about it," Mavis agreed.

Harriet put a hand on each of their arms and nodded toward Carla. Tears were running down the young woman's face.

"What am I going to do?" she blubbered.

"Oh, honey, he didn't mean you," Mavis soothed.

"He's exhausted and angry, so he's lashing out at Mavis and I and Harriet," Beth said. "I'm sure he wasn't talking about you."

"He's *so* angry," Carla said, her tears slowing.

"He needs you to take care of Randy. And to cook and shop for him," Harriet reminded her. "I'm sure he didn't mean you. He was talking about the rest of the Loose Threads. It's me he's mad at. I could have warned him, and I didn't, and I told you not to. I'll make sure he understands that."

Aunt Beth handed Carla a tissue. Mavis held her arms out.

"Give me that baby. I'll take her up to the nursery and sit with her while you pull yourself together."

Carla handed the now-sleeping baby to her, and Mavis climbed back up the servant's stairs.

"Connie is up in the parlor with Wendy," Lauren said as she came in from the dining room. "I told Sarah and Jenny the meeting was over, and they should leave."

Robin followed her. "I'm going to go over to the hospital and see what I can find out about Neelie."

"Good idea," Harriet said. "Let us know if you hear anything that could help explain all this."

Robin left the way she'd come, and Harriet watched her and Sarah and Jenny get into their cars and pull out of the driveway.

Connie came down the back stairs with Wendy.

"Mavis and I were talking upstairs. We were thinking it might be a good idea if Carla and the two babies come to my house for lunch and dinner and maybe even stay the night. Just to give Aiden time to cool down and come to his senses. I have a crib and high chair, and we can bring the portable crib from here."

"That's not a bad idea," Beth said. "What do you think?" she asked Harriet.

"I agree. A little peace and quiet might do him some good. But what do I know? I thought keeping him in the dark about Neelie was a good idea."

"Is that self-pity I hear?" Aunt Beth chided. "The boy is overwhelmed. Let's give him some space, let him get some rest and then see where we are."

"I'll go up and pack," Carla said in a small voice and stood up.

Aunt Beth put her arm around the young woman's thin shoulders.

"Don't worry, we'll get this sorted out. You're going to be fine. Aiden isn't going to put you out on the street. He was just taken by surprise with Neelie being here and all."

"I'll go feed Randy," Harriet said, and went out the back door without waiting for agreement from anyone. She felt like she might vomit and didn't want to do it in front of her friends.

She stopped as soon as she was out of sight of the kitchen, leaning against the back corner of the garage. She took a deep breath, trying to regain control. She'd never had a man, or anyone else, for that matter, display such naked emotion in front of her, and it had shaken her to her core. And it had never occurred to her she might cause Carla to lose her job.

Chapter 14

H arriet spent more time than she needed to feeding and playing with Randy. She wanted to give Mavis, Connie, Carla and the two babies time to load up and leave. When she returned to the kitchen, only Aunt Beth remained.

"I figured you were waiting until everyone left," Aunt Beth said. She was loading Aiden's dishwasher with cups from the aborted meeting. "What do you say we swing by Pins and Needles and see if we can schedule a room for Monday afternoon? We can pick up some children's fabric and make a couple of baby quilts for Joseph, since we can't work on our dog blocks yet."

"I suppose," Harriet said.

"Would it help if we went by Tico's on the way home for some lunch?"

Harriet forced a smile. "We could try it and find out."

✂- - - ✂- - - ✂

They chose several pre-printed panels each, large pieces of fabric anywhere from three-quarters to a full yard with an over-all image printed on it. For larger panels, a quilter could simply choose a backing fabric, layer the batting in and start the quilting process. The panels could also be made to look more original by adding a border of simple pieced blocks. Harriet and Beth each had large enough collections of fabric in their at-home stashes they didn't need to purchase more for the pieced blocks.

"That's bizarre," Marjory Swain said from her perch by the cash register when Aunt Beth finished telling her about the events at Aiden's house that morning. Harriet had gone to the back of the store where Marjory kept the larger spools of thread used on long-arm quilt machines. She didn't really need more thread, but she also didn't want to relive the ordeal through the telling. She brought her spools of thread to the counter as her aunt finished the tale.

"Don't you worry," Marjory said with a glance at Harriet. "It will sort itself out. These things always do."

Harriet tried to smile.

"Come on," Aunt Beth said. "You'll feel better after you eat."

✂- - - ✂- - - ✂

The two women rode in silence for the few blocks it took to arrive at Tico's Tacos.

"Hey, chiquitas," Jorge greeted them as they came through the door. "Are you dining in or taking out today?"

His warm smile touched Harriet.

"We'll be staying," Aunt Beth answered.

Harriet was in front, but she was pretty sure Aunt Beth was raising her eyebrows or nodding her head or in some other way communicating silently to Jorge.

"Right this way," he said, and led them into the large private dining room. No one was at either of the two large picnic-style tables that sat in the center of the room.

He left briefly, then returned with a basket of chips and a large stoneware bowl that contained three avocados, a tomato, a small cup of salsa and a lime. He emptied the bowl's contents onto the table and pulled a paring knife from the pocket of his apron.

"So, what's the trouble, chiquita?" he asked Harriet as he began to peel the avocados.

"There's no trouble."

"I keep telling you—you are no good at lies. You know you'll feel better after you tell me. Besides, maybe I can help. It has been known to happen, you know."

"Okay, fine," Harriet said, and picked a chip out of the basket. "Do you want to hear about the unconscious woman we found, or would you like to go straight to Aiden's fit?"

80

"How about you start at the beginning?" Jorge suggested as he continued creating the guacamole as they watched. "I got time."

Harriet recited the events of the morning, concluding her story just as Jorge set the finished bowl of guacamole in front of her. She buried her chip in the chunky dip.

"This is fabulous," she said and closed her eyes.

"Do you really think Aiden would leave a pregnant woman in Africa?" Jorge asked.

"Well, not if he knew about it," Aunt Beth said bluntly, "but the timing is such she would have gotten pregnant just before he left."

"I don't believe it," Jorge said. "Aiden is like a son to me, and I taught him and Julio better than that."

Jorge's son Julio was an environmental lawyer in Seattle, and he and Aiden had been inseparable since kindergarten.

His eyes flashed with anger. "I don't know who that woman is or whose baby she has, but it is not Aiden's. You can put money on that."

"I should have known that," Harriet said, tears welling in her eyes.

"Now, chiquita," Jorge said, his face softening. He handed her a clean napkin from the table. "We'll get this straightened out."

"So far, we aren't getting anywhere," Aunt Beth said, and dipped a chip into the guacamole. "Every time we turn around, we find another question."

"Let me get you something to drink," Jorge said, scooping the avocado and lime peels into the empty salsa container with one large hand. "Limonada?"

They both nodded, and in a few minutes, he was back with three large glasses of freshly made lemonade.

"Now," he said, "back to our situation. That woman was in here last night, after all you quilters had come and gone. This time, she was with a different man."

"What man?" Harriet asked.

"A stranger," Jorge replied. "A black man—someone I've never seen before. If he's from around here, he doesn't eat Mexican."

"How did they seem?" Harriet asked. "Did they seem friendly?"

"Did you hear anything they were talking about?" Aunt Beth asked.

"I think they were arguing, but they didn't want anyone to hear. They were leaning toward each other—you know how people do. Their heads were close together. They stopped talking every time someone came near their table."

"What makes you think they were arguing?"

"Please, chiquita," he said in an injured tone. "Give an old man some credit. I know arguing when I see it, even if they were trying to keep it quiet."

"I wonder who he is," Aunt Beth said, and took a sip of her lemonade.

"He didn't have an accent like she did," Jorge said. "I made a point of going by the table—you know, asking how their dinners were."

"We're not convinced her accent is real," Harriet said. "Mavis heard her yelling at someone in the grocery store, and she didn't have one."

"What do you think is going on?" Jorge asked. "Did she come to town to try to scam Aiden? Surely she'd realize he'd know if he had fathered a baby."

"We didn't," Harriet pointed out. "Maybe she knew him in Africa and made some assumptions about a relationship he did or didn't have."

"We're going to have to find out what Aiden knows," Aunt Beth said. "If he knows this woman, maybe he can figure out what game she's playing. If he's never met her, it's a whole different ballgame."

"Don't look at me," Harriet said. "He's not speaking to me anytime soon."

"We need to give him some time to cool down. That and time to rest. He'll come around.

"Now," Jorge said as he stood up. "What would you ladies like to eat?"

Harriet had her favorite green enchiladas, and Aunt Beth went with a chicken tostada. They spoke only a few words while they ate.

They were nearly finished when the door opened, and Jorge ushered Robin in.

"Hi," Harriet said. "What's up?"

"I wish I were here to eat," Robin replied, looking at the remains of the guacamole. "Unfortunately, I just left the hospital. Neelie Obote died."

"How?" Aunt Beth asked.

"From what?" Harriet asked at the same time.

"Here, sit down," Beth said and patted the bench beside her. "Start at the beginning."

Jorge returned with a glass of iced tea and a small plate of raw vegetables. He set both in front of Robin. The Loose Threads were frequent-enough customers he knew their preferences.

"As you know, I went to the hospital after we all left Aiden's." She picked up a carrot stick and took a bite. "No one would tell me anything, but that was to be expected. She was in the emergency room, and at first it seemed like everyone was hustling around. The ER was pretty quiet today.

"After a while, it seemed like people weren't moving as fast. Then the doctor came out and spoke to me. He asked if I knew Neelie, and if I knew her next of kin. I explained how I knew her—or didn't know her, as it were. He's new, so he isn't one of the doctors we know. He didn't want to tell me what had happened, but he had no one else, and I think he got that I was going to wait there until someone told me something."

"And?" Harriet prompted.

"He said Neelie had been in a diabetic coma, and that she had passed away. He asked me if I knew anything about her management of her diabetes. I said no and asked him if there was something unusual about what had happened.

"He wouldn't tell me, but his silence spoke volumes. We need to call Darcy and see if she's heard anything," she concluded, referring to Darcy Lewis, a local criminalist and part-time Loose Threads member.

"I think we're better off not knowing," Harriet said. "I mean, she's a stranger, and it appears she was up to no good. It's sad that she died, and I don't know what that means regarding the baby, but all signs point to the fact she was attempting some sort of scam."

"I'll call Mavis and Carla when we're done here," Robin said. "There's probably no point in trying to call social services until Monday."

"What do you think they'll do with the baby?" Harriet asked.

"I think that will depend on whether they can figure out if she has relatives in Africa. If they can't find anyone for her, then I imagine she'll go into foster care here."

Chapter 15

By the way," Robin said when she'd finished eating the plate of vegetables and a small bowl of guacamole Jorge had provided, "I called DeAnn to see how things are going."

"I'll bet she is just over the moon," said Beth with a smile.

"I guess."

"What?" asked Harriet. "Is there a problem?"

"I'm not sure. Like I said, I called, and DeAnn said things were okay, but I could hear the little girl screaming in the background, and DeAnn sounded like she was really stressed. I didn't want to press too much, but she finally did admit that things were a little rougher than she had anticipated. The child has been screaming nonstop since she got there."

"Did she talk to Joseph?" Harriet asked. "He's her social worker, isn't he?"

"Yes, she did call. He said sometimes children who come straight from the orphanage have a little rougher transition. I guess the kids usually go into foster care for a while first."

"Do you think she wants any help?" Aunt Beth asked.

"I'm not sure she'd ask for it, but I think she's going to need some relief, especially if the little girl keeps crying."

"Maybe I'll stop by on the way home from church tomorrow," Aunt Beth said. "Just to see how it's going."

Robin sighed. "I think that would be good. I'm going to go check on Mavis and Carla and Neelie's baby tomorrow, see if anyone's contacted them about her or anything."

"Let us know what you find out," Harriet asked.

"Maybe I'll give Phyllis a jingle when I get home and see if she has any ideas," Beth said. "I'm sure Joseph is good at his job, but Phyl has been doing this a lot longer than he has. I'm sure she's seen it all."

"I guess it couldn't hurt," Robin said and stood up. "I better go—I just thought you would want to know about Neelie."

"Thanks," Harriet said. She turned to Aunt Beth. "Shall we go?"

"Yeah, we've got some dog blocks to work on."

Chapter 16

Harriet was rearranging a grouping of red-toned blocks on her design wall for what felt like the thousandth time when she heard a knock on the outside studio door. She got up to answer, but she was only halfway across the room when it opened and Aiden walked in.

"What have you gotten me into?" he demanded. He raked his fingers through his black hair.

Harriet was speechless as he paced across the room and back.

"The police came to the clinic to question me—the *police*, for crying out loud. I was with my patients, so they told me to come in tomorrow morning. They said if I didn't show up by noon, they'd come get me. What have you done?"

He strode across the room again.

"If you want to talk to me, you better take it down a notch," Harriet said in a cold voice, her stomach tensing. She turned and went into the kitchen. She was slamming the lid on the teakettle when he followed her and sat on a stool at the bar. He took a couple of deep breaths then spoke in a controlled voice.

"Harriet, could you please tell me what's going on here?"

She told him what had happened in his absence then described Neelie's death as clearly as she could. His jaw tensed, and his lower left eyelid twitched spasmodically, but he didn't say anything until she'd finished.

When Harriet had been quiet for most of a minute, he spoke, the tension still clear in the stiffness of his posture.

"So, none of this seemed the least bit odd to you?" he spat.

"Of course it seemed odd. It seemed *crazy*, and yes, we assumed it was some sort of scam. But we had to think about the baby."

"The one you just assumed must be mine," he said. "Because it had blue eyes. Do you have any idea how many black children are born each year with blue eyes? Blue eyes are the result of a genetic mutation that took place ten thousand years ago. Every blue-eyed person relates back to that common ancestor. They crop up everywhere, in every country and every race."

"Thanks for the biology lesson, but that isn't why she was living at your house. She told us the baby was her sister's child. That her sister had died, but before she did, she asked Neelie to bring your child to you."

"And you didn't question it?"

"We tried, but it was her sister's dying request."

"You should have known I wouldn't get a woman pregnant and then just leave."

"I *didn't* think you would do that. Lauren has been trying to find out about Neelie's sister, but, Aiden, in the meantime, there was a baby involved. Carla said she wasn't being fed properly."

"So, now you're going to blame Carla for this?"

"Unlike you, I'm not blaming anyone for anything. I'm trying to find out who these people are, and I want to find out the truth, whatever that is."

He stood up and began to pace again.

"Could you stop the pacing, please?" The kettle whistled, and she poured water over a teabag in her mug. "Would you like some tea or coffee?"

"Coffee," he said and sat down.

Harriet got out her single-cup coffee filter unit and set it on the mug Aiden usually used at her house, then scooped ground coffee into the filter section and poured boiling water over the grounds.

"You do realize you've never really told me about your time in Africa. I mean, you've mentioned your research and being in multiple villages, but for all I know, you could have been married and divorced three times while you were there."

"Oh, please," he said as he accepted the cup she handed him.

"Think about it. You know everything about my dead husband—his lies, his disease, his death. And you certainly know about my parents. Anyone who uses the internet could know about my parents, but I told you how they warehoused me in boarding schools—all of it, the good, the bad, the ugly.

"Yet all I know about you is what happened to your mother, and the immediate aftermath of her death, and that's only because I lived through it. I have no idea if you went to Africa because your girlfriend since high school broke your heart, or if you were a serial dater."

"Thanks for the vote of confidence."

Harriet reached across the bar and put her hand on his arm.

"I know in my heart you're a good person. You wouldn't knowingly leave a pregnant woman without support."

"That's big of you."

"There is still a lot of room for a baby scenario. You could have agreed with your pregnant-by-someone-else friend to take responsibility for her child if something happened to her, never imagining it would happen this soon."

Aiden's shoulders sagged.

"Didn't think of that, did you?" she said with a self-satisfied smirk.

He sat in silence, sipping his coffee.

"Carla and I figured, with the help of Aunt Beth and the Threads, that the baby was safer where we could keep an eye on her and Neelie, at least until we could figure out what was going on. We were also hoping you'd get back and shed some light on the situation. We had no way of knowing Neelie would die while she was staying at your house."

Aiden wasn't ready to concede he'd overreacted, but Harriet could see that his anger was receding. She took the top off her ceramic cookie jar, pulled out three home-baked chocolate chip cookies and put them on a plate. Aunt Beth nagged her about her weight, but Mavis and Connie restocked her cookie jar on the sly, always with admonishments to not abuse their gift.

89

"Thanks," he said when she set the plate in front of him.

"Let's go back to the start." Harriet watched his face for a return of his earlier anger. "Do you know a woman named Nabirye Obote?"

He paused so long before answering she was afraid he wasn't going to, but finally he did.

"Yes, I know a woman named Nabirye Obote. She worked for a national initiative for clean water in Uganda. We crossed paths because I was trying to get the villagers to take better care of their animals, and she was trying to get them to keep their water sources clean. We were organizing the same groups of people, so we decided to work together."

"Was she pregnant that you know of?"

"No!" he all but shouted. "No," he repeated more quietly. "She was pretty clear about the need to improve things in Uganda and appalled by the infant mortality rate. In Uganda, eighty-five of every one thousand children die before their first birthday, and the average life-expectancy at birth is only fifty-two years.

"Besides, she had been educated in England. I always got the sense she was paying some kind of debt to her home country. She was planning to return to Oxford to pursue graduate studies so she could affect things at a higher level."

"Did you know Neelie Obote?"

"No, I didn't know she had a sister." He took another sip of his coffee. "You're not getting the right picture here. Nabirye and I worked closely together on our joint sanitation project. We talked a lot when we were working on our presentation, but that was because she spoke English, as well as all three of the major Ugandan languages. I mainly speak Lugandan, which is spoken in the south, but in the north I needed help translating, and Nabirye was there.

"She is very intense about her country and her cause. When we spoke, it was always about water, animals or how to help her people. She could have twelve sisters and that many husbands, too. What we did together was a small part of my work. Most of the time, I wasn't even in her home village."

"So why on earth would she leave her baby to you?"

Aiden ran his hands through his hair and then stared at them in his lap.

"I don't know how many ways I can say this. Nabirye certainly didn't have *my* baby, and I seriously doubt she had anyone else's baby, either."

"Then why did Neelie say she did? And more important, where did she get the baby?"

"Maybe it's hers."

"Carla doesn't think she takes care of Kissa the way a mother should or would."

"There are lots of bad mothers in this world."

"I suppose," Harriet said.

They sipped their drinks in silence.

"We should be able to prove Nabirye isn't dead easily enough," Aiden said.

"That's what Lauren and I were thinking. She couldn't find any death reports for her or birth reports for the baby. But she did come up with an online video clip that shows Nabirye talking about clean water. It looks like it was taken pretty recently. It's on my computer right now if you want to look."

He followed her into her studio. She turned on her computer and pulled up the clip. As soon as it started, he pointed at the screen.

"That's her," he said. "See, she's alive and not pregnant."

"I'm guessing that if it were simple to call her, you would have already suggested that option."

Aiden put his hands on her shoulders and turned her to face him.

"You're kidding, right?"

"Right," she said, even though she'd been serious.

"The villages I worked in didn't have consistent electricity, much less telephones or cell towers. Of course, they have those things in the capitol city, but she's not there very often. I can call and leave a message for her at the water project headquarters, but it's anyone's guess when she'll get it. It could be weeks, maybe longer."

"Hopefully, we'll have this figured out long before that, but just to cover all our bases, maybe you should go ahead and make that call."

Aiden looked at the black plastic-encased sports watch on his wrist.

"I've got to give another round of antibiotics to my worst cases at midnight, so I'm going to see if I can grab a couple of hours sleep before I have to go back. If you think of anything else that could help me with the inquisition in the morning, give a call."

Harriet was relieved to see a brief flash of his normal humor.

"I know I have no right to ask," she said, "but could you please call Carla? She's terrified of losing her job."

"Why on earth does she think that?"

"I have no idea," Harriet said with as straight a face as she could manage. "You can find her at Connie's," she said when she could speak without smiling.

✂- - -✂- - -✂

She walked him to the door then went back into the kitchen, where Fred immediately began weaving figure-eights around her ankles. She went to the refrigerator and took out his can of cat food, scooping a generous tablespoon into his dish.

"Things are looking up," she told him. "Aiden may not have forgiven us just yet, but he's starting to thaw."

Fred made satisfied smacking noises as he ate. If he had an opinion as to Aiden's state of mind, he kept it to himself.

Chapter 17

Harriet drove her aunt to the ten o'clock church service the following morning and then on to DeAnn's house when church let out. Aunt Beth had called DeAnn the night before and left a message with her husband David about their intention to visit. He encouraged them and confided to Beth that any ideas she might have about calming the baby would be greatly appreciated no matter what DeAnn might say.

Harriet noted Mavis's powder-blue Lincoln Town Car in the driveway as she pulled in to the curb in front of DeAnn's brown two-story bungalow. DeAnn met them at the door, her index finger against her lips in the universal sign for quiet.

"Mavis finally got her to sleep," she whispered. She was clutching a damp baby blanket.

They quietly followed her into the the living room, where Mavis held the sleeping child. She nodded as they continued through the dining room and kitchen into the breakfast room.

"Would you like some tea or coffee?" DeAnn asked.

"You sit down and rest a minute," Aunt Beth said. She poured herself a cup of coffee from the pot on the counter then filled the teakettle that sat on the stove and turned the flame on. With easy familiarity, she got a mug and put a teabag in it.

"So," Harriet said. "How's it going?" She could guess how it was going from the dark smudges that shadowed her friend's eyes.

DeAnn laughed. "I think it's going about as bad as it can go. Iloai has cried pretty much nonstop. Mavis is the first one who's been able to get her calm enough to fall asleep."

"I'm sorry," Harriet offered.

"It's okay," DeAnn said. "We were prepared in our adoption class for this possibility."

"Still, it can't be easy," Aunt Beth said "You want some coffee?"

DeAnn nodded, and directed her to a green mug with the Foggy Point Video logo on its side. Beth filled it and handed it to her.

"Somehow, when they described crying, tantrums and difficulty sleeping in our class they sounded so manageable." She took a sip of her coffee. "Iloai has done all of that and then some."

"You'd think she'd be loving life here after being raised in an orphanage," Harriet said.

"If she's never known anything else, this sort of change could be unnerving, though," Aunt Beth said. "Think about it. She's used to being surrounded by a lot of children, and she probably hasn't had much adult attention. She might be having sensory overload."

"Is that her blanket?" Harriet asked. DeAnn was still holding the tattered beige quilt.

"Yes." DeAnn laid the small quilt on the kitchen table and spread it out. "She's been chewing on the corner here," she said, and pointed to a damp section. "I was going to try to stabilize the edge there, where it's coming apart, while she's asleep."

Aunt Beth held out her hand, and DeAnn handed her the quilt.

"Huh," Aunt Beth mumbled as she examined it.

"What?" Harriet and DeAnn asked in unison.

She turned the small quilt around.

"Look at the embroidered images," she said. "See how the color of the thread is starting to fade there at the top?" She pointed to the upper left corner. "Then look at this one."

DeAnn and Harriet leaned closer to examine the spot she was pointing at.

"The thread does look darker in the middle of the quilt." Harriet ran her hand over the surface, pausing to carefully feel the area where each of the embroidered squares joined. "It almost looks like the embroidered pieces were added after the quilt was finished. See how the bottom half of the quilt has plain fabric with no embellishment? I think the stitched blocks were made and added on to the quilt over a period of time."

"Someone may have donated a UFO," Aunt Beth suggested, using the acronym most quilters used for their unfinished quilts or "objects." "The volunteers probably took the top the way it was and put it with a backing. Feels like they used fabric inside in place of batting," she added.

"That makes sense," Harriet said. "They probably don't have much use for warm quilts in Africa." She looked at the embroidered designs again. "The imagery is interesting. Look." She pointed at the block in the upper right corner. "It looks like a woman holding a baby in her arms."

"These lines look like waves," Aunt Beth said, rubbing her forefinger over several parallel rows of blue stitching.

"Lots of different charities donate quilts to orphanages," Harriet mused. "They could have come from anywhere in the world."

"I suppose," Aunt Beth said.

"Not to change the subject," DeAnn said, "but I heard Aiden had a meltdown at the Threads meeting yesterday."

"That's putting it mildly," Aunt Beth told her, mouth twitching into a smile.

"We had round two last night," Harriet admitted.

"Was he any calmer?" Aunt Beth asked.

"By the time he left, he was better, but only a little. The police had come to the clinic to ask him about Neelie."

"Why are they questioning *him*?" DeAnn asked. "He wasn't even here."

"I don't know. He put them off until later today. I'm guessing it has to do with her staying at his house and being found on his property."

DeAnn picked up her napkin and twisted it like a rope.

"Carla's going to freak out when they question her. Since she's the one who let Neelie stay there, they definitely *will* question her."

"Yeah, but we didn't stop her," Harriet said. She started to run her fingers through her hair then stopped herself when she recognized Aiden's habit.

"She's down for the count," Mavis announced as she came into the kitchen. The teakettle whistled and she took a mug from a black iron rack on the counter and put a tea bag in it.

"Could you pour mine, too?" Harriet asked.

"I know the agency told you to put her in a crib," Mavis continued when she'd poured the tea. "but I couldn't hoist her over the rails, so I put her on the bed."

"Frankly, if she stays asleep, I don't care," DeAnn admitted. "Joseph suggested the crib, since that's what they had at the orphanage. I guess they don't move to beds until they literally can't fit in the crib."

"She's worn out," Mavis said. "Poor little thing."

"Speaking of worn out," Aunt Beth said, "we'll get out of your hair so you can get some rest, too."

"I'm going to go back up and sit in that big rocker you have in Iloai's room," Mavis said. "I brought my dog appliqué with me, and there's light enough in her room I can work on it while she sleeps. That way you can get a real nap."

"Speaking of the dog blocks, we better go call everyone and figure out when we can meet. We need to see where we are," Aunt Beth said when they'd talked through their block options one more time without coming to any new conclusions.

"Let us know if we can do anything," Harriet added and stood up. She gathered the used cups from the table and took them to the sink.

"She's going to have a tough few weeks ahead," Aunt Beth said when they were back in Harriet's car.

"I hope it's only a few weeks," Harriet said. "Do you have time to preview my dog block before you go home?"

"Oh, honey, I always have time for you."

"Nothing else going on, huh?"

Beth laughed.

Chapter 18

They continued the discussion about dog quilt possibilities as Harriet drove into her neighborhood. A maroon sedan was sitting at the top of her drive, adjacent to the front door. Harriet parked her car, and as she and Aunt Beth got out, two people, a man and a woman, left the sedan and walked toward them.

The woman opened a leather badge case, displaying both a gold shield and an identification card.

"I'm Detective Morse, and this is Detective Sanders. Are you Harriet Truman?" Detective Morse looked like she was in her mid-to-late forties. She wore navy blue slacks with a blue print cowl-necked blouse. She had pulled on a matching navy blazer as she approached. Detective Sanders wore gray slacks with a white shirt and maroon tie. His sleeves were rolled up to just below his elbows.

"I'm Harriet, and this is my aunt, Beth Carlson. What's this about?"

"We'd like to ask you some questions, if you have a few minutes. Could we go inside?"

Harriet looked at her aunt. Beth nodded, and Harriet led the pair to the studio entrance.

"What's this about?" she asked.

The two detectives looked at each other.

"Did you know a woman named Neelie Obote?" Morse asked.

"I'm not sure I'd say I *knew* Neelie Obote. I spoke to her, and I visited the house she was staying at a few times."

"And why was that?" Sanders asked. "Can we sit down?" He gestured toward the two wingback chairs in the receiving area for her quilting clients.

"Is there somewhere private *we* could go?" Detective Morse asked Aunt Beth.

Harriet looked helplessly at Aunt Beth. She wasn't anxious for them to be separated, but that was clearly the intent.

"It's okay, honey," Aunt Beth said. "We haven't done anything wrong." She led the detective to Harriet's kitchen.

"Now," Sanders said when he was seated. "Why was it you were at the house where Miss Obote was staying?"

"My...friend," Harriet said, stumbling over the word *boyfriend*, "Aiden Jalbert lives there. It's his house. And my friend Carla lives there, too."

"So, this is some sort of boarding house?" the detective asked. "Or commune?"

"No!" she said a little too loud. "No. Nothing like that. Aiden inherited a very large home, and he hired Carla to be his house-keeper. Neelie came looking for Aiden—he was a friend of her sister when he was in Africa. She didn't have a place to stay, and didn't know anyone else in Foggy Point, so Carla let her stay until Aiden came home." She purposely avoided mentioning Kissa.

"And where was Mr. Jalbert?"

"It's Dr. Jalbert. He's a veterinarian. He had to go to eastern Washington to work on an animal hoarding case. He was gone for a few days."

"Did Miss Obote say why she was looking for Dr. Jalbert?"

"She said her sister had just passed away and had asked her to bring something back to America for Aiden."

"Do you know what that something is?"

"Yes." Harriet gulped.

"You could save us both a lot of time by just telling me what Neelie brought from Africa. You're a horrible liar, and I will find out in the end, and then you'll be on my short list of suspects."

"A baby," Harriet said with a sigh. "She brought a baby. She claimed it's Aiden's—Dr. Jalbert's. But it's not."

"And you know this how?"

"He told me," she blurted before she could stop herself, realizing too late she'd just put Aiden on the suspect list.

"So, he came back from eastern Washington, and Miss Obote confronted him with a baby?"

"No," she said and paused to craft her next answer.

The detective let the silence grow.

"To my knowledge, Dr. Jalbert did not meet Neelie. He came back to Foggy Point, but he brought a lot of sick and injured dogs with him, and he's been taking care of them night and day since then."

"Does Dr. Jalbert have the baby now?"

"No, as I said, to my knowledge, he never met Neelie."

"Did he tell you that?" Detective Sanders was holding a small notebook in one hand and a mechanical pencil in the other, but he wasn't writing anything.

"Yes, he told me he'd never met her, and I believe him."

"When you spoke to Miss Obote, what did you talk about?"

"She asked several of us if we knew Aiden. She grabbed my phone from me when she overheard me talking to him. Another time, she looked ill, so I asked her if she was diabetic, and she didn't answer, but she did drink the juice I gave her, and it did seem to perk her up. Stop me if you already know any of this."

"Whoa, slow down. Back up to the part where Dr. Jalbert talked to Miss Obote on your cell phone."

"He didn't talk to her. She grabbed my phone and babbled into it, but in the process, she dropped it and it was broken."

"So, you two struggled over possession of your phone?"

"I wouldn't call it a struggle. I was talking on my phone, and someone grabbed it from me from behind. Of course I made a grab to get it back. It fell and broke."

"So, you were angry at Miss Obote?" Sanders persisted.

"No, I wasn't angry. I was confused. I didn't know why this virtual stranger would grab and break my phone."

"Let's go back to Miss Obote's diabetes. You say you talked to her about it?"

99

"I asked her if she was diabetic. She seemed a little shaky when she came to Dr. Jalbert's house. I asked her, and she didn't answer, so I got her a glass of orange juice and she drank it."

"Then you concluded Miss Obote was diabetic."

"You could say that. She drank the juice, and after a little while she seemed better, so, yes, I concluded she was a diabetic."

Detective Sanders continued in this manner for another thirty minutes, asking a few new questions but always circling back to whether Aiden knew Neelie and knew about baby Kissa. He finally seemed satisfied and suggested they join his partner and Aunt Beth in the kitchen.

Harriet led the way, and when they entered the kitchen, Aunt Beth and Detective Morse were drinking tea and laughing like old friends.

"Oh, honey, I was just telling Jane here about that nine-patch quilt you made. The one with the panel pieces you cut apart. Is that somewhere handy?"

"Sure," she said. "It's upstairs. Shall I go get it?" she asked and looked at Detective Morse.

"If it isn't too much trouble, I'd love to see it."

Detective Sanders rolled his eyes at the ceiling but didn't say anything.

Harriet went upstairs and came back with a green quilt draped over her arm. She unfolded the large wall hanging and held it up. She had taken a fabric panel with a variety of wildlife images printed on it and cut it apart, rearranging the images and then surrounding them with nine-patch blocks in coordinating and contrasting colors.

"You're right," Detective Morse said, "that would be the perfect thing to do with my fairy panel. Thanks for showing it to me," she added.

Harriet wondered if this was some quilting variation of good cop/bad cop. It was clear which one she'd just met.

"We generally meet on Tuesdays," Aunt Beth said. "Think about coming if you get a chance."

Chapter 19

You invited her to the Loose Threads meeting?" Harriet asked when the detectives were back in their sedan and preparing to leave. "What were you thinking?"

"I was thinking here is a lady who likes to quilt and doesn't belong to a group. Besides, it can't hurt to have a detective where we can keep an eye on her."

"It could backfire big time."

"She seems like a good person."

"Yeah, well, he seemed like a total jerk bent on connecting Aiden to Neelie and her death."

"Honey, you know he's just doing his job. Someone has to ask the hard questions, and you know better than anyone they have to question everyone."

"So, what did she ask you?"

"Probably the same thing he asked you. She wanted to know if I knew anything about Neelie, and if I knew anything about her health. Of course I told her no."

"You didn't mention our suspicions about her being diabetic?"

Aunt Beth picked up the detective's used cup and carried it to the sink.

"I didn't mention it because it was your theory, based on your observations. Besides, I didn't want to give them anything to work with."

"Well, that ship has sailed," Harriet said. "I spilled all about Neelie appearing diabetic, and I tried not to tell him about the baby, but I wasn't prepared to lie about it, and he pushed."

Aunt Beth was silent for a moment. "I better warn Connie," she said and picked up the kitchen phone. She spoke quietly for a few minutes then hung up. "We're going to keep the baby moving while the detectives are doing their interviews. She's too little to speak, and we don't want them thinking about calling Children's Services."

"We should at least try to find out whose baby she is," Harriet pointed out. "I need to call Aiden. He needs to know what to expect from the detectives."

She made the phone call, apologizing for waking him up, and gave him the short version of her interview. He reported he'd put in a call to Africa but reiterated he didn't expect a reply anytime soon.

"Aiden's calming down," Harriet reported to her aunt. "Having the rest of the clinic help with the rescue dogs is reducing his stress level. I can hear it in his voice."

"Speaking of stressful things, what are we going to do about our auction quilts?" Aunt Beth asked.

"To tell the truth, I haven't given a thought to any of the quilts but my own, and I've barely thought about it."

"Have you had any breakthroughs with yours?"

"It's showing promise, I think my idea is going to work, but I need to find the right fabric combos. I think with tumbling blocks, the texture needs to match. Of course you have to have three intensities of color, but I think the prints need to be the same scale or feel or something. That's the part I'm struggling with right now."

"I'm afraid to say what I'm doing out loud, for fear it'll show up on the Small Stitches design wall before I even show it to anyone."

"Do you really think they're stealing our ideas?"

Aunt Beth looked over the top of her reading glasses.

"Of course they're copying our work. I talked to Glynnis at church. She didn't admit it, but she said Frieda was determined the raffle quilt was going to come from the Small Stitches this year."

She went to her canvas bag and pulled out a quilt block. She held it up for Harriet's approval.

"Very clever," Harriet said.

Before she could continue, Beth cut her off.

"Don't say its name," she cautioned. "Your studio may be bugged."

Harriet laughed. "I know we ate lunch at Tico's yesterday, but do you feel like going back today?"

"You know I'm always up for a meal there, but what are you up to?"

"I was thinking about what Jorge told us yesterday. He said Neelie was talking to a black man he didn't recognize. We don't get that many new people in Foggy Point, especially this time of year. Don't you think it's a bit of a coincidence that he showed up at the same time Neelie did? I'm wondering if they're partners in the baby scam. Maybe it's his baby. I want to ask Jorge a few more questions."

"When this business is settled, and we finish our raffle quilts, we're going to take a week and just eat salad and fruit."

"Really?" Harriet asked.

"Bet on it."

Chapter 20

"Two days in a row," marveled Jorge. "Don't get me wrong, I'm always happy to see you two, but this is not like Señora Beth."

"She's making us eat salad all next week to make up for it," Harriet said with smile. She ducked to avoid Aunt Beth's purse, which had been swung with mock fury.

"Come in," Jorge said and put his arm around Harriet's shoulders. "You want a table or a booth?"

"A booth is fine," she said and followed him as he led them to an unoccupied booth then went to the kitchen to fix their guacamole. He returned a few minutes later with the creamy green dip and a basket of warm tortilla chips.

"Do you remember the man you told us about, the one who was talking to Neelie? Have you seen him since?"

"Oh, sure." He turned his head slightly to the right. "As a matter of fact, he's here now."

Harriet looked. She spotted the man, sitting by himself in the last booth in the row on the opposite side of the seating area.

"He's been sitting there for a couple of hours, drinking coffee and calling people on his phone. Judging by the look on his face, things aren't going well."

"I'll be right back," Harriet said, and was up and out before Aunt Beth could protest.

She walked to the booth at the back where the man sat, cell phone pressed firmly to his ear. A dark-brown leather jacket covered the opposite seat. She waited at the end of the table until he realized she was there and abruptly punched the end button on his phone and laid it on the table. She waited, and when he didn't say anything, she did.

"May I speak to you for a moment?" she asked.

"It's a free country," he mumbled.

Harriet looked pointedly at the jacket-covered banquette. The man sighed, straightened in his seat then used his foot to pull his jacket from the bench and into his hands. She slid into the seat.

"Did you know Neelie Obote?" she asked without preamble.

The man's jaw tightened. "What's it to you?"

"I know you spoke to her a few days ago, so don't even go there. The police questioned me earlier about her death. "

The man lowered his head into his hands and began to weep.

"She was my wife," he said without looking up.

"What?" Harriet said it a little too loudly, and before she could stop herself.

"We hadn't been together lately, mind you, but she was my wife," he repeated, and raised his head, looking like he'd aged ten years since she'd sat down.

"Maybe you better start at the beginning. Who are you, what was Neelie doing here and why did you follow her?"

The man sighed deeply, and Harriet wasn't sure he was going to answer.

"I'm Rodney. Rodney Miller." He offered his hand across the table, and she took it.

"I'm Harriet Truman," she said and waited.

He raised his eyebrows. "Like in Harry Truman?"

"Like in I have weird parents. We're distantly related to *the* Harry Truman but not in any way that matters."

"That's cold," he said.

"Yeah, tell me about it."

Rodney leaned back in his seat.

"I don't know what Neelie was doing here. We'd been having troubles, and she'd been staying with her girlfriend Jasmine in East Bay."

As a former California resident, Harriet knew the place Rodney referred to was in San Francisco, and the east side could mean Oakland, Berkeley or one of several other communities.

"She's kind of a free spirit, you know what I'm saying? She was young to be married, and I'm older than her, but I thought if we were married, I could settle her down some. I was talking to her every day on her cell, trying to get her to come home so we could work on things.

"Then she just up and disappeared. She was gone for a month or better, took all my cash, too. Then she calls Jasmine and says she's in Foggy Point, Washington, and she needs money. Jasmine called me, and here I am."

"What about the baby?" Harriet asked.

"What about it?" Rodney said, a sly note creeping into his voice.

"Whose baby is it?"

"What business is it of yours?" he asked and leaned back. Clearly, he sensed he was in the driver's seat.

Harriet sighed deeply. She'd met people like him in boarding school. Not physically like him, of course, but with the same "what's in it for me" attitude.

"How much?" she asked.

"I'm offended," he said in a mocking tone.

"How much is it going to cost me to cut to the chase?" She gave him a hard look she hoped conveyed that this was a one-time offer.

"A hundred," he said and waited to see how his opening bid had been received.

"We're done," Harriet said and started to rise.

"Look, I'm stuck here. I was going to get my money back from Neelie, and now she's gone. What am I supposed to do?"

"Fifty dollars, take it or leave it."

"Lessee it," he said in an injured tone.

Harriet pulled three bills from her wallet but held them in her hand.

"She brought a baby here and said her sister in Uganda asked her to bring her daughter here to the baby's father," she said. "Who does the baby really belong to? Is it yours?"

"No, it's not mine. Neelie can't take care of herself—I wouldn't give her a baby on top of everything else. And a sister?" Rodney leaned toward her. "I never met no sister. And that's the truth."

She could tell by the look on his face that at least the last statement was true. He didn't know about the sister.

"How can I get in touch with this Jasmine?"

"I wish I knew. Jasmine's phone don't work, and no one's seen her in a while, but that's Jasmine for you. That's why I didn't like Neelie staying with her."

"So, you were just looking out for Neelie's welfare. Is that your story?"

"That's the truth," he said and snatched the bills from Harriet's hand.

"If you think of anything else, call me," she said and pulled a business card for her long-arm studio out of her pocket and handed it to him.

"You got your money's worth. You want to talk more..." He rubbed his thumb across his first two fingers in the universal sign for money.

Harriet turned without another word and returned to the booth, where Aunt Beth had nearly polished off the guacamole. Before she could say anything, Jorge brought a fresh bowl of dip and swept away the spent one.

"You're making your aunt nervous," he said and laughed, then lowered his voice, a fellow conspirator now. "Did you learn anything good?"

"He fed me a line about being Neelie's husband, and how he was looking for her to keep her out of trouble. I'm not sure I believe anything he said, except that he seemed surprised by the baby and sister. I don't think he knew about either one. That's telling, if he's really her husband."

"Or if he knew her at all," Aunt Beth added.

"Maybe he's her pimp," Jorge offered.

"He doesn't seem flashy enough," Harriet said. "Of course, my knowledge of pimps is limited to Hollywood portrayals."

They all looked at Rodney now.

"He doesn't look like husband material," Jorge countered.

"Not for a normal person, but when people are running a complicated con they often have at least one partner." Harriet said.

"That I can believe, but you'd think he'd have cleared out when she died."

"He said he wants to recover the money he claims she took from him," Harriet said. "If he's smart, he'll use the money I gave him and take the next bus out of Foggy Point."

"He's not that kind of smart," Jorge said. "You can see it in his eyes. If there's money and any chance he can get it, he's going for it."

"That's another reason we need to keep that baby out of everyone's reach until this sorts itself out," Beth said. "I don't know how, but she figures into this."

"You ladies want to try my new special tacos?" Jorge asked. "They're marinated pork with a special hot sauce. Just for you, I'll put a green salad on the side instead of beans and rice."

"Perfect," Aunt Beth said with a smile.

Jorge headed to the kitchen without waiting for Harriet's response. She sighed. Aunt Beth wasn't her mother, but she was more like a mother than her actual parent. She wondered if all mothers attempted to control their daughter's weight as openly as Aunt Beth did hers.

Harriet wasn't what anyone would call thin, but she wasn't exactly fat, either. She'd gotten heavier after Steve died, but that weight had come off since she'd returned to Foggy Point.

"Did your detective say anything about why they were investigating Neelie's death?" Aunt Beth asked, jarring her back to reality.

"No, he didn't, why? Did yours?"

"She gave me a generic line about investigating the death because Neelie wasn't from here, and therefore, they didn't know if she'd been in a doctor's care, and anytime an otherwise healthy person dies, they investigate."

"And you didn't believe her."

"I'm with you. I think that girl was diabetic. She should have had one of those testing gadgets, and she probably had needle marks or, if not that, then medication at least."

"They wouldn't be assigning two detectives for anything less than murder," Harriet said, ending the discussion.

Jorge brought their meals, and they ate in silence.

"We need to confirm that," Harriet said after a while. "Doesn't Connie's daughter-in-law work at the hospital?"

"Yes, she does, although I'm not sure how much she'll be able to tell us even if she does know. You know how they regulate everything medical these days. I'll call Connie when we're done eating, and see if the gossip wheel has been turning." Beth didn't like talking on her cell phone in public places.

"Maybe we should drive by on our way home. We could check her quilt block progress while we're there."

"I doubt she's gotten much done if she still has Carla and the babies there, but we should check on them, in any case."

They finished their taco dinners and placed generous tips under their plates to counter Jorge's ongoing unwillingness to accept money from Harriet and, by association, anyone she was dining with.

"You ladies come back again," he said from his post by the front door. "And don't forget to tell me what's going on. You never know when an old man can help."

They assured them he would be the first to know any breaking news. Jorge pulled a white paper bag from under the counter that held the cash register.

"Since you look like ladies on a mission, I took the liberty of preparing some flan to go. I put an ice pack in the sack, so it should be good until the end of your adventure." He winked at Harriet. They both knew Aunt Beth would never have agreed to dessert no matter how long they had stayed at the restaurant.

Chapter 21

Connie opened the door to her tan stucco house when she saw Harriet pull into the driveway.

"Would you two like some tea?" she asked once they were inside.

"Sure," Beth said.

"Things seem calmer than I expected," Harriet said as Connie led them through the living room and into her spacious kitchen at the back of the house.

"Baby Kissa is a little dreamboat," Connie said. "And Carla and Wendy went back to Aiden's. They went to feed the dog, and Aiden was just coming home, and they talked, and now she's back there."

"Where is Kissa?" Harriet asked.

"Rodrigo is pushing her around the neighborhood in the stroller," she said and laughed. "That would be the new stroller he went out and bought this morning. She definitely has Grandpa Rod wrapped around her little finger."

"Makes you feel sorry for DeAnn and her family, doesn't it?" Harriet said.

"Mark my words," Aunt Beth said sagely. "There's something not right about that situation."

Harriet explained the other reason they'd stopped by unannounced.

"I'll call Zoe right now and see if she knows more, but she already told me the forensic nurse had been called when the body came in."

Forensic training for nurses was a relatively new phenomenon in hospitals, having only been recognized as a specialty in the late 1990s. Their specialized job was to be sure all possible evidence was preserved when a person was brought into the hospital in a condition that suggested a crime had been committed. A major part of their caseload was battered women and children, but most of them were also ER nurses, so they used their skills whenever a suspicious case came through the doors.

Beth took over the tea preparations while Connie called her daughter-in-law.

"Uh-huh," she said, after the usual greeting and a quick run-down of what they wanted. "Of course we wouldn't tell anyone...You're sure about that?...Okay, thanks, honey." She hung up and turned to Harriet and Beth. "You have to swear you won't tell anyone else," she told them, "She said the lab results showed levels of insulin that were way too high to be accidental. And she had needle marks on the back of her shoulder."

"I thought so," Harriet said. "She *was* a diabetic."

"I'm not sure we can conclude that, honey." Aunt Beth said. "Someone could have killed her with insulin even if she wasn't a diabetic."

"Yeah, but how much more convenient if she was and took injectable insulin? How could anyone prove she didn't accidentally overdose?"

"In the back of her shoulder?" Beth asked.

"That only matters if she doesn't have other needle marks on her."

"They'll figure it out," Connie said.

Beth looked at Harriet.

"What?" Connie asked.

Harriet quickly explained the visit they'd had from the two detectives.

"They're grasping at straws," Connie said. "Don't you worry—we all hardly knew the woman. And anyone who met that

111

young woman could see she was troubled. They'll dig around in her background and find out what really happened."

"How about we talk quilt blocks for a minute," Beth suggested, ending their speculation about Neelie.

"Let me show you what Lauren and I have been working on," Connie said and headed for her sewing room. She was back a moment later with a small stack of blocks she handed to Harriet.

"These are great," Harriet said and passed them one-by-one to Aunt Beth after she'd looked at them.

The two women had made several variations of doghouse blocks. They had started with a basic schoolhouse-type traditional block and then, in some cases, put miniature pieced blocks on the building side while on others they had fussy-cut dog faces from novelty fabric and stitched them in window frames in the side of the doghouse.

"We're still working on it," Connie said. "We tried using landscape prints, so the grass was green and the sky had clouds, but they looked too busy. Lauren is working on that idea still, seeing if she can minimize the problem by making the blocks bigger."

"All of these look good," Harriet said. "Don't show them to anyone."

Beth peered over the top of her reading glasses.

"Until we figure out how the Small Stitches are stealing our ideas, we need to be careful."

"Lauren and I were talking about that," Connie said. "She thinks we should leave Sarah out of the next meeting."

"What?" Beth said.

"That's not a bad idea," Harriet said.

"We can't start accusing our own members of being a spy," Beth protested. "Especially without any evidence."

"Think about it a minute," Connie said. "The Small Stitches meet where Sarah works. They could be getting into her stitching bag when she leaves the front desk."

"If they're clever, they could create a diversion so she'd *have* to leave the front," Harriet added.

"Lauren and I were just thinking if we meet somewhere other than Pins and Needles, and leave Sarah out of the loop, we can find out if our ideas really are being stolen. We can check and see what they do next, and then we'll know. Lauren said she can make up a reason to go check the computers at the senior center when the Stitches have their next meeting."

Connie sat down and picked up the cup of tea Beth had made for her.

"Lauren and I were also talking about DeAnn's little girl," she said, cutting off any further discussion of Sarah and spying. "I told her about the quilt the baby brought with her. She wants to research it and see where it leads."

"Sounds like a good idea," Harriet said.

"Maybe you can call and tell her that, chiquita," Connie said with a hopeful look.

"Fine, I'll call her when I get home."

Talk turned to a wedding quilt Connie was making for her niece and continued until they were interrupted by the arrival of Rodrigo and the now-sleeping Kissa. He wheeled the stroller gently into the kitchen.

"She's out cold," he said in a stage whisper.

"She's the happiest little baby." Connie shook her head. "Too bad DeAnn's new little one isn't the same."

"Maybe we should send Rodrigo over to work his magic." Aunt Beth said.

"Rodrigo *is* good," Connie said, and patted her husband's arm, "but Kissa is a goodnatured, happy little one. Unfortunately, the same can't be said for DeAnn's daughter."

Rodrigo wheeled Kissa through the doorway to the living room. He looked back at the women.

"Excuse me, I have a baby to take care of." He was humming as he disappeared into the next room.

Harriet's brow furrowed, and her gaze became unfocused.

"What are you thinking?" Aunt Beth asked.

"I was wondering if DeAnn's daughter is having a language problem. She's old enough to be talking, but no one here can understand her and vice versa. Kissa doesn't have that problem because she isn't of an age to be speaking, is she?"

"Kissa should have a dozen words or so," Connie said thoughtfully. "But, you're correct—Iloai should be using simple sentences by now. Maybe she's upset because she can't communicate."

"This must be a fairly common problem in international adoptions," Harriet said. "I wonder how they handle it."

"We can check with Phyllis tomorrow," Aunt Beth suggested.

"There might be another way," Harriet said slowly.

Aunt Beth and Connie stared expectantly at her.

"Iloai is from Uganda, isn't she?"

"I think that's what they said," Beth said.

"Aiden is fluent in the main language there. Even if Iloai is from a different region, the language would probably be similar enough the sound of it might be calming to her."

"It's worth a try," Connie said. "At this point, DeAnn is probably willing to try anything."

"I'll give him a call and see if the waters are continuing to thaw," Harriet said.

"I see," said Connie. "You have ulterior motives." She smiled at Harriet.

"I hadn't thought about that," Harriet objected, but she could see neither her aunt nor Connie believed her.

Beth looked at her watch. "We better get going if you're going to talk to Lauren *and* Aiden."

"Thanks for the tea," Harriet said.

"De nada," Connie replied and ushered them out of the house.

Chapter 22

"Y ou call Aiden, and I'll call DeAnn," Aunt Beth suggested as Harriet drove up the driveway and parked. "I'm guessing Aiden will want to help, so I'll just give her a heads-up."

Harriet unlocked the door to her studio and led the way into the kitchen. Fred jumped off the bar and started weaving through her ankles. She picked up the kitchen phone and dialed Aiden's cell number. She cradled the handset between her left ear and shoulder while she opened the refrigerator and put the flan away then retrieved Fred's can of cat food.

"Hey," she said tentatively when Aiden finally answered.

"What's up?" he asked, his tone neutral.

She quickly described the problems DeAnn and her husband were having with their new daughter and asked if he'd be willing to try talking to her in Lugandan, to see if she'd respond with anything but tears.

"As it happens, this is your lucky day," he said with a hint of his previous charm. "The dogs were all stable when I left, and Dr. Johnson has the vet tech spending the night with them. I assume you've got me scheduled to appear already."

"Not yet," Harriet said and tried not to laugh. "Aunt Beth's working on it, though."

"Give me the address, and I'll meet you there in a half-hour."

"Thank you," she said, and when he didn't say anymore, she hung up.

We're on, she mouthed to her aunt, who was talking on her cell phone in the hallway that led from the kitchen to the stairs.

"Okay," Beth said into her phone. "Looks like we're good to go—we'll see you in a few minutes." She said her goodbyes to DeAnn and hung up. "They're ready to try anything, as we suspected."

"Hopefully, it will help," Harriet said. "I wonder if we should have Connie bring Kissa over to DeAnn's?"

"What for?"

"I know the two babies are different ages and stages of language, but Kissa should still react to Aiden speaking her native tongue. I was just thinking it would provide a sort of control for our test."

"We don't know *where* Kissa is from, really, do we?" Beth asked.

"All the more reason to have her there—we can kill two birds with one stone. If Kissa doesn't react at all to Aiden, it would go a long way toward proving she has nothing to do with Africa."

Aunt Beth called Connie, and she quickly agreed to bring Kissa to DeAnn's.

✂ - - - ✂ - - - ✂

Mavis opened the door when Harriet and Beth arrived at DeAnn's.

"Come on in, the party's just getting started."

She ushered them into a greatroom-style family room. Connie sat on a beige overstuffed sofa with Kissa in her lap. DeAnn's two sons were dangling toys in front of Iloai, and for the moment, it was keeping her distracted.

DeAnn entered the room, combing her wet hair with her fingers. She'd obviously just gotten out of the shower.

"Thanks for coming," she said to the group in general.

"Aiden should be here any minute," Harriet said.

"He's here," Aiden said from the door to the family room. "I knocked, but no one answered, so I let myself in."

"Please, come in," DeAnn said and ushered him to an overstuffed chair at an angle to the sofa the babies were sitting on. He avoided eye contact with Harriet.

He rattled off a string of words Harriet assumed were Lugandan—she spoke seven languages, but she'd never tackled any of the African tongues. Iloai kept batting at the toy DeAnn's son was holding in front of her, but Kissa turned and looked at Aiden.

"*Mata?*" he said and looked at Kissa.

"*Cupa,*" she babbled and reached toward him.

"Does she have a bottle?" he asked Connie.

She handed him a plastic bottle of milk, and he held it in front of first Iloai then Kissa.

"*Hina,*" said Iloai in a clear little girl voice.

"*Cupa, cupa,*" Kissa said in an increasingly frantic tone.

Aiden handed her the bottle. He looked at Iloai and pointed at his mouth.

"*Mumwa,*" he said.

Iloai looked at him and, again in her clear little voice, said, "*Ngutu.*"

Connie pulled a second bottle from Kissa's diaper bag and handed it to Iloai. The little girl took it and started drinking from it.

"I'm sure she drinks from a cup by now, but children often regress when they're stressed, especially in the presence of a smaller child."

DeAnn sat down beside Iloai and slowly eased the child onto her lap. The little girl nestled into her arm and drank from the bottle.

Aiden sat back in his chair and tented his fingers, resting his chin on them. After a few moments, he sat forward again.

"Okay," he began. "I'm no expert in linguistics, but this one…" He pointed at Kissa, who was now dozing in Connie's arms. "She seemed to understand what I was saying, to the degree you can tell what babies understand. I was saying *milk* and *bottle.*

"That one," he said, pointing to Iloai, "didn't react to the Lugandan words but countered with other words I didn't recognize. I'm not fluent in the other two languages spoken in Uganda, but I'm familiar enough with them I don't think she was speaking either of them."

"So, what does that mean?" DeAnn asked.

"It means we were sold a bill of goods," DeAnn's husband said. He had slipped into the room unnoticed.

"I wouldn't jump to conclusions based on what I say," Aiden said. He stood up. "Hi, David," he said and offered his hand. DeAnn's husband shook it.

"Thanks for coming by and trying to help. Iloai here is having a real rough time, and we're at a loss about what to do for her."

"For what it's worth—and keep in mind, this is just based on my own experience in Uganda, and Africa's a big place," Aiden said. "But I've seen a lot of Ugandan children, and Iloai doesn't look like them. She doesn't really look *African* to me."

"That's strange," Harriet said. "If she isn't from Africa, why would it matter? Why wouldn't they just say where she *was* from?"

"That's exactly what we'll be asking Joseph at Little Lamb in the morning," David said.

"He should be able to settle things quickly enough," Aunt Beth said. "Maybe they just made a mistake with her paperwork."

"Or maybe she just doesn't look typical for her region," Aiden offered. "Is there anything else I can do for you?" He looked at DeAnn and then David. They both shook their heads. "Sorry I couldn't be more help." He stood up. "I've got a dog I need to check on," he said, contradicting what he'd told Harriet earlier, and left.

Mavis got up and followed him out. She was gone for a few minutes.

"Aiden would like to speak to you outside," she told Harriet when she returned, and sat down in the chair he had vacated.

Harriet felt a mixture of anger and humiliation. This was the part of small-town life she hated. Her aunt's friends all felt like they had the right to interfere in her personal life.

Still, it wasn't going to help the two little girls for her to cause a scene by refusing to go, so she picked up her purse and left. If she were to be honest with herself, she didn't like being at odds with Aiden and really did want an opportunity to talk to him, but she'd wanted it to be his idea.

He was leaning against her car when she came through the front door and onto the porch. He was staring at the toe of his shoe

118

as if some alien life form were emerging from it. His silky black hair had fallen forward over his eyes.

"You want to go get a cup of coffee?" he asked when he finally looked up.

"Sure," she said, and followed him to his vintage Ford Bronco.

Chapter 23

H ow are the dogs doing?" she asked when they were in the car and Aiden had pulled away from the curb.

"Most of them will rebound. They all have skin lesions of one sort or another. Most of them have dental problems that are a result of poor nutrition, poor conditions and, in some cases, poor bloodlines. One of the reasons we brought them back is so we could clip and shave them under better conditions."

"Why do people do that to animals?" Harriet said.

"I don't know—it's an illness. The weird part is that the people don't look crazy to the outside world. These people in Ephrata worked outside the home, and I bet if you asked people they worked with, they wouldn't have a clue."

Harriet started to relax. It felt good to be talking to him about normal things again, not that dog hoarding could be considered normal. But it was his job, and she liked hearing him talk with such passion about it.

"The local authorities might not have found this situation if it hadn't been for an alert UPS driver. The family worked hard at keeping people away from their house. The kids were homeschooled, and they weren't allowed to have friends over.

"The mistake they made was letting the kids have computer access. One of them ordered a video game and gave the street address and—enter the UPS guy. The parents were out, and the kid answered the door. The driver took one whiff and called nine-one-one. He thought he was reporting a child welfare case, and I guess he was, but he had no idea what was inside the house and in the outbuildings around it."

"I'm so sorry, Aiden. This must be awful for you."

They rode in silence the rest of the way to the coffee shop. He'd driven them to The Steaming Cup, the same place she'd had her phone altercation with Neelie. She watched his face as he parked in the small lot, looking for any indication he'd done it on purpose, but she saw none.

She ordered a hot caramel apple cider at the counter.

"That sounds good," Aiden said. "I'll have the same thing."

A group of teenagers were sprawled on the upholstered chairs, so he led her to a table across the room. He pulled out her chair for her then sat in the one opposite.

"Nice place," he said.

Before Harriet could say anything in response, the barista delivered their steaming whipped cream-topped drinks.

"I know Mavis made you ask me to coffee, but you know as well as I do she's going to know if we don't talk," Harriet said when the silence had stretched to the breaking point.

"You want to talk?" Aiden said, and looked into her eyes. "Tell me this—was that baby Connie was holding the one that's supposed to be mine?"

Harriet stared back at him, then turned in her chair and started to stand up. He grabbed her wrist.

"I'm sorry," he said. "Stay, please."

"No, *I'm* sorry," Harriet said. "But that doesn't seem to be good enough for you, and at this point, I don't know what else to say." She pulled her wrist from his grasp but returned to her seat.

Aiden raked his hand through his hair. "I'm sorry, really. Mavis is probably right."

Harriet sat up. "Exactly what did she say?"

"Basically, she said to get over myself."

"She must have said more than that." She tried to suppress a smile. "She was out there with you for a while."

"Oh, yeah, she said a lot," he said with a rueful smile. "But she meant 'get over yourself,' and by the way, you can stop enjoying this so much."

"I should have handled things better," Harriet said in a serious tone.

"How? Some crazy lady shows up with a baby she claims is mine. As Mavis pointed out, they don't hand out babies at the local Walmart. Most rational people would assume that if someone arrives on your doorstep with a baby it probably is *their* baby, or whoever they claim it is."

"Thank you, Mavis," Harriet said.

"I said I'm sorry."

"I guess I'm glad you finally understand."

"That's the hard part," Aiden said and took a drink of his cider. "I still don't understand what's going on, if it's still going on. Why would someone show up with a baby and claim it was mine, when obviously I'd deny it and a simple DNA test would prove it."

"That's what we've been trying to figure out. If Kissa really is from Africa, it would take some time to get her and then come back here with her. Even you didn't know you were going to be out of town when she arrived, so she must have been planning on confronting you."

"But again—why?"

"Assuming she wasn't completely nuts, the next obvious motive is money. She didn't have any—that was why we let her stay at your house. We were worried about her ability to care for Kissa."

"Do you think she thought I'd feel sorry for her and give her money?"

"That would be pretty risky. You might have dismissed her out of hand. No, I think she had reason to believe you would take responsibility for Kissa. Maybe she really did think the baby was yours.

"Do you think Neelie's sister might have been conning her?" she continued. "Maybe she didn't want her baby and figured Neelie wouldn't have the money to return to Africa with her."

"If you're talking about Nabirye, I'm telling you, she didn't have that or any other baby. I'll be surprised if that woman turns out to have been her sister or any other sort of relative. I still haven't heard from her, but that's not unexpected. When she's able to call, she can confirm her part, or lack of part, in this drama."

Harriet sipped her cider, and Aiden did the same.

"I was just thinking about what Mavis said."

"That I need to get over myself?" he asked, and smiled.

"No, the part about not being able to pick up a baby at Walmart. If the baby isn't her sister's—and you say that's not likely—then where did she get Kissa?"

"Unfortunately, if you know your way around Africa, and you aren't a highly visible American pop icon, you can get a baby and the papers to go with it for a few well-placed bribes."

"That's sad."

"That's life in undeveloped countries."

"I wonder what's going to happen to the baby."

"I was going to ask you about that." He covered her hand with his. "I didn't realize Connie had been certified to do foster care." He looked at her. "She did get certified, right? Tell me you ladies didn't kidnap that child."

"I don't think it's kidnapping when someone gives you a baby."

"What, exactly, would you call it?"

"More of a failure to return." She gave him what she hoped was a winning smile. "You aren't going to turn us in, are you?"

"Are you serious?"

"Carla said the baby was undernourished, and we were afraid if we told the police about her, she would be put into a series of foster homes where they wouldn't take care of her."

Aiden laughed. "Are you listening to yourself? Carla is now the expert on baby health and the rest of you were…what? Going to keep the baby until she's eighteen? You've all have been watching a little too much TV if that's your image of our foster care system."

Harriet had the good grace to blush.

"They have a program at the clinic that pairs up dog owners with foster kids who need a dog for the canine Four-H program. All the foster care parents I've met have been selfless, caring people who either don't have children of their own at home or always have room for one more around their table."

"I didn't say it was a well-thought-out plan."

"I can't believe Robin went along with this. As a lawyer, doesn't she have an obligation as an officer of the court to report a crime in progress?"

"I think the rule about not having to incriminate yourself trumps her officer of the court status. Besides, we haven't committed a crime. We were asked to take care of Kissa, and we are. When someone asks for her, we'll hand her over."

"Isn't that what's known as a sin of omission?"

"Repeat—are you going to turn us in?"

"My only professional obligation is to protect any animals involved, so no, but I'd encourage you to let the police know you have her."

"I'll tell Aunt Beth," Harriet said, and took a long swallow of her cider, effectively ending the discussion.

"How's the raffle quilt coming?" Aiden asked, switching to a safer topic.

"You'll have to ask the Small Stitches. So far, we haven't come up with anything that's even suitable to be used as dog beds, much less the silent auction, and forget about being chosen for the raffle."

"What happened? From what I understand listening to the talk around the clinic, the Loose Threads always produce the quilt chosen to be used in the raffle."

"In the past, there were no rules as to what sort of quilts could be donated. Aunt Beth said the last few years the Threads have used Foggy Point as their theme. This year the auction committee decided that since the event is benefiting dog adoption, the quilts should reflect that topic.

"Mavis and Connie tried to argue they should be making quilts that had the greatest value to the raffle ticket-buying public, but they didn't get anywhere with that, and now we're all stuck with the dog theme."

"I'm sure you ladies will come up with something wonderful," he said with a smile. He reached across the table and took both her hands in his. "I'm glad we're done fighting," he added, and Harriet raised her left eyebrow but kept her mouth shut. "I've missed you."

"I missed you, too," she said. She knew they probably looked like two lovesick teenagers staring into each other's eyes, but for once, she didn't care.

They were interrupted when Joseph Marston passed carrying a ceramic cup of coffee, a teaspoon and three packets of raw sugar. He sat down at the next table. Neither of them had noticed him come in nor had he seemed to see them.

"Hey, Joe," Harriet said as she stood and took the two steps to his table. The dark smudges under his eyes were darker, if that was possible. He nervously tapped the spoon on the tabletop.

"Oh, hi, Harriet," he said absently. "I didn't see you. Thanks again for working on those quilts."

His eyes were red-rimmed, and it was obvious quilts were the last thing on his mind.

"Is everything okay?" she asked him. "You seem upset."

"I'm fine," he said in a loud voice, and then repeated it in a softer tone. "I'm fine. Things are just a little hectic at the agency."

Aiden had started to stand when Joseph had raised his voice, but Harriet glanced at him and gave her head a barely perceptible shake. He eased back down but continued to watch Joseph intently.

"Do you have a lot of adoptions in progress?"

"No, no more than usual. I told you, everything is fine."

"Could I ask you a question about DeAnn's child?"

"You can ask, but I probably can't answer—you know, confidentiality."

"I just wondered where the child is from."

"What do you mean, where she's from? I know DeAnn told you—she's from the orphanage in Uganda. I heard you all talking about it when I was eating my cake the other day. What difference does it make, anyway? She's here now."

Harriet was surprised by his aggressive tone. She didn't know Joseph well, but everything DeAnn had said about him had led her to believe he was meek almost to the point of ineffectiveness.

"It's just that she seems to be having trouble settling in."

"And what? You thought if she was from a different country that would explain it? The adoption process is rough on kids, no matter how much you try to handle them with kid gloves. We're ripping them out of a familiar situation, however grim, and taking them halfway around the world and placing them with strangers who don't look like them or talk like them. The surprise isn't that they start crying. It's that they ever stop."

"I'm sorry—"

"Don't even say it. I know, you were just trying to help." He said this last bit in a mocking tone.

She had planned on asking him a few questions about the quilt Iloai had but could see she wasn't going to get any useful information out of Joseph Marston—not tonight, anyway.

"It was nice to see you again," she said in a failed attempt at civility.

She stepped back to the table and slid into her chair, leaning toward Aiden. He leaned in to meet her.

"That was weird," she whispered. "I'll tell you when we leave."

They drank their cider, making small talk as they finished. Harriet kept an eye on Joseph. He fidgeted with his teaspoon then tore his empty sugar packets to shreds. He took a cell phone from his pocket, flipped it open and dialed, then slammed it shut without completing the call.

"He's sure acting like a dog with a bad case of fleas," Aiden commented. "Who is he, anyway?"

"He's the social worker at Little Lamb. He handled DeAnn's adoption," Harriet murmured.

"Seems like a nervous little twit."

"Something's bothering him. Let's go," she said.

Aiden took their cups and set them in the gray tub on the collection cart then followed Harriet to the door, his arm draped protectively across her shoulders. Once they were in his car, she recounted her interaction with Joseph Marston.

"It was all rather strange," she said. "Just a couple of days ago, he was at the shower waxing poetic about children and adoptive parents. Today, not so much."

"Maybe you just caught him at a bad time. As you're well aware, every job comes with its own unique stresses."

"I suppose, but I still think it was weird."

"Shall we go get your car?"

Mavis's Town Car was parked in Harriet's driveway, and the lights were on in her studio when she pulled in. She parked and went to the door. It opened before she'd even reached for the knob.

"So?" Mavis said as she stepped aside to let Harriet into her own house.

Aunt Beth was sitting in one of the wingback chairs, a cup of tea balanced on her knee. Mavis settled into the other chair, leaving Harriet to pull a wheeled chair over from her work area.

"So what?" she teased.

"Are we back to normal?" Mavis pressed.

"After your little 'chat,' did you expect anything less?" Harriet asked with a smile.

"Now that my boys are getting settled, I'm a little rusty, but I guess I got the job done, huh?"

"'Get over yourself' I think was the phrase."

"I didn't put it quite that way, honey, but that was the general idea."

"Well, he got the message, and frankly, I think if he hadn't been so stressed over his dogs, he would have figured it out himself eventually."

"Never pays to take that kind of chance." Mavis looked at Beth. "Remember Eula Jackson?"

"Of course."

The two older women nodded in agreement about Eula, whoever she was. After a moment's silence didn't produce additional information, Harriet finally spoke.

"Okay, I give—who was Eula Jackson, and what happened to her?"

"Eula was dating Ollie Swenson, and they had a misunderstanding about where they were supposed to meet for dinner, and they each waited all night at a different location, and they both were mad, and neither one was willing to approach the other, and they never spoke again," Mavis recounted.

"I take it she ended up a lonely old spinster?" Harriet prompted.

"No, she left town with the Fuller Brush man. They got married and had four daughters. If I'm not mistaken, they still live in Angel Harbor," Aunt Beth said.

"And Ollie joined the navy and never came back. We heard he settled in Montana with a woman he met in San Diego."

"So, basically they all lived happily ever after?" Harriet asked bewildered.

Beth and Mavis looked knowingly at each other and then at her.

"They were perfect for each other," Beth said, and Mavis nodded in agreement.

Harriet laughed. "You two are crazy. You do know that, right?"

"You watch your tongue," Beth scolded. "Besides, Mavis did get you and Aiden back together, right?"

Harriet shook her head and went into the kitchen to make a cup of tea.

Chapter 24

The house phone was ringing when Harriet came downstairs and into her kitchen Monday morning. It was Connie. She and Lauren had convinced Mavis and Aunt Beth the Threads should meet without Sarah to test their theory she was leaking their designs to the Small Stitches. The Threads were meeting at her house at ten o'clock.

"I'm in," Harriet said. "As long as I'm not the one who has to deal with Sarah when she finds out."

Connie assured Harriet she would take care of Sarah and that Harriet should just worry about bringing a winning dog design. Harriet laughed and said she would see her in an hour and a half.

Fred was doing his usual morning dance around her ankles, so she dished up his breakfast. She'd spent her morning shower time thinking about DeAnn's situation. Phyllis and Joseph had pretty much said the same thing—any child who was taken from a familiar living situation and thrust into a strange one, no matter how much nicer the new one was, would feel the stress of the change. Logically, she understood the explanation, but something didn't feel right. Why, in that case, was Kissa so calm. Hadn't she traveled halfway around the world, too? Could it just be the difference in their personalities? Maybe Kissa came from a family. Maybe Neelie *had* been her mother.

She had a hard time believing that last thought.

She kept coming back around to the quilt Iloai clung to. There had to be something they could learn from it. She picked the phone up again and dialed Mavis.

"Do you think I could spend some time with the quilt Iloai brought with her?" she asked when she'd connected with her friend. "Maybe I could stitch it to a piece of flannel, to stabilize it."

"I think that's a great idea. I took a rag doll over this morning," Mavis said. "I had a couple left over from a batch I made last spring for the church bazaar. That baby grabbed onto the doll like a life preserver. She dropped the blanket. You could check with DeAnn, but I'll bet she'll think it's a good plan."

Harriet thanked her and rang off, then called DeAnn, who confirmed Iloai was sufficiently distracted by the doll she probably wouldn't miss her blanket until bedtime. She agreed that anything Harriet could do to keep it from falling apart would be welcome.

"Robin stopped by this morning and was just telling me you're all going to meet at Connie's at ten. If you want, I can send it along with her. Just promise me you can have it back before eight o'clock."

"That shouldn't be a problem. I'll work on it as soon as the meeting is over."

Harriet fixed a piece of toast and a cup of tea and took both into her studio. She cut out two more sets of diamonds then played with her block layout until she'd tried every variation twice. She still wasn't happy with it, so she pinned the pieces onto a piece of paper instead of sewing them.

"What am I going to do, Fred?" she asked as she came back into the kitchen. "It's not time to go, but there's not enough time to do anything else."

Fred jumped onto the counter in front of her and pressed his face into her hand.

"Do you have to drool when you do that?" she asked and wiped her hand on her jeans. "If that's your best idea, I'm leaving."

She put another small spoonful of food into his dish, gathered her purse and quilting bag and left. It was her turn to drive, so she headed for her aunt's.

Beth had moved into a cottage on the Strait of Juan de Fuca. It was smaller than the Victorian home Harriet now occupied, but it did have three bedrooms and a garden space that was much more manageable. Harriet took a shortcut over Miller Hill and arrived at Aunt Beth's a few minutes later.

"You're early," Beth said as she opened the door before Harriet could knock. When Harriet didn't move immediately, her aunt grabbed her arm and pulled her inside. "Don't just stand there, make yourself useful. Fetch my quilting bag from my sewing room, will you?"

She retreated to the bathroom to brush her teeth.

Harriet went to the upstairs bedroom turned into a sewing room. Colorful quilt blocks were stuck to the design wall. Beth had tried several different color combinations, and Harriet assumed the winner was in the bag, so to speak. The requested canvas tote hung by its handle from the back of a wooden chair. She grabbed it and went back downstairs. Aunt Beth was standing by the front door with her purple rain jacket draped over her arm.

"What's the hurry?" Harriet asked.

"Since you're so early, I thought we could stop by Little Lamb and chat with Phyllis. I tried to call her, but her phone was busy. When I tried later, her machine answered, so I left her a message."

"Okay. Do you think she'll be able to tell us anything new?"

"Oh, I don't know," Aunt Beth said with a sigh. "I feel like we have to try *something* to help DeAnn. Phyl has a lot of experience with adoption, so if there's anything to be done, she can tell us."

Harriet waited for her aunt to buckle her seatbelt then headed her car back up over Miller Hill and on to downtown Foggy Point.

Phyllis was sitting at the reception desk in the front room of the Little Lamb Adoption Agency office, shuffling papers without looking at them. A tendril of her cotton-candy hair hung limply across her forehead. She looked up when the door's warning bell chimed as Harriet and Beth entered, her eyes wide.

"Hi, Phyl," Beth said. "Is everything all right?"

"No, everything is not all right," Phyllis snapped.

Harriet and Beth stood in shocked silence.

"I'm sorry," Phyllis said with a sigh. She hoisted her bulk to a standing position. "It's just Joseph."

"What about Joseph?" Harriet asked.

"He didn't show up for work today. He's not answering his house phone or cell phone." She again shuffled the papers she still clutched in her hands.

"Maybe he just overslept," Aunt Beth offered.

"He's never overslept before, especially when he was supposed to be taking a baby to Angel Harbor this morning. I had a courier pick up a baby at the airport in Seattle. Joseph was supposed to meet him at seven and take the baby on to the adoptive family. The courier arrived, and no Joseph."

Aunt Beth looked around the office. "So, where's the baby?"

"Jennifer had to hustle in and take over for him," Phyllis said, referring to the other social worker she employed. "Fortunately, none of her clients is at a critical stage today. I was just trying to find the paperwork for the meeting she was supposed to do this morning so I can fill in for her." She collapsed into Jennifer's chair. "This is just not like Joseph."

"Is there anything we can do to help?" Beth asked.

"No. Why are you here? I'm sorry, I don't mean to sound rude, but were we meeting?"

"Oh, no, we wanted to ask you something," Harriet said. "We can wait until a better time."

"If you were going to ask me what to do about DeAnn's new daughter, I'll tell you what I told Connie and Mavis when *they* each called me—tincture of time. That's all she can do. Love the child and wait for her to settle in. I know it seems like an eternity now, but I guarantee that a month from now it will seem like that girl has always been a part of their family.

"I do hope you know that if we were seeing any problem with a placement, we would be intervening. Joseph has been monitoring the situation, and he told me he hasn't observed anything out of the ordinary. Of course, that was before he disappeared." Phyllis covered her face with her hands.

"I'm sorry we bothered you," Harriet said, and ushered her aunt toward the door. "I hope you find Joseph." She waited until they were back in her car before she spoke. "Was that weird or what?"

"She did seem a little stressed," Beth agreed, stating the obvious.

"A *little* stressed? She seemed more than a *little* stressed. I don't know her like you do, but she seemed pretty upset to me."

"Normally, she's pretty steady. I think she's really worried about Joseph. It does seem weird he would no-show like that."

"Aiden and I saw him last night, and he was acting pretty strange." Harriet recounted her encounter with Joseph. "It was weird the way he said 'what difference does it make, anyway' when I asked about the child being from Uganda."

"That young man has always been a little odd," Aunt Beth said. "I'm not sure what a social worker is supposed to be like, but he's a little high-strung, if you ask me."

They talked through the morning's strange encounter two more times before they got to Connie's house, but they didn't come to any useful conclusions.

Robin pulled up to the curb at the same time they arrived.

"Hey, you guys," she said when they were out of their cars. She was dressed as always in black yoga pants, their longer length her only concession to the cooling weather. "I have something for you." She pulled the tattered baby blanket from her bag and handed it to Harriet. "I hope this tells you something."

"How are things going over there?" Beth asked.

Robin held her hand up, fingers spread, and rocked it back and forth.

"Iloai is sleeping a little, but more from exhaustion than anything."

"I wish there was more we could do," Harriet said.

"Fixing her quilt will help, and if you can figure out anything about her origins from it, all the better."

"We better get inside," Aunt Beth said. "It looks like Jenny is already here." She gestured toward a late-model BMW sedan parked in Connie's driveway.

Baby Kissa was balanced on Connie's hip when she opened the front door and welcomed them inside, Connie's knitted lace shawl wrapped around both of them. Kissa smiled when Aunt Beth made a silly face for her.

"Has anyone called you about her yet?" Robin asked.

"Not so far," Connie said.

"The longer this goes on, the more I worry about it. We can plead ignorance for a few days, but eventually, that won't cut it. It's obvious we have a baby here who doesn't belong to any of us. If anything happened to Kissa, and she had to go to the hospital, and you gave permission to treat her, that would be another whole set of problems."

"I'll call Phyllis when our meeting is over and see what she thinks," Connie said. "Maybe she can help me get certified as a temporary foster home. Besides, she must have experience dealing with children who don't have normal documentation."

"I'm not sure I'd call Phyllis today," Harriet offered, and then explained their encounter that morning.

"That's strange that Joseph pulled a no-show," Robin said. "Delivering a child to adoptive parents isn't the kind of thing a social worker flakes on without a real good excuse."

The doorbell rang, ending the discussion as Carla and Lauren both arrived. Connie took drink orders from everyone then handed Kissa off to her husband.

"Let's go into the family room and get started," she said when Mavis had arrived and the drinks had been made and distributed. Jenny pulled a plastic bag from her quilting tote that turned out to be chocolate chip cookies.

"I thought a little chocolate might help us think," she said with a smile as she handed the bag around.

Connie brought a large flannel-covered foam-core panel from her sewing room and set it in front of the fireplace, leaning it back against the mantle—her version of a portable design wall. One by one, the assembled women put their block or blocks on the board.

"Things are starting to look up," Aunt Beth said.

Carla and Robin had taken Beth's and Mavis's idea of fussy-cutting the dog image from a print fabric and surrounding it with solid fabric of the same color as its original background, and then using the resulting isolated image to make the center of their star blocks.

"That technique looks better in the stars then in our snowballs, don't you think?" Beth said to Mavis.

"I agree," Mavis concurred. "I think the snowballs with the smaller-scale print and the solid corners are the best of our lot."

"They'll make a serviceable quilt, but they aren't going to win any prizes," Beth said. She stuck her print snowball block next to Mavis's on the board.

"I like Lauren's doghouse," Carla said in a quiet voice. "Connie's, too," she added. "It looks hard to do, though."

Lauren and Connie had worked with their landscape and dog prints, carefully cutting out dog faces and raw-edge appliquéing them into the door opening of the doghouses.

"It was easy," Connie told Carla. "I cut out the dog face with my embroidery scissors then glued it to the doghouse door with a glue stick. I used clear nylon thread in my machine and ran a narrow zigzag stitch around the face and, voila!" She pointed at her block.

"I can't help but notice a big blank spot where Harriet's blocks should to be," Lauren said and looked straight at her. "Aren't you supposed to be working on the super-secret design that is going to guarantee a win?"

Harriet pulled the paper mock-ups of her block from her bag and pinned them to the design wall. One was a basic tumbling block using medium-scale dog prints; the other included one side that had been cut to position a dog image on the block face.

"The color scheme isn't quite right yet, but I think you guys can see the general idea."

"I think this has real potential," Jenny said thoughtfully.

"Did everyone bring patterns and instructions for their blocks?" Mavis asked.

The group nodded and murmured their assent. Each person would do two blocks from each pattern, and then the original pair who had designed the block would assemble the quilt top.

"What shall we do about the dog bones?" Jenny asked, referring to her complicated appliqué block.

"I'm game," Harriet said.

Connie, Mavis, Robin and Beth also volunteered to make the difficult blocks.

"I'd be willing to try," Carla said. "I'm not sure the result would be usable, though. I'm still getting the hang of inside curves."

Her face turned pink as she finished speaking.

"That's okay, honey," Mavis said. "I had trouble with that myself when I was a beginner."

"If we made them larger, we could do six blocks, each one with a different dog breed in the middle of the bone wreath, and it would make a nice wall hanging," Jenny said.

"That sounds good," Aunt Beth said. "Harriet, are you ready to hand out patterns for your tumbling blocks?"

"Not yet, but I'll make sure everyone has them by tomorrow night."

"So, how are we going to handle Sarah?" Robin asked.

"I can check up on the Small Stitches," Lauren volunteered. "The senior center staff is still having trouble with the new software. It's totally simple, but their employees don't want to use it. One of them is sabotaging the system. I'll probably still be going there this time next year."

"We still have to tell Sarah *something*," Robin said. "She's going to start wondering if we suddenly aren't having meetings, which is how it's going to seem to her if we keep meeting without her."

"I think we should let her run with her dog-bone design," Lauren said with a wicked smile.

"No one would believe we were really making a quilt from that block," Mavis said.

"If the Small Stitches are willing to steal to try to win, they might bite," Lauren argued. "And we know Sarah thinks it's a great design. She won't be able to keep quiet about it."

"So what, exactly, are you proposing?" Aunt Beth asked.

"I think we should ask Sarah to make several variations of her block with different backgrounds. If the Stitches are stealing our ideas, they should show up with Sarah's very distinctive bone design."

"But what about Sarah?" Carla asked. "What's going to happen when we don't make her quilt?"

"If Lauren verifies the Small Stitches are making the same quilt, we'll tell Sarah they copied her work and we therefore aren't going to do the same quilt."

"What if they *don't* copy her block?" Harriet asked. "What do we do about Sarah?"

"That won't happen," Lauren said. "If it does, just leave her to me."

Right, Harriet thought. That wouldn't be pretty, but frankly, she had bigger fish to fry at the moment—like who had killed Neelie, and who might be next.

"Are you ever going to tell Sarah's dad they have a saboteur?"

"Oh, right, Harriet, I'm just some mercenary computer hacker who is collecting beaucoup bucks from Sarah's simple, unsuspecting parents."

"I didn't say that," Harriet said, trying hard to keep her voice neutral.

"It's what you meant, though. For your information, I've told them every way I can, including in writing both on paper and in an e-mail, which, by the way, they didn't read since they are among the worst when it comes to not using the computer system. They want the employees to use it, but not themselves.

"They refuse to consider the possibility one of their slavishly devoted work crew could do such a thing. So, I go each week and undo the mischief and collect my customary fee each and every time. And no, I don't feel a bit guilty about it."

Harriet didn't know what to say. She'd didn't think she'd ever met Sarah's parents, but if they were anything like Sarah, she could see how Lauren's situation might have developed.

Lauren shook her head in disgust and turned away.

The meeting went on for another thirty minutes as the women exchanged the details that would insure each quilter would produce blocks that were all the same size and shape.

"We should get going," Aunt Beth said when the discussion finally ebbed. "I'd like to stop at the police station on our way home."

"Something I should know about?" Harriet asked, her curiosity piqued.

"Detective Morse called and asked me if I had the pattern for a slash-and-stitch baby quilt I showed her the other day. I told her I could drop it by today. Is that okay with you?"

"In principle, its fine, I just don't like the idea of you cozying up to a police detective, given what's going on."

"She's a *quilter*," Aunt Beth said, as if that fact over rode everything else.

"Fine," Harriet said. "Let's not linger, though. I don't want them thinking they get to question us again just because we're in the building."

"You worry too much," Beth said and picked up her purse and bag.

Harriet put on her gray hoodie and picked up her stitching bag. Connie walked them to the door and was about to open it when it swung wide and Rodrigo burst in waving a piece of paper.

"We're legal," he shouted. He handed Kissa to Connie. "You are legal, my little one," he said and kissed the baby on her fuzzy head.

"What happened?" Robin asked as she came into the entryway, followed by Carla and Jenny.

"I didn't want to say anything until I checked it out, but years ago, when I first started working for the county, I used to go on domestic abuse calls with the police, to translate. Since there were often kids involved, and it sometimes took hours and sometimes a couple of days to sort things out, Connie and I got certified for short-term foster care.

"It was mainly to give me official standing so I could remove the kids from the scene as quickly as possible. We had a list of Spanish-speaking foster care homes, and if the children had to be removed, I would arrange for them to stay there, but once or twice we kept kids overnight at the office."

"I didn't realize we were officially certified," Connie said.

"It was a special circumstance," Rodrigo said. "They didn't expect us to take the children home, so they didn't do all of the home inspections that typical foster parents go through."

"So, what does this mean for Kissa?" Robin asked.

"It means she has been temporarily declared a ward of the county and released to our care until they can investigate her circumstances," Rodrigo said.

"Why didn't you say anything?" Connie asked and batted her husband's arm in mock annoyance.

"I didn't want you ladies getting into any more trouble than normal. Besides, I know people—I knew I could ask a few pointed questions, and if I didn't like the answers, they wouldn't press the matter. As it turns out, it was easy. Kissa and I picked up the papers while you all were meeting."

"I'm glad someone was sensible about this," Robin said. "Now we just need to figure out who she really is."

"And more to the point, who her mother was," Harriet said.

"Or is," Lauren said, joining the group in the entry at last. "We don't know that Kissa isn't a kidnap victim."

A collective groan came from the assembled group.

"Didn't think of that, did you?" With that, Lauren brushed past Jenny, Carla and Mavis. "Ciao," she said, and went out the door.

"Do you really think she was kidnapped?" Carla asked Harriet.

"I hope not, but I guess anything's possible."

"Let's go," Aunt Beth said. "We've got work to do."

Harriet and Beth said their goodbyes and followed Lauren out the door.

"Lauren's right, you know," Harriet said when they were settled in her car. "Kissa could be a kidnap victim." She headed toward downtown Foggy Point and the police station.

"Let's not borrow trouble. She's in legal foster care for the moment. She could as easily be Neelie's or her sister's baby. We don't know. I'm sure the county will explore all those possibilities. You need to concentrate on fixing Iloai's quilt and making up your patterns for the dog quilt."

Harriet hated it when her aunt treated her like she was still a child dropped unexpectedly into her kitchen by her globetrotting parents, but she was right.

"Okay, a quick stop at the police station, and if it's okay with you, I'd like to stop in Pins and Needles and see if she's got flannel backing that's a better match for Iloai's quilt than the off-white I have."

"That sounds good. I need to get more fabric to make borders for the rest of Joseph's quilts, and this will save me a trip."

Chapter 25

Harriet parked on a side street half a block from the police station. You could no longer park directly in front of the station, as those spots had been turned into an elaborate planter system that was in reality a concrete buffer to protect the station in the event terrorists arrived in Foggy Point and decided to storm the FPPD.

Aunt Beth just shook her head as they threaded past the floral displays.

"You never know," Harriet told her. "Foggy Point could become a target."

"I'm sure you're right," Aunt Beth said with just a touch of sarcasm. "There's a real possibility terrorists would bypass the Trident nuclear submarine base in Bremerton and come on into Foggy Point."

"It could happen," Harriet said and laughed.

They reached the door, and Harriet held it for her aunt. The room they entered was beige, from the worn linoleum underfoot to the plastic ceiling tiles. The chairs had to have been there since the nineteen-fifties and belonged in a museum, not a working police station, but things were slow to change in Foggy Point.

Harriet heard him before she saw him.

"You tell the de–tec–tive I want to know what he's doing about my wife," Rodney Miller said, emphasizing each syllable of the word. "Someone killed her, and she needs justice. No one cares, but she needs justice." He banged his fist on the bulletproof glass that separated him from the receptionist. "She was my wife," he said and started crying.

"Can I help you?" the receptionist called to Aunt Beth.

"*I* need help," Rodney shouted. "Why ain't you helping me?"

"I came to see Detective Morse," Aunt Beth said in a firm voice.

"What do *you* need a detective for?" Rodney said to her. "She supposed to be finding out who killed Neelie."

Detective Morse started to come through a door into the waiting area, but Rodney lunged for her, and she quickly closed the door and went back into the part of the reception area behind the glass. A moment later, two patrol officers came in the front doors. Harriet recognized Officer Jason Nguyen from previous encounters, but she'd never seen the second officer, a muscular young man with a military-style crewcut.

The two men flanked Rodney, grasping his arms. Rodney countered by slithering out of his leather jacket in an attempt to escape. The two officers were ready for the move and grasped his now-bare wrists, quickly pulling them behind him and applying handcuffs.

"Calm down, Mr. Miller," Officer Nguyen said in a firm voice. "I know you're upset about your wife, but this isn't helping."

"No one will tell me anything. An' they ain't doing anything. Neelie's dead. *Dead!*"

"That's not true," Nguyen assured him. "The detectives are following several leads, and the lab is processing evidence, but until they get some results, there's nothing to tell. That doesn't mean they aren't doing anything."

Harriet wanted to know what they were doing, too, but it didn't seem like the time to ask.

"If you don't stop coming in here and screaming at our receptionist, we're going to have to put you in a cell and charge you with disorderly conduct. I don't want to do that, but if you can't control yourself, I will."

The second officer had remained silent till now.

"Take a deep breath," he said softly, and Rodney did.

He relaxed, and they sat him in one of the chairs in the waiting area.

"You okay now?" Officer Nguyen asked after Rodney had been quiet for a few minutes.

Rodney nodded.

"Okay," said the other officer. "We're going to walk you outside and undo the cuffs. I promise, as soon as we know anything about what happened to your wife, we'll give you a call. We've got your cell phone number."

Rodney looked at him intently then said "Okay," and let them lead him out of the station.

After another minute had passed, Detective Morse came through the side door again.

"Sorry about that," she said. "I feel sorry for that poor man, I really do."

"So, are you still working on the case?" Harriet asked. Aunt Beth nudged her, but it was too late—her question was out there.

"I wish what the officer said was true, but the fact is, we don't have any leads. The lab is processing what little forensic evidence we have, but we don't have much to go on. Ms. Obote isn't from around here, so we don't have any known associates to question. I probably shouldn't be telling you this, but we don't even know for sure where the actual crime scene is. If you ladies can add any more to your statements, that would be helpful, but even if you'd seen her collapse in Dr. Jalbert's yard that wouldn't help much."

"It seems like she came to town to con Aiden," Harriet said. "She was waiting for him to return from eastern Washington. I don't understand why someone would kill her. She hadn't even made her play yet."

"Why do you think Ms. Obote was going to con Dr. Jalbert?"

"She had a baby she claimed was her sister's, and that her sister had died and asked her to deliver the baby to Aiden. I told this all to Detective Sanders."

Detective Morse raised her left eyebrow.

"Did you, now?" she said, more to herself than to Beth and Harriet. "I take it the baby is not Dr. Jalbert's."

"No," Harriet said in a firm voice. "He knew nothing about it, and in fact says he'll be very surprised if it's Nabirye Obote's baby."

"Where's the baby now?" Detective Morse asked.

"She's in foster care," Aunt Beth answered quickly.

"Well, this is something, anyway. Tell me the name of the baby's alleged mother again."

Harriet told her. "Aiden has a call in to her. He did work with her in Africa before he came back to Foggy Point," she added.

"It's strange Mr. Miller didn't mention a baby."

"He claims he knew nothing about the baby or the sister in Africa," Harriet said.

"You've spoken to him?" Morse asked.

Harriet ducked her head. "I did run into him at dinner one night," she said sheepishly.

"I'm pretty sure you've heard this before, but you need to let the police do the detecting. People who commit crimes are dangerous. Officer Nguyen told me you've had some experience with that. He said you got a nasty bump on the head. Next time, you might not be so lucky. If you hear anything, see anything or, heck, even *think* anything related to this case, you call me immediately." She pulled a business card from her shirt pocket and wrote a number on the back. "That's my cell number. Call me."

Harriet felt like a little girl in the principal's office.

Detective Morse turned to Aunt Beth, who handed her a thin pattern book.

"Here's that pattern you asked about."

"Thanks," she said and leafed through the booklet. "This looks perfect for my sister's baby. And by that, I mean it looks like I could finish it in time."

"If you need any help, give me a call," Aunt Beth said. "I'm in the phone book."

"Thanks for taking the time to drop it by. And please, keep your niece out of the detecting business, for her own sake."

"Will do," Beth said and nudged Harriet toward the door.

"Will do?" Harriet repeated when they were back at the car.

"What did you want me to say? I wasn't about to tell her I was your accomplice. Then she'd never tell us anything."

"If I'm not mistaken, she *didn't* tell us anything. We told *her* stuff."

"She will," Aunt Beth said. "Once she trusts us. You saw how she acted when you talked about the baby. That Detective Sanders is keeping things from her. She'll talk to us because he's trying to make her look incompetent, or at least less competent."

"Typical male ego," Harriet mused.

"She's going to need allies, and we could use her insider knowledge."

"She could just be playing us."

"I don't think so," Beth said. "It's only a couple of blocks to the quilt store. You want to walk?"

Harriet looked up at the cloudy sky. "Sure, why not."

Chapter 26

D o you want to work on your baby quilt in the studio while I fix Iloai's?" Harriet asked when they had made their purchases and were returning to the car, bags in hand.

"I'd love to, but I left that stuff at my house. You'd have to drive me back by there first."

"It's not like you live in Seattle," Harriet said with a smile. "Let me throw my flannel in the washer at my house before we leave." She'd purchased two and a half yards of a pale-gold flannel so she'd have plenty of extra fabric to account for the shrinkage flannel is so notorious for.

The town of Foggy Point strictly enforced its twenty-five-mile-an-hour speed limit everywhere within the city limits. Deer wandered freely in the residential neighborhoods, and the city council had enacted the low speed limit law not long after cars edged out horses and buggies as the favored mode of transportation. The law had withstood the passage of time without a single challenge. Even so, Harriet had Aunt Beth home and back and installed at a work table with her fabric, ruler and rotary cutter in less than an hour.

Harriet spread Iloai's quilt on her big cutting table. She carefully examined the embroidered areas at the top of the quilt and then the blank fabric at the bottom. She picked loose a couple of stitches along a seam that joined two imaged areas. As she'd suspected, pre-sewn blocks had been appliquéd to a background fabric. She brought a bright, natural-light floor lamp to the table and shone it on the quilt. A magnifying glass was attached to the stem of the lamp by means of a flexible arm. She swung the lens over the quilt and took a close look at the background fabric.

"This is kind of interesting."

"What do you see?"

"It looks like whoever made this turned a piece of fabric inside out to make the background."

"Haven't you ever done that to get a color you wanted? I have."

"I've done it when I was piecing something and needed a small amount of an odd color or in appliqué, but never for a whole top or backing. This looks almost textured."

"Well, don't just pick at it, undo a whole section and look."

"What if it falls apart?"

"You're fixing it anyway. I wouldn't take it apart up where the embroidery work is—do a bottom corner."

Harriet turned the quilt around and then carefully, starting in the lower left corner, picked the stitches apart for six inches in each direction. When she had the top fabric loosened from the backing, she folded it back, revealing the reverse side of the fabric.

"Whoa!"

"What?" Aunt Beth got up from her work table and joined Harriet.

"Wow," she said. "Mavis and Gerald had matching shirts made from fabric very similar to that."

"Really?" Harriet looked at the navy blue-on-off-white Hawaiian print.

"Yeah. His sister went on a cruise of the South Pacific and brought them back shirts."

"When was that?"

"Oh, gosh." Beth looked at the ceiling while she thought. "It must have been in the late sixties. Maybe the early seventies."

"This isn't real bark cloth."

"Of course not," Beth said. "I don't think real bark cloth is produced in that kind of quantity. Back in the fifties, a cotton imitation bark cloth became popular for interior decorating...and Hawaiian shirts."

"Do you know where in the South Pacific the shirts came from?"

Beth stared at her.

"Don't look at me like I've grown a horn in the middle of my forehead," Harriet said with a laugh. "You know all kinds of bizarre stuff."

"I'm not sure if that's a compliment or an insult. I'll call Mavis and see if she remembers."

She went to her purse and extracted her cell phone. She spoke for a few minutes then dropped the phone back into her purse.

"She said she could drive the shirts over," she announced.

"Why am I not surprised she still has them?"

"I'll have you know they've come in very handy as a last-minute costume more than once through the years."

"What's Mavis up to?"

"Can't be much if she's coming here. I better go put the tea water on."

"I'll go throw my flannel in the dryer."

Mavis arrived fifteen minutes later with the shirts draped over one arm and her quilting bag and purse on the opposite shoulder. Harriet greeted her and then led her to the kitchen, where Beth had tea and snickerdoodles ready.

"Where did the cookies come from?" Harriet asked. The smell of sugar and cinnamon was almost unbearable. She wanted to eat them all herself.

"They're in the freezer in the garage—I thawed them in the oven. I didn't think you'd mind if I left some there when I moved. I labeled them 'green peas.' You never know when you'll need a cookie, although now that you know they're there, I suppose I should move them to protect you from yourself."

"I'm not twelve, you know." Harriet said and glared at her.

"These are delicious," Mavis said around a bite of cookie. "Nothing better than a warm cookie."

"Shall we go look at the shirts?" Harriet suggested when they had finished their tea.

The three women clustered around the end of the cutting table as Mavis flattened one of the shirts next to the small quilt.

"Boy, they do look very similar, don't they?" Harriet said after she'd examined both carefully.

"That's what I was saying," Aunt Beth said.

"Do you know where, exactly, your sister-in-law bought these shirts?" Harriet asked Mavis.

"Let me think. Her cruise originated in Sydney, Australia. I know she went to Fiji and Vanuatu and then Samoa, I think. It could have been any of those places. Or knowing her, it could have been at the airport in Sydney, although they seem a little nicer than what they sold in airports in those days."

Harriet turned the quilt and folded it so only the embroidered portion showed.

"You know, these images make more sense if you think about the South Pacific when you look at them." She rubbed her finger over a line of green stitching. "This looks like it might have been a palm tree." The stitching was broken where she indicated.

Beth leaned in for a closer look. "I think you're right."

"If Iloai is from one of the islands in the South Pacific, why would they say she was African?" Mavis asked.

"That would be the question," Harriet said.

The women stared in silence at the quilt and shirt. A knock on the outside studio door interrupted their reverie. Harriet crossed the room and opened it.

"I know where Iloai comes from," Lauren said as she brushed past.

"The South Pacific?" Aunt Beth said.

Lauren's shoulders slumped, and the animation left her face.

"You knew?" She paused. "Why didn't you tell me?" she said, anger replacing her earlier excitement. "You knew I was researching this."

"We just figured it out," Harriet told her. "Literally, right before you walked in. Would you like some tea, now that you're here?"

"Yeah, sure, I guess."

She set her purse on the floor by one of the wingback chairs and took off her caramel-colored barn-style jacket. Harriet went into the kitchen and returned a few minutes later with tea and two cookies.

"Okay, Harriet's back, so now—how did you come to the conclusion Iloai is from the South Pacific?" Mavis asked.

"It was simple," Lauren said. "I should have thought of it sooner. You think you're so smart, you should have thought of it."

"Thought of what?" Harriet asked.

"Her name," Lauren said. "I ran her name through a name database. It tells you the origins of any name you type in. Iloai isn't an African name. It's Samoan."

"Wow," said Harriet.

"I know, it makes no sense," Lauren said. "Why lie about something like that?"

"Maybe there's some sort of monetary advantage if the child comes from Africa," Mavis said.

"Or maybe there are immigration quotas that have been exceeded in one place but not in the other," Beth suggested.

"I suppose there's always the chance her parents emigrated from the South Pacific to Africa and then died or became otherwise unable to care for her," Harriet said. "It seems kind of farfetched, though."

"That would explain the language thing, too," Aunt Beth said.

"I wonder if Phyllis ever found Joseph," Harriet said. "If anyone knows the answer to all this, it should be him."

"I'll call Phyl," Aunt Beth offered. She went to the phone and dialed.

"I guess I better put this quilt back together," Harriet said. "We said we'd return it before bedtime."

Beth turned back to the group.

"No answer," she announced. "I tried the office, her home number and her cell phone and nada."

"If Joseph is still missing in action, she's probably hustling to cover his appointments as well as her own."

"Anyone need a refill?" Aunt Beth asked and headed to the kitchen with her cup.

"I'll come with you," Mavis said.

"So, what do you really think is going on?" Lauren asked, and sipped her tea.

"I'm not sure, but I'll tell you this—I don't think it has to do with immigration numbers or emigrating dead parents. I also think it's curious the social worker who could clear this up has been acting a little strange and is currently missing from his job."

"Yeah, that is weird. But then, I've always thought that guy was a little strange."

Harriet threaded a needle with beige cotton thread and began re-stitching the seam she'd pulled out on the child's quilt.

"I better get back to work," Lauren said when she'd finished her tea. "I was just finishing at the senior center when I had my epiphany. I used their computer to look it up. I'm with you about the immigration angle, but I'll see what I can find out when I get back to my own computer. Maybe I can at least eliminate some things."

"That would be useful," Harriet agreed.

"Later," Lauren said as she set her cup down and picked up her coat and purse. She went out the door without another word.

Aunt Beth and Mavis returned and settled in to their own work, Mavis making dog quilt blocks and Beth continuing with her functional dog quilt for the shelter. Harriet re-sewed the seams she'd opened and repaired the ones that had torn apart before retrieving the new piece of flannel from the dryer.

"You going to attach that flannel bag style?" Mavis asked, referring to the method of laying the front sides of two pieces of fabric together and sewing the perimeter, leaving a small open area and then turning the result inside out.

"Yeah, I thought I would do that then top-stitch the edge. I think I'll quilt around the perimeter of each of the embroidered blocks then stitch over the quilting that was done in the blank half. Whoever made it obviously assumed the quilting would be covered up." She held it up, showing Mavis the simple grid pattern that had been done on the lower half of the quilt.

"I think I'll just use my sewing machine. There's no real reason to take the time to put it on the big machine."

"I agree," Beth said. "Especially since you need to get that back in…" She looked at her watch. "…a couple of hours."

"I better get busy," Harriet said.

Chapter 27

The light coming in through the front window was beginning to wane when the trio heard a knock on the studio door followed by Aiden opening it and coming in. Harriet had Iloai's quilt on the big table again, clipping threads and generally giving it the once-over. Aunt Beth straightened in her chair and rubbed her lower back with a sigh.

"This looks like trouble," he said with a smile.

"What?" Harriet asked.

"Whenever the Loose Threads brain trust gets together, it's trouble."

"We aren't the brain trust," Mavis said. "That would be Lauren—just ask her."

"I came by to see if anyone wanted to go get pizza. I have a couple of hours before the next round of meds starts for the rescue dogs."

"How are they doing?" Beth asked.

"Some will be ready for adoption soon, but there are a lot that still have a way to go, and there are a few that will have to have on-going treatment that could last years."

"That's so sad," Beth said.

"I'm just thankful you all do such a good job of raising money at your auction so we can take care of them. Unfortunately, a lot of

152

places would have euthanized many of these dogs to avoid the cost of rehabbing them."

"Hopefully, we'll get a good turnout this time," Mavis said. "The community is usually very generous, but the economy has been so bad these last few years."

"Someone will want to pay top dollar for the beautiful quilts you ladies make," Aiden said with a broad grin.

"Always the charmer," Aunt Beth said.

"So, how about pizza? Are you ladies in?"

"Sounds good to me, if you don't mind having a couple of old hags tag along with you and Harriet," Mavis said.

"You beautiful ladies aren't hags," Aiden said in a shocked tone.

"Like I said." Beth rolled her eyes. "Always the charmer."

"I'm in," Harriet said, "I'm starving."

"Mamma Theresa's okay with everyone?"

"Is there anywhere else?" Mavis replied.

"Not if you want good pizza," Beth said.

"I think I'd better take my own car," Harriet said. "I've got to go by DeAnn's and drop this quilt off when we're done. In fact, I better go call her and let her know."

"Speaking of your communication problems," Aiden said when she had finished her call. "I hope you won't think I'm being too forward, but it worries me that you're driving around without a way to call for help."

She started to protest, but he held his hand up to silence her. With the other, he pulled a box out of the pocket of the blue fleece jacket he was wearing over his customary surgical scrubs and handed it to her.

"I took the liberty of getting you a replacement phone. All you have to do is plug it into your computer to transfer your phone book." He pretended to duck. "Okay, you can hit me now."

A range of emotions swept through Harriet. Her knee-jerk reaction to anyone making decisions "for her own good" was anger. On the other hand, she needed a phone and had dreaded having to go to the phone store and fight through the myriad options, upgrades and other sales-related pressures such a trip would entail.

In the end, gratitude won.

"Thank you so much," she said. She pressed the on button and smiled when she saw that he'd already programmed his own number into the directory.

Never one to miss an opportunity, Aiden closed the distance between them and pulled her into an embrace.

"We'll meet you there," Aunt Beth said as she and Mavis gathered their purses and coats and hustled out the door.

Aiden kissed her gently on her lips.

"I'm glad we're not fighting anymore."

Harriet tensed in his arms, but he put his finger to her lips.

"Let's enjoy the moment, okay?"

She smiled and put her arms around his neck, pulling his head down for another, deeper kiss.

"Okay, we better go while we still can," he said when they finally broke contact.

Harriet picked up her coat and followed him out the door.

✄ - - - ✄ - - - ✄

"We took the liberty of ordering," Mavis said when Aiden and Harriet arrived at the restaurant and joined them at their table.

"We got a large pepperoni and one that's half artichoke, black olive and feta cheese and half Mamma's combo."

"Sounds good," Aiden said and took a drink from the large water glass that had already been set at his place. "Hey, I heard back from my friend in Africa."

"Why didn't you say something?" Harriet asked, her voice rising slightly.

"I figured you'd get all excited and then I wouldn't get a kiss when I gave you the phone."

She started to argue and then realized he was once again teasing her.

"I forgot," he continued in a more serious tone. "She called when I was with a patient, and the phone connection wasn't very good."

"Well?" Aunt Beth prompted.

"As I suspected, she had no idea what I was talking about, and she definitely has not had a baby—now or ever."

"Does she have a sister?" Harriet asked.

"She does, but it's more complicated than that."

"What does that mean," Beth asked.

"She has a full sister who is married and lives in Uganda, and she's seen her recently. The complication is that in Uganda, it's not unusual for men to have more than one family, each in a different village. Her father had at least two other families, and she's met several of her half-siblings. I was trying to ask her about Neelie when our connection was dropped."

"So, we don't really know anything," Mavis said.

"We know Neelie's maybe-sister who worked with Aiden didn't send him a baby, so for sure that much was a scam. We're not any closer to knowing who Neelie really was or why she targeted Aiden."

"We also don't know who baby Kissa really is," Aunt Beth added.

"Baby steps, ladies," Aiden said as their pizza arrived and their waitress set it on a two-tiered rack at the center of their table. "One fact at a time is what I say."

"That's easy for you—you don't have a motherless baby in your midst."

"True, but I still think caution is advised." He slid a piece of pepperoni pizza onto his plate.

"The police aren't any further along in their investigation," Beth said and proceeded to recount the trip to see Detective Morse while the other three munched on their pizza.

"We ran into Neelie's so-called husband," Harriet added when her aunt had finished the account of their police visit without mentioning Rodney. She described the action they had witnessed.

"That's weird," he said. "I just saw a guy who fits that description on my way through town on the way to your house. He was on the street in front of Little Lamb. It looked like he was trying to talk to Joseph, but Joe wasn't having any of it. He pulled his arm free and hustled into the building."

"You saw Joseph?" Harriet and Mavis said at the same time.

"Yeah, didn't I just say that? He was arguing with that Rodney guy in front of Little Lamb. Why are you so shocked?"

"He was a no-show at work this morning. He left Phyllis in a real pickle," Mavis said.

"Didn't I hear somewhere he still lives with his mother?" He slid another piece of pepperoni pizza onto his now-empty plate.

"He lives in his mother's *house*," Mavis said. "It's that pink Victorian we pass on the way to DeAnn's. She remarried a couple of years ago and hasn't been seen in these parts since."

"He takes care of the place for her," Beth added. "She and Mr. Moneybags are living in a villa somewhere in Europe, according to Phyllis."

"It was Joseph's grandma's house before that." Mavis continued her local history lesson. "His mother lived there with her mother until the old lady went into the senior home. His grandmother was born in that house. *Her* mother died young, and she lived there and took care of her father who, if I'm not mistaken, was in the merchant marine. When she married, her husband moved in."

"It must be nice," Harriet said.

Aiden's cheeks turned red. "I have nothing to say about that," he said and took a bite of his pizza.

"It's not the same thing at all," Harriet protested when she realized what he was thinking. He was, after all, living in *his* mother's house. "You inherited your house when your mother died. That's completely different."

"Living in Momma's house when she's still alive is a whole different kettle of fish," Mavis concurred.

"We think we know where DeAnn's new daughter is from," Harriet said, changing the subject, to Aiden's obvious relief. She explained their conclusion that Iloai was from somewhere in the South Pacific.

"Have you tried talking to her in her own language?" he asked.

"Not yet," Harriet said and wiped her mouth on her napkin. "We just figured it out. Besides, there are more than a few islands with more than a few possible languages."

"Maybe you can record the child talking and put it through a translation program," he suggested.

"Now you're sounding like Lauren," Mavis said.

"Was that a compliment?" He grinned. "I'll take it as one. I only know about the translation programs on the internet because of my time out of country."

"I can't believe it took us so long to figure it out," Harriet said.

"I can," Mavis said. "Joseph told DeAnn she's from Uganda. Why would you give it another thought? People tend to believe what other people tell them until incontrovertible proof is shoved in their face."

"I should have recognized that 'Iloai' isn't a Ugandan name," Aiden said. "But I didn't put two and two together."

"You've had distractions, though," Harriet said.

"True, but that's what I'm saying. Everyone has their own stuff going on, so you don't question information unless something happens that makes you doubt it."

"Good point," Aunt Beth said. "So, what else are we taking at face value that we should reexamine?"

"Everything about Kissa," Mavis said. "She's a delightful child, but I don't think we can believe anything Neelie said about her."

"At least *she* has a Ugandan name," Aiden said. "I encountered more than one Kissa while I was there."

"I think Rodney falls into the question-everything category, too." Aunt Beth said.

"He does seem genuinely upset about Neelie's death," Harriet said. "But I agree—I think he knows a lot more about Neelie and what she was doing in Foggy Point. But that doesn't mean he knows everything."

Aiden looked at her, and then at Aunt Beth and Mavis, in turn.

"So, what's next, ladies? I'm not sure I want to know the answer, but I can't help it."

"Someone needs to tell DeAnn what's going on," Harriet said.

"I'm not sure that's our place," Aunt Beth protested.

"I think she needs to know anything we find out that can help her ease her daughter's transition," Harriet countered.

"It's just guesswork on our part at this point," Beth said. "We need to talk to Phyllis or Joseph and see what they have to say about it."

157

"If someone pulled a switch at the other end, Phyl and Joe might not know any more than we do," Mavis pointed out.

"So, what do *you* think we should do?" Harriet asked her aunt.

"I say we leave DeAnn out of it until we can get some confirmation her child is not from Africa. In the meantime, we keep trying until we can talk to Phyllis or Joseph."

"We need to get hold of Rodney and see if we can get anything else out of him," Mavis said.

"That should be easy," Harriet said. "He's all about money and who's going to pay him. We just need to figure out where he's staying."

"Nabirye said she would e-mail me a list of her half-siblings," Aiden added. "It won't be quick, since she was calling from a field phone. We have to wait until she gets somewhere that has computer access or a fax machine."

Mavis slid another piece of the artichoke pizza onto her plate.

"I've got plenty of quilting to keep me busy," she said. "We need to get our blocks made and get on to making quilts. That auction is just around the corner."

Aiden polished off his pizza and wiped his hands on his napkin.

"I've got to go flush some wounds," he said and stood up. "Thanks for dining with me, ladies."

Harriet stood and walked him to the door.

"This should only take me an hour or so. Can I call you when I'm done? Maybe come by and…?" He waggled his eyebrows in a suggestive way.

"You're incorrigible,"she told him with a smile. "Yes, you can call or come by. I have to stop by DeAnn's and drop off the little girl's quilt that I repaired, then I'll be home working on my dog blocks."

"Later," he said and leaned in for a quick kiss before going out the door.

Harriet returned to the table and sat down again.

"I should get going, too," she said. "As soon as I finish this." She picked up her half-eaten piece of pizza.

"We all need to get going," Mavis said. "We've spent so much time trying to outwit the Small Stitches that, if we're not careful, we won't have anything finished in time for the auction, prize-winning or otherwise."

"I hear you," Beth said. "Let me get a box for our leftovers."

Chapter 28

Harriet zipped her hoodie as she walked to her car. A cold gust of wind slammed into her from the side, sending a shiver down her spine. There was a definite nip of fall in the air.

She had moved back to Foggy Point from California in the early spring and had so far been able to avoid shopping for cold-weather clothes; she could tell her hoodie wasn't going to cut it much longer, and she would have to make the drive to Seattle to buy some real winter wear.

Joseph's house was dark when she passed it, save for a pale-yellow glow in one downstairs window. She slowed and tried to look down the driveway to see if his car was there, but the drive curved around behind the house where it most likely ended in a detached garage that had been a carriage house in former times. It was an arrangement common to most of the Victorian houses in the area.

She toyed with the idea of stopping but looked at the time and decided she'd better go on to DeAnn's and deliver the now slightly less tattered quilt.

She pulled up to the curb in front of DeAnn's house and couldn't help but notice a familiar car parked in front of hers.

"Are you just now delivering Iloai's quilt?" Lauren asked. "DeAnn's already getting the girl ready for bed. It's hard to tell without speaking her language, but I think she's missing that quilt."

Harriet sighed. "Yes, I'm delivering the quilt. What are you doing here?"

"You don't have to get your knickers in a twist. I was only stating the obvious. And if you must know, I downloaded a list of basic words from all the major South Pacific languages and gave them to DeAnn so she can try some of them."

So much for taking it slow, Harriet thought.

"Mavis and my aunt were hoping to not bother DeAnn with our idle speculation until we'd been able to verify the facts."

"I wouldn't want to contradict the Delphic Oracle and her sidekick, but DeAnn was grateful for the help, and for your information, she's tried out the languages and Iloai responds to Samoan."

"That's great," Harriet said in a tone that didn't sound sincere to either one of them.

"Gotta go," Lauren said with a smirk. "I've got quilt blocks to make."

"Two steps forward, one step back," Harriet muttered. "See you," she said louder and headed for the front door.

DeAnn greeted her on the porch.

"Did Lauren tell you?" she asked. "She figured out Iloai is Samoan."

"That's great," Harriet said, with feigned enthusiasm.

"She narrowed it to somewhere in the South Pacific and brought us lists of words from each of the local languages. We hit the jackpot on the third try. I said *ina*, which means *drink*, and her face lit up like we'd never seen. She started babbling and clapping her hands. David is on his way to the bookstore in Port Angeles—they have a Samoan/English dictionary. The owner is going to keep the store open until he gets there.

"What am I thinking, leaving you standing out here in the cold on the porch?" She stood aside so Harriet could enter. "Come in. Would you like some tea?"

"No, thank you," Harriet said. "I have the quilt." She pulled it from her canvas bag and held it up.

"This looks wonderful. Let's go give it to her. She's in the family room with the boys. They're trying to learn how to pronounce the list of words by getting her to say them."

Iloai was sitting on the edge of the overstuffed sofa between DeAnn's sons. She slid to the floor at the sight of her quilt, and ran over to grab it from DeAnn as soon as they came into the room.

"You sure you don't want some tea?" DeAnn asked again.

"Okay, I guess I could drink a small cup. I need to go back and work on my blocks for the auction. We've wasted a lot of time deciding on our designs, so we're going to have to hustle to get the quilts done."

"I'm sure it's not helping that I'm not contributing anything," DeAnn said as she led the way to the kitchen.

"That's not the problem," Harriet assured her. "Really. Our trouble has been the Small Stitches copying our designs. Plus, none of us has had a great inspiration. I guess too many of us are cat people," she finished with a laugh. "We have a plan, of sorts, finally. Now we all have to make our blocks and get the quilts put together."

"I wish I could contribute something. This..." She spread her arms to indicate her house and the people in it. "...has been pretty all-consuming, though."

"Don't worry," Harriet said, and took the cup of steaming tea DeAnn offered her. "You just focus on your new daughter."

"I wonder why Joseph thought she was from Africa," DeAnn said. "It seems like a big thing to get confused about."

"Mavis and Aunt Beth and I were wondering the same thing at dinner tonight."

"You knew?"

"Not for sure, but we were just figuring it out when Lauren came by and told us what *she'd* figured out."

"She forgot to mention that part," DeAnn said with a knowing smile.

"Well, like we were saying, it seems strange that, with all the work involved in setting up an adoption, you could mistake the location of the orphanage you were getting a child from."

"You could maybe understand it if they had just confused one African country with another, but Samoa is half a world away, isn't it?"

"We came up with a few scenarios that could explain it, but if you ask me, they were pretty far-fetched. There's something else going on here. We just have to figure out what."

"There's one more thing that's been bothering me," DeAnn said, looking down at her hands as she spoke. "If Iloai has been living in an overcrowded orphanage most of her life, why is she so anxious to be anywhere but here? Are we that terrible by comparison?"

A tear fell onto her napkin, and she wiped her cheek with the back of her hand.

"No, that's not possible." Harriet reached across the table and squeezed her hand. "There are things we don't know yet, that's all. We'll get to the bottom of this, and in the meantime, you're not alone. The Threads are all here for you—whatever you need, whenever you need it, let one of us know. And just in case, one of us will be checking on you every day."

Mavis and Aunt Beth would have been proud if they'd heard her, Harriet thought.

The two women sipped their tea while DeAnn dabbed at her tears with her napkin.

"I can tell you one thing," she said when she'd regained her composure. "I'll be at the door to Little Lamb Adoption Agency tomorrow morning, and I *will* have some answers."

"You better call before you go if you're hoping to talk to Joseph. My aunt and I stopped by there this morning, and he hadn't showed up. Phyllis was pretty worried."

"Great," DeAnn said and leaned back in her chair, her face tilted up at the ceiling.

"I better get going," Harriet said. "I've got blocks to work on."

"Thanks for fixing Iloai's blanket and…and for everything."

Harriet got up and carried her teacup to the sink. She rinsed it, then picked up her bag and purse and headed to the front door. DeAnn followed.

163

"I'll let you know if we hear anything about Joseph," Harriet said, and went out into the chilly air.

She slowed once again as she drove by Joseph's house on her way home. The same downstairs window glowed yellow. She had almost passed the stately Victorian when she thought she saw a shadow move across the illuminated space, blocking the light for a second. She pulled into the next driveway she came to and turned around, parking at the curb in front of Joseph's house.

No more shadowy movement interrupted the light, so Harriet got out of her car and went up to the front door. Joseph's house was not the common style people think of as Victorian; his didn't have the broad porch or steep roofs with gingerbread trim. Only the fact Harriet had spent several of her boarding school years in France allowed her to identify the squared-off roof lines and tall narrow construction as the mansard style of Victorian. That particular design put the window Harriet was looking for directly above a large rhododendron shrub, just beyond reach from the porch.

She knocked on the door, waited then knocked again, but no one answered. She knocked a third time and listened for any sound that might indicate Joseph was inside. Nothing.

She stood for a moment trying to decide what to do next. She put her hands in the pockets of her sweatshirt and felt the smooth surface of her new cell phone. She pulled it out and pressed the wake-up button then dialed information and asked the operator for Joseph Marston's home phone number. She was connected, and a moment later could hear the distant sound of a phone ringing somewhere inside the house. She hung up when the voice mail came on. If Joseph was inside, he wasn't interested in having company.

Harriet stepped back off the porch and pushed between the bushes to the window. Concealed by the shrubbery was a cement window well that provided access to a lower floor window protected by an ornate wrought iron grill. She had stepped onto the cement surround, preparing to look in the lighted window, when she thought she saw a flicker of movement through the lower window in her peripheral vision. She wasn't sure if she'd really seen anything, but decided she'd better check it out, just in case.

The blow to her back, when it came, did two things. It knocked the wind out of her, and it forced her down into the window well, twisting her ankle. Pain shot up her leg, and she tried to cry out, but without air in her lungs, no sound came out.

Tears streamed down her cheeks as she struggled to breathe and, at the same time, move her body to relieve the pressure on her ankle. In her shock and pain, she couldn't hear anything but her own wheezing attempts to make her diaphragm work again.

She'd just managed a partial breath and was struggling to lift herself out of her cement prison when a heavy weight hit her from above and crushed her back into the window well. She sucked in a ragged breath, thankful she was finally able to breathe again.

Something large had been thrown into the window well on top of her, and the space wasn't big enough for both. She wriggled around until she could get her arms in front of her and her knees under her, then she pushed with all her strength. She managed to heave whatever had been thrown on top of her off to the side and squeeze past it and out of the confined space.

A sharp pain shot across her low back where she'd been hit the first time. It was dark behind the shrubs, but she could see well enough to determine the "something" that had been shoved on top of her was most probably a person.

A wave of nausea hit as she tried to stand and put weight on her ankle. She immediately crouched down, taking the weight off her damaged leg. Whoever was lying in a heap at her feet was dressed in dark clothes. It was a man.

She carefully scooted around the body then reached into her sweatshirt pocket and, miraculously, found her cell phone still there. She pulled it out and pressed the wake-up button, which lit up the screen, illuminating the immediate area. She held the phone next to the man's face to see if she could detect signs of breathing and almost dropped it. She'd been assuming it was Joseph, but it wasn't—it was Rodney Miller. And he *wasn't* breathing.

Harriet staggered to her feet and, with great effort, turned Rodney onto his back. She knelt beside him, carefully positioning her damaged ankle, then tilted his head back and began chest compressions, but nothing happened. His skin felt cool to her touch; eventually, that fact seeped into her brain, and she realized he probably hadn't been breathing for a while.

She pulled her cell phone from her pocket one more time and dialed 911.

"Police," she said into the phone in response to the operator's question. "There's a man here, and he's not breathing…Harriet. Harriet Truman…It doesn't matter where I live. I'm at Joseph Marston's house with a dead man," she screamed.

Shortly thereafter, she heard the sound of sirens, distant at first but drawing closer. She reached out toward Rodney then snatched her hand back before taking a deep breath and making herself reach out again.

"What secrets have you been keeping, Rodney?" she asked his supine form as she patted the outside pockets of his leather jacket, but all she found was a half-empty pack of sugar-free gum.

"I want you to know, I'm really sorry someone did this to you, and I'll do my best to figure out who did it and bring them to justice." She continued talking, more to calm herself than anything else. "Help me out here. You must have something that can help me."

She pulled the right sleeve of her sweatshirt over her hand and carefully opened the front of Rodney's jacket. She tugged the left side up, revealing the inside breast pocket. She tried to reach into it with her fingers covered by the sweatshirt, but it became clear the shirt and her fingers weren't both going to fit. The sound of sirens was so loud the trucks had to be on Joseph's street already. She gave up and used her bare fingertips to extract a small black notebook and stuffed it into the pocket of her sweatshirt, zipping the pocket shut.

The fire engine and its companion paramedic truck were the first to arrive. Harriet forced herself to her feet and pushed through the rhododendron branches, waving to the First Responders. The chubby blond paramedic who had come to Aiden's when they'd found Neelie came straight to her and began assessing her injuries. An older man went through the branches and knelt next to Rodney. Harriet could see his feet below the leaf line as he rose a moment later and came through the bushes again, shaking his head as he came toward her and her attendant.

"Can you tell me what happened?" her paramedic asked her.

She described the hit to her back and the resulting fall into the window well.

"Let's have a look at your back," he said, pulling a pair of bandage scissors from the leg pocket of his navy blue cargo pants. He slipped a penlight from his shirt pocket, turned it on and held it in his teeth.

"Whoa, there," Harriet said and blocked his hand. "I can take my shirt off—you don't need to cut it."

"Actually, I do," the blond guy said. "I don't want you moving around that much until we see what we're dealing with."

"I don't have that many clothes," she protested. It was a weak argument, and it was her own fault that she hadn't attended to her fall clothes shopping yet.

"How about we slip off the hoodie, and I can cut your shirt close to the seam so you can sew it back up if you want to."

Harriet agreed with a sigh and shrugged to help him slide her hoodie off. True to his word, he cut her shirt along the seam line from waist to armpit and then along the sleeve seam.

The paramedic gently probed her lower back where she'd taken the blow. She winced and reflexively pulled away from the pain of his touch.

"I think the doctors are going to want to get an ultrasound and probably an MRI of your kidney area," he said. "Let me get your blood pressure." He took her blood pressure, listened to her heart and lungs and probed her back, more gently this time. He called to the other paramedic, "We're going to need the gurney here," he said. He turned back to Harriet. "Let's have a look at that ankle,"

He unlaced her shoe and carefully peeled it off her foot. He pulled his scissors out again and cut her sock off. Harriet's foot hurt so much she didn't protest.

"Looks like a nasty sprain," the blond said, shining his penlight on her ankle.

She looked down, but he had already flicked the light off.

167

"I don't think it's broken," he offered. "I saw you stepping on it when you came through the bushes when we first arrived. I don't think you could have done that if it was broken, but I'm sure the docs will want an x-ray to make sure."

"Can I make a phone call?"

"Sure. Let's get you on the gurney first."

Harriet wasn't sure which call she dreaded the most—Aunt Beth or Aiden. Both were going to involve long lectures.

"What happened to Rodney?" she asked, finally thinking beyond her own immediately pain.

"It that the man we found on the ground?"

"Yes," she said impatiently. "He's dead, right? What happened to him?"

"He is dead, but that's all I know."

Of course he didn't know, she realized, he'd been with her since arriving.

"Can you find out?"

"Not really," he said. "Once we determine a person has died of unknown causes, our job is to preserve the evidence. We can't go near the body until after the police are through. And by the way, when you make your calls, have your people meet you at the emergency room. The police aren't going to want anyone else contaminating the scene."

The other paramedic had wheeled the gurney next to where Harriet sat on the ground. He came around to her side opposite the blond.

"Be careful," the blond told him, "she's got a big bruise on her back. She might have internal injuries."

The second paramedic rolled his eyes, obviously annoyed at the suggestion he would be less than careful with any patient. Harriet got the sense this was an ongoing conflict.

She struggled upright and was attempting to balance on her good foot when the two men in blue broke their staring contest and remembered there was a third person present.

"Here, let us help you," the blond said.

Both paramedics put an arm under hers and supported her weight, grasped her under her thighs and lifted her onto the gurney when they had her positioned close to its padded surface. The blond then released the brake and began pushing her across the grass to the driveway where they had parked their emergency response truck.

Harriet asked the blond for the phone from her sweatshirt pocket—she was covered with a blanket and strapped down and hadn't put it back on after her field exam.

Aiden came striding up before the paramedic could comply.

"What happened here?" he demanded.

"This wo—lady…called us, and we found her by the bushes over there," the paramedic stammered and stopped pushing the gurney.

"How bad,"

"Sprained ankle and a bruise over her kidney. She needs x-rays and probably an MRI." The blond man's cheeks turned pink.

"Did you get the prescription cat food I told you about?" It became clear why patient confidentiality had just sailed out the window.

"Not yet, but I will as soon as I get paid," the paramedic said in a rush.

"Good man," Aiden said. "I think you'll find she'll stop pulling her hair out after she's been on the new food for a couple of weeks."

"I am here, you know," Harriet said.

"I'm too mad at you right now to risk speaking to you," Aiden informed her.

"It makes one wonder why you bothered to come."

"I heard the call on our police scanner, and I recognized the address," he said before she could ask the obvious. "Or at least, I was pretty sure. I called your house, and you didn't answer, and I called DeAnn, and she said you'd left almost thirty minutes ago. I decided I'd retrace your route, which we both know goes right past here. I was hoping I'd find you waiting for Triple A to come fix a flat tire or something equally lacking in danger, but I saw your car at the curb and the fire engines and here we are."

"Rodney's dead," Harriet said before he could launch into a lecture.

"What?"

"Rodney's *dead*," she repeated, and pointed with her chin toward the spot where he still lay on the ground.

"How? What happened? Why Joseph's house?"

"I don't know what happened," she said. "I saw someone move past the window, but no one answered the doorbell. I was going to look in the window, but just as I was about to, someone hit me from behind. A moment later, Rodney's body fell on top of me."

"He fell on you?"

Harriet sighed. "He was already cool when I tried to do CPR on him, so I think he was dead before I got here."

"Why were you out in the bushes? Wouldn't it have been easier to look in one of the windows on the porch?"

"That wasn't where I saw motion. The window just above the rhododendrons is where I saw something move."

Aiden looked back at the house. "The window is dark. How did you see something moving?"

She tried to twist around, but he stilled her with a hand on her arm.

"That window was lit when I drove by. I noticed it on my way to DeAnn's, so I was driving slowly when I went back by on my way home. Someone crossed in front of the window."

Aiden looked at the dark house again.

"I didn't make it up," Harriet insisted. "There was light in the window, and someone was in the room. We need to get some answers from Joseph, and I thought he was home."

"I believe you," Aiden said. "Someone else had to have been here, or Rodney wouldn't have gone airborne after he was already dead."

"Unless she made the whole thing up," Detective Sanders said, joining them.

"I suppose you think she clubbed herself in the kidney and sprained her own ankle, too?"

"She could have fallen down the stairs when she was carrying the body out of the house. And by the way, who are you?"

"Dr. Aiden Jalbert," Aiden said in his professional voice, extending his hand, forcing Sanders to either shake it or appear rude.

He cleverly left out the DVM part of his title, Harriet noticed, correctly guessing Sanders would defer to someone he thought was a people doctor.

"We need to get Ms. Truman here to the hospital for an MRI, if you'll excuse us," he continued. "You can question her after we've run our tests."

His bluff worked. Sanders stepped back, and the blond paramedic pushed Harriet to the waiting emergency vehicle.

"You can meet us at the hospital, Dr. Jalbert," he said with a smirk.

"Could you call my aunt?" Harriet called as she disappeared into the ambulance.

Chapter 29

A part of Harriet was impressed by the speed with which the paramedics and then the emergency room staff transferred her into a cubicle in the hospital's trauma unit. The other part wondered how many more years it was going to take to get pain relief of any sort. The ER doctor explained they would not be giving her major painkillers until they finished assessing her injuries.

Aunt Beth and Mavis were waiting in her hospital room when the nurse's aide finally brought her in, after every possible test that could be done had been.

"Oh, honey, are you okay?" Aunt Beth asked. "They wouldn't tell us anything."

"Aiden got called back to the clinic. Apparently, one of his patients took a turn for the worse," Mavis told her. "He said to tell you he'll be back as quick as he can."

"Are the detectives here?" Harriet asked, her voice weak from exhaustion and pain.

"No, we haven't seen any police, detectives or otherwise." Beth said. "All we know is Aiden called and said you'd been hurt and to meet him here."

"He said you were at Joseph's house and that someone had died," Mavis added.

"Rodney," Harriet said.

"Oh, thank heaven," Aunt Beth said. She picked up the plastic cup of water from the bedside table and guided the straw to Harriet's mouth, urging her to drink. "Well, not that Rodney's dead, of course. I thought when Aiden said you'd found a dead man and you were at Joseph's house…well, I assumed it was Joseph."

"Aiden went back to wherever they had you before he told us who it was you found," Mavis explained.

"And they wouldn't let us in the emergency area. They said you were off getting scanned or x-rayed or something," Aunt Beth said.

"It's okay, you're here now." She started to cough but checked it when sharp pain radiated through her back. Her face must have turned the color of her sheet.

"So, what happened?" Aunt Beth asked, having waited until the color returned to Harriet's face. "Why were you at Joseph's house?"

"A light was on, so I stopped. I saw a shadow cross the window. Someone was in the house."

"Why did you go alone? You could have been killed." Tears filled Aunt Beth's eyes.

"Somehow going up and knocking on the door of someone I know in Foggy Point didn't seem like a big risk. This is Washington State, not Washington, DC. "

"If I'm not mistaken, you weren't found on the front porch," Mavis pointed out.

"I started out on the front porch. When no one came to the door, I went over to the lighted window to see if I could get Joseph's attention. When I got to the window, I discovered it was just above a basement window well. I thought I saw something moving through *that* window, so I bent to look and then I was hit from behind."

"So, why are you worrying about a detective being here? If you were just looking in a window and then *you* got attacked, that makes you the victim here, right?" Mavis asked.

"You could have been killed," Aunt Beth said again.

"Not according to Detective Sanders," Harriet said. "He thinks I hit myself in the back, fell, sprained my own ankle, and somehow killed Rodney, too."

"He doesn't!" Shock was clear in Mavis's voice.

"Aiden ran interference so he didn't get very far, but that was the road he was going down."

"Well, that's just ridiculous," Aunt Beth said.

"Did *Joseph* kill him?" Mavis wondered.

"I have no idea," Harriet said. "One minute I was trying to look into the basement window and the next I was getting whacked in the back. I fell into the window well, and when I was trying to get out, someone threw Rodney on top of me."

"Do you think he dropped from above?" Mavis asked thoughtfully.

"I don't see how. The roof is the only thing above that window, and it's three stories up. With that weird shape—flat on top but steeply sloped sides below, I can't see how that would work. My guess is, someone did a fireman's carry with him over their shoulder then just flopped him onto me. I was below grade in that cement well, remember."

"Who would want Rodney dead?" Aunt Beth wondered.

"I'm not sure we know enough about the man to answer that," Mavis said.

"That's true, but I don't think it's a coincidence he was found at Joseph's house," Harriet said. "Aiden saw him at Little Lamb earlier tonight, and we know he was frustrated with the police. What we don't know is why he thought Joseph had the answers he was after."

She shifted slightly and winced as pain shot up her back. Aunt Beth gave Mavis a long look.

"We don't need to solve this tonight," Mavis said.

"I had a thought about our quilting deception," Aunt Beth said, changing the subject. "We need to make up a couple of ugly dog-bone quilt blocks and make sure anyone who might encounter a Small Stitch member has one. As awful as that block looks, they might become suspicious if Sarah is the only one working on them. We need to sell them on the idea we're all making blocks for that quilt."

"Harriet for sure will need one, since she'll probably be asked to quilt a few of theirs before the auction," Mavis said.

"Don't even think about how you're going to keep your quilting schedule. My shoulder is doing much better since it's had time to rest," Aunt Beth told Harriet, referring to the reason she'd retired from long-arm quilting. "I can run the machine while you recover. You just focus on getting better."

Harriet felt her eyelids beginning to droop under the influence of the drugs the doctors had finally given her. The next thing she knew, her aunt and Mavis were gone, and Aiden was sitting in the chair beside her bed, in her darkened room, holding her hand.

"How are you feeling?" he asked softly when he realized she'd awakened.

"Like I've been trampled by a herd of wild horses." She tried to smile.

"What am I going to do with you? Putting yourself in harm's way—again."

"I wasn't *trying*. Somehow, it didn't occur to me going to Joseph Marston's house was putting me in harm's way."

"Yeah, but you did know he'd been acting weird lately."

"Yeah, and hindsight is twenty-twenty," she said. "Can we not talk about this right now? Do you know what's wrong with my back?"

"The doctor told your aunt you have a renal contusion as a result of blunt-force trauma."

"In English, please."

"Your kidney is bruised, but thankfully not broken. And you have a sprained ankle. You can expect a full recovery if you rest until your injuries are healed."

"It sure hurts more than just a bruise."

"The tissue of your back is also bruised, and they think you have a cracked rib. And by the way, a bruised kidney is nothing to be taken lightly. You're lucky you're not in the operating room having that kidney removed."

"Did anyone say what I was hit with?"

"Not that I've heard," he said. "But then, I was gone for a while."

"Is your dog okay now?"

"I'm sorry I had to leave, but I'm the only one in our clinic trained to handle the skin grafting. It still could go either way, but we've done everything we can. Like a lot of them, he has an infection. He had large sores on his back, and he's just a little fellow. It's just sick. These hoarders are so delusional, they can't see how horrible their animals' conditions are."

"I'm sorry," Harriet said.

"No, *I'm* sorry. I shouldn't be talking about this when you've got your own problems."

"It helps, actually. I mean, I'm sad about your dogs, but thinking about them keeps me from thinking about Rodney and Neelie and Joseph."

"Do you think Joseph did this to you?"

"I don't know what to think. I *was* at his house. But why would he want to hurt me?"

"I doubt whoever did this was trying to hurt you. They just wanted to keep you from seeing what was going on in the basement."

"Which leads us back to Joseph. It's his basement. Assuming his mother and stepfather are still out of the country, he's the person who has access to the space. I suppose it's possible someone else was using it, but that still means he at least had knowledge of what was going on there."

"Here's a wild idea," Aiden said. "How about we just let the police figure it out?"

"That's fine with me. I'll leave them alone if they leave me alone."

"It doesn't work that way, I'm afraid. But let's take one thing at a time. Let's you and me concentrate on getting you better."

Chapter 30

Harriet felt better when she woke up the next morning. In spite of near-constant interruptions by the nurses, the pain medication had allowed her to fall back to sleep easily.

Sunlight streamed into her room, illuminating the falling dust particles in the air. Aiden was gone, and her guest chair was empty. She reached for the glass of water on her bedside table and found a folded piece of paper standing like a tent in front of her glass.

"Aiden is checking on his dogs and Mavis and I are in the cafeteria having breakfast. Call us when you're awake," the note read. It was signed by Aunt Beth. Harriet glanced at the clock and was surprised to see that it read nine-thirty.

"Oh, good, you're awake," a red-headed nurse said as she came into the room. "I'm Heather, and I'm your day nurse. How are you feeling?"

"I've been better, but all things considered, I'm not too bad."

"We aim to please," Heather said in a cheery voice. "I'll call for your breakfast and see if the doctor okayed shower privileges."

"I thought I'd do that at home later when you let me out."

"Nice try," Heather said without missing a beat. "The doctor wants to keep you for at least a full twenty-four hours. You checked in just after midnight, but we don't check people out in the middle of the night, so your clock started at seven this morning. You might as well settle in and enjoy the room service. The doctor will be by later today to check your injuries and answer any questions you have."

"Great," Harriet mumbled.

"What was that?"

"Thanks," she said in a louder voice. "I said thanks."

Heather gave her a genuine smile and left the room.

✂ - - - ✂ - - - ✂

"Well, the dead have arisen," Mavis said to Aunt Beth as the pair came back into Harriet's room.

Harriet had just finished her hospital breakfast. The scrambled eggs were soft and fluffy, and the toast was crisp and warm. The orange juice tasted like it was fresh-squeezed, or at least was pure juice.

She was lying with her sprained ankle propped up on pillows and her head only slightly raised. She tried to scoot into a more upright position, but the pain in her side stopped her efforts.

"Is my sweatshirt here somewhere?" she asked.

Mavis and Beth looked around the room, and then Mavis got up and went to the tiny closet in the wall opposite the bed.

"Here it is," she said and brought over Harriet's gray hoodie.

"What are we looking for?" Aunt Beth asked.

"Check the pockets," Harriet said.

Aunt Beth did as directed and, after one false start, retrieved Rodney's small black notebook.

"What have we here?" she said and riffled the pages before handing the book to Harriet.

"I'm not sure, but I found it in Rodney's pocket. I think it's the same book he had out when we saw him in Tico's making phone calls. Hopefully, it's going to tell us something about why he and Neelie were in Foggy Point." She opened the book and scanned the first few pages before flipping quickly through the rest. "Well, it isn't exactly a memoir," she said. "It's names and phone numbers and a very few cryptic notes."

"Did you really think he was going to carry his 'dear diary' around in his breast pocket?" Mavis asked.

"A girl can hope." She paged through the book again, more slowly this time. She stopped and pointed to a name and its corresponding phone number, tapping the page. "Jasmine. I'm pretty sure that's the person Neelie supposedly was staying with after she left Rodney and before she came here."

"One way to find out," Aunt Beth said.

"My purse," Harriet groaned. "My purse is or was in my car in front of Joseph's house before...all this." She gestured to encompass the room.

"Don't worry," Mavis said before she could get too worked up. "Your aunt and I went by Joseph's early this morning and brought your car here. We'll take it home when we leave tonight."

"And," Aunt Beth said as she got up and went to the small closet, "we brought your purse in with us, and your cell phone's there on the bedstand." She brought the purse to the bed.

"We also took the liberty of bringing your stitching bag in," Mavis added.

"After we gathered up the materials for an appliquéd dog block and put them inside," Beth finished.

"Let's start with the cell phone," Harriet said. She winced as she leaned toward it. Aunt Beth moved it within her reach. She dialed the number, but the phone sent her directly to Jasmine's voice mail. She left a brief message asking for a call back.

"Well, that's a dead end," she said.

"She might call back," Aunt Beth said. "In the meantime, you can rest."

Harriet started to protest but was interrupted by the arrival of a large spray of yellow flowers that obscured the person carrying it. Phyllis carried the cut-glass vase filled with yellow lilies, roses and sunflowers into the room, staggering a little from the weight, and set it on the windowsill. The fragrance from the lilies immediately filled the space.

"I hope it's okay that I barged right in without knocking," she said. "That vase is heavier than it looks, with the water and all."

"Come in," Mavis said. "Here, sit down and take a load off." She got up and offered the easy chair she'd been sitting in to her larger friend. "And of course you're welcome."

"Thank you," Harriet said. "I appreciate the flowers. You shouldn't have, but I'm grateful that you did."

Aunt Beth beamed her approval of Harriet's courtesy.

"How are you feeling?" Phyllis asked. "I came over as soon as I heard."

"Mavis and I have been remiss, as you can see—yours are the first flowers," Aunt Beth said.

"Just out of curiosity, how did you find out I was here? I mean, I checked in during the middle of the night."

"If Joseph's across-the-street neighbor hadn't been worried about him and called, I *wouldn't* have known," she said, the smile leaving her lips. "That, and the fact Joseph was a no-show again today. I don't mind sharing that I'm really starting to get worried about the boy. His neighbor was afraid something had happened to him, and knew he worked at Little Lamb. Her concerns, coupled with my own, caused me to call the police when I'd hung up.

"I'm sorry you were hurt, Harriet, but I have to say I was relieved the dead man they took from that house wasn't Joseph."

"Did you know the dead man?" Harriet asked.

"I'd never even heard of him," Phyllis said. "And I hope the same is true of Joseph."

Harriet knew it wasn't but decided there was no point in worrying Phyllis any more than she already was. Besides, the flowers were beautiful.

"Can I get anyone some coffee or tea?" Aunt Beth asked. "I'm going to the cafeteria."

Phyllis and Mavis put in their orders, and Aunt Beth left to get them.

"How are you ladies coming with your quilts for the auction?" Phyllis asked.

"The usual," Mavis said. "We're behind where we'd like to be, but we'll pull it together by auction time."

"I don't know how the Stitches are doing," Phyllis admitted. "I missed our last meeting because of Joseph." She looked at her hands in her lap. "He's left me in a real pickle, that boy."

"It'd be a lot easier on all of us if this year's organizing committee hadn't decided on this dog theme nonsense. We'd get a lot more money for the quilts if we'd done it like we always have, with any design being acceptable," Mavis complained, not for the first time.

"The last block design the Stitches were looking at was pretty ridiculous, if you ask me," Phyllis looked up when she said this but went back to studying the gold signet ring on her right pinkie finger. "A bunch of dog bones," she added.

Harriet exchanged a glance with Mavis, but she didn't let on that the dog-bone design meant anything to her.

Chapter 31

Y ou didn't let on?" Aunt Beth asked, even though Mavis had indicated they hadn't, when they recounted the discussion they'd had after Phyllis had gone back to work. "I talked to Lauren yesterday," she continued, "after we got home from pizza and before all this. She said she was hidden behind a desk, fixing a loose wire, when Glynnis and Frieda came into the office. It was just as we suspected—they looked around and made sure no one was looking, or so they thought, and then they went through Sarah's bag."

"We knew they had to be doing that," Mavis said. "But somehow, I'm still shocked."

"Is it shock or outrage?" Harriet said. "I hate that we have to spend so much, or even any, time on all this subterfuge."

"Who are you, and what did you do with my niece?" Aunt Beth asked. "You middle name is Intrigue—or am I mistaken?"

"I may like a good puzzle as much as the next guy, but not where our quilts are concerned," Harriet protested.

"Be that as it may," Aunt Beth said, "it's where we find ourselves, so we need to do our parts to make sure the Threads retain their dominance in the event."

"Can I be dominant tomorrow?" Harriet asked. She yawned. "I think I need a nap."

As if on cue, Nurse Heather came into the room.

"Time for our patient to get some rest," she said in a cheery voice.

"Is this place bugged?" Mavis asked.

Nurse Heather raised her eyebrows and tilted her head slightly to the side.

"Of course it is." Mavis answered her own question.

"We prefer to think of it as patient monitoring," Heather said.

"Come on, Mavis," Aunt Beth said. "We need to make sure everyone who needs to has a decoy dog-bone block on display. Besides, we need to catch the rest of the Threads up on last night's doin's"

"We'll be back in a couple of hours, honey." Mavis gathered her bags and followed Beth out of the room.

Harriet fell into a dreamless sleep that ended when a doctor she'd never met came in an hour and a half later to check her progress.

"Hi, I'm Doctor Eisner."

Harriet noted his blond hair, brown eyes and stocky build and the irrational thought he was the polar opposite of Aiden came unbidden to her mind. It has to be the drugs, she thought. That and the fact he looked as young as Aiden, if not younger, if that was possible given the man had to have at least eight years of college and medical school and all that other stuff doctors had to do.

"How are you feeling?"

"Better, I think." She gasped when he touched her lower back.

"That's what I thought, still pretty tender."

"Only when I breathe," she said with a weak smile.

"Well, you're smiling, that's a good sign. I've looked at all your scans, and you have a nasty bruise on your kidney, but it doesn't appear to be lacerated. I'm keeping you one more day to stabilize your fluids and control the load on your kidneys. And I'd like to see the blood in your urine gone before we let you go.

"Your ankle looks like a straightforward sprain, but since your reputation precedes you, we're going to put you in a non-walking cast for a week that will insure you stay off it, and at the same time give your kidney time to heal. I'm serious—you have to rest."

The smile froze on Harriet's face, and she didn't say anything for a minute.

"That's good news," Dr. Eisner said. "If you'd been hit any harder, we'd be in recovery right now, talking about how you were going to live with one kidney."

"I'm sorry. I didn't mean to seem ungrateful. I've just got a lot of work to do, and this isn't going to help." *And I need to find out who did this to me.*

"I'll be back to see you tomorrow. Get some rest. The nurses can give you pain medication if you need it. Just use your buzzer."

"Thanks," she said and yawned, sleepiness once again taking control of her body.

"If you follow our advice, stay off your foot, control your liquids, and get plenty of rest, in a few weeks, you'll be as good as new."

Harriet was asleep before he'd finished his warning.

✂ - - - ✂ - - - ✂

The doctor was serious about Harriet getting rest, and although she used every argument she could come up with to change his mind, he prevailed. He cut her visitation time to ten minutes per hour every other hour for the duration of her stay. Aunt Beth and Aiden both grumbled about being excepted from those limits, but the doctor was adamant.

Just as he'd said, Harriet was there for another full day, and had to admit she did feel more rested as a result of his strict policy. Nurse Heather told her she would have probably been there another *two* days otherwise.

Chapter 32

An unmarked police car was parked in Harriet's driveway when Mavis pulled up to the studio door. She and Beth had decided the Town Car was better suited than Beth's Beetle to transport their patient home.

Harriet was maneuvering out of the car and onto her crutches when Detective Morse got out of the unmarked and approached her.

"How are you feeling?"

"Like you care?" Harriet snapped.

"She's doing much better, thank you," Aunt Beth said and glared at her niece.

"I was hoping we could talk."

"So you can ask me why I called nine-one-one after I killed Rodney, whacked myself in the back and jumped into the window well?"

"That's only one theory," Morse said in a weary voice. "I'd be interested in hearing what actually happened."

"Come on, honey," Mavis said as she came around the car. "You need to get inside and put your foot up." She carried Harriet's purse along with her own and their quilting bags.

"We put the gray chair and ottoman in the studio," Aunt Beth said, referring to the upholstered easy chair and its footstool, which she'd gotten Aiden to move from the upstairs TV room. She put her hand under Harriet's elbow to help her negotiate the steps.

"Your aunt and I figured it would be easier if you only had to climb the stairs at bedtime," Mavis explained.

Harriet stopped. "I know you're trying to help, but these crutches are hard enough with one driver."

Beth released her niece's elbow and backed up a step.

"Fine," she said.

"I'm sorry. This is hard for all of us."

"Just go on inside," Beth said. She turned back to Detective Morse. "I'm not sure this is a good time."

"There isn't going to be a good time," Morse told her. "There is now, here, with me, while Detective Sanders is in court on another case, or we can wait until later when he's not otherwise engaged and is available to give his full attention to this matter."

Beth sighed. "I'll put the tea on."

Harriet hobbled into the studio, carefully crutching to the large gray chair. Aunt Beth had set three bed pillows on the ottoman. She gasped as she tried to lean down and pick one up.

"Oh, honey, let me do that," Mavis said and arranged the pillows at Harriet's direction then helped her sit in the chair, propping her injured leg.

When Harriet was settled, she indicated Detective Morse should take one of the wingback chairs. Mavis and Beth had removed two of the worktables from the corner and created a new sitting area with the gray chair, the two wingback chairs and the piecrust table from the original space.

"Nice touch," Harriet said, looking down at the hand-braided circular rug the chairs sat on. Mavis had brought it over from its storage spot in her garage, a product of yet another craft hobby that had fallen out of style, along with the macramé plant holders and painted ceramic geese she and Beth had made in the late nineteen-seventies.

"We thought it made the area look a little warmer," Mavis said, also looking down at the rug.

Detective Morse cleared her throat. "Would it be okay if we talk about what happened?"

"I'll go check on the tea," Mavis said, heading for the door to the kitchen.

"Do you want to start at the beginning?" Detective Morse asked when she and Harriet were alone.

"There's not a lot to tell. I went to Joseph's, he didn't answer the door, I saw movement in a window, went to look in the window, got whacked in the back, sprained my ankle and had a dead guy fall on me."

"We can make this easy, or we can make it hard, but I'm not going anywhere until I get all my questions answered to my satisfaction."

"Okay," Harriet said, drawing the word out. "What more do you want to know?"

"Why did you go to see Joseph?"

Harriet explained that she hadn't planned the stop and had only done it in response to the movement in the lighted window.

"Who did you see move across the window?"

She explained again about the shadow, and that she only saw movement in the ground-level window with her peripheral vision.

"I wish I had more to show for all my injuries," Harriet said when Detective Morse had run out of questions, "but like I said at the beginning, I stopped on a whim. I don't even know Joseph all that well. I had just been at our friend DeAnn's house. She and her husband recently adopted a little girl, and Joseph is their social worker. We had a question for him, and he's been sort of hard to find, so when I saw the light I thought I'd stop by and see if he was in."

"You said, 'we' had a question. Who're we?"

"DeAnn, me, the Loose Threads—we," Harriet said.

"Does your quilt group always get involved in each other's business?"

"Keeping in mind that I'm a recent returnee to the area and the group and therefore have a limited amount of data on the subject, I'd say from what I've seen that's exactly how the Loose Threads operate, and also from what I've seen, it isn't just them, it's most of Foggy Point."

"I'm not from this area, either," Detective Morse admitted with a half-smile. "But that's how it seems to me, too."

"With a network like this, it makes you wonder why no one can find Joseph," Harriet mused.

"I wouldn't say no one can find him. We just haven't found him *yet*. It's entirely possible he's just out of town and doesn't know anyone is looking for him. Other than owning the house where the dead man fell on you, he hasn't done anything. Unless you know something about him I don't. Or maybe you'd like to tell me what it was that you and your group were so anxious to find him for."

"As I said before, he's the social worker handling DeAnn Gault's adoption of a little girl from Africa, only we're beginning to suspect the child isn't from Africa."

"That's strange," Morse said.

"That's what we thought," Aunt Beth interjected as she carried in a tray with teacups and a teapot on it. She set it on the side of the ottoman that wasn't occupied by Harriet's feet. Mavis followed, carrying the sugar bowl and creamer.

"We can't figure out why someone would claim a child was from a third-world country if she's really from a depressed island in the South Pacific."

"Unless Joseph was playing with immigration numbers," Harriet said. "But I don't even know if that makes sense."

"Maybe their paperwork got mixed up," Morse suggested. "Do you know if anyone else in the area adopted a child of the same age in the same time frame? Maybe there's another family out there that has the African child when they were expecting an island child."

"DeAnn had received quite a bit of information about her child before the adoption went through, including pictures," Harriet countered.

"Moving on," Morse said. "What was..." She looked at her notes. "...Rodney Miller doing at Joseph's house?"

"Other than dying?" Harriet asked.

"Yeah, other than that."

"We already told you about that," Aunt Beth said as she distributed teacups. "He seems to have followed Neelie here for his own reasons."

"Which we were never able to figure out," Harriet added. "The last thing I'd heard about him was that someone had seen him arguing with Joseph in front of Little Lamb, and then he was dead at Joseph's house. What happened in between is anyone's guess."

"You're sure you don't know anything else about Rodney Miller or Neelie Obote?"

"If we did, I'd tell you," Aunt Beth said.

"What happened to the baby?" Morse asked.

"Which one?" Mavis asked, and offered the cream and sugar to each person in turn.

"The one Neelie brought to town."

"She's in foster care," Aunt Beth said. None of the women felt inclined to identify Connie as the foster mother.

"Two people who know each other come to Foggy Point and die within days of each other, you have to believe there's a connection," Morse said thoughtfully.

"Rodney told anyone who would listen he was Neelie's grieving husband," Harriet said.

"That's great, except there's no legal proof the marriage existed," Morse said. "And believe me, we've checked. If they were married, they didn't file a license in this country."

"Is it possible the Neelie-and-Rodney story is simply one of domestic violence?" Aunt Beth asked. She picked up her cup and sipped. "She and the baby were trying to escape, and he followed them here. He kills her, and someone sees him do it, and that someone else kills him in retaliation."

"Anything's possible," Morse said. "But, believe it or not, most people who witness a murder actually call the police."

"Is that it?" Harriet asked.

Detective Morse raised her left eyebrow.

"If you're done with your questions, I have a few of my own."

"I can't guarantee I can answer, but if I can..." She trailed off with a sigh.

"Okay, first, I'd like to know if you know what was used to hit me."

"A blunt object?" Morse offered.

This time both Mavis and Aunt Beth glared at the detective.

"Okay, okay, I suppose it can't hurt to tell you we think you were hit with a baseball bat. You can thank your friend Darcy

Lewis for that." Morse referred to the pixie-faced criminalist who also was a part-time Loose Thread member. "She was the one who found the bat in the garage behind the house. It was leaning against a set of golf clubs along the back wall. Darcy noticed that the clubs, the workbench and virtually everything else in that bay of the garage was coated with a thick layer of dust and cobwebs."

"Everything except the bat," Mavis finished for the detective.

"Exactly." Morse picked up her cup and took a long drink.

"I don't suppose there were any prints on the bat," Harriet asked.

"It obviously had been wiped down, but Darcy got a partial print off the end." Morse didn't look hopeful.

"That's good, isn't it?" Harriet asked.

"It looks like it's a child's print." Morse said.

"A *kid* hit me?"

"Probably not," Morse said. "The print most likely belongs to the actual owner of the bat. If we could identify the kid, it might give us a circle of adults with access to look at, but unfortunately, there isn't a huge database of children's fingerprints to compare it to."

"I thought the grade school did a big drive to collect all the children's fingerprints to use in case of child abductions," Mavis said.

"Unfortunately, not all fingerprints are created equal. If they aren't taken by someone the forensic lab has trained, they often are unusable—smeared or flattened beyond recognition."

"That's too bad," Aunt Beth said. "I suppose almost anyone could have wielded a bat. I mean, any household that has or has had children in it is likely to have a bat and ball."

"You begin to see the scope of our problem."

"Have you been able to verify the identification of Neelie or Rodney?" Harriet asked.

"No. We've interviewed quite a few people, and no one has known anything other than that two people we have in the morgue used the names Neelie Obote and Rodney Miller."

"This is all making my head hurt," Harriet said, and leaned that head against the back of her chair. She closed her eyes for just a moment.

Chapter 33

It was dark when Harriet woke with a start. She was still sitting in the gray chair, but she was alone in the room, and she'd been covered with a plaid flannel log cabin lap quilt. Fred rose up from his spot next to her left thigh and meowed.

"Where is everyone?" Harriet asked her cat. He meowed again.

"I'm coming," said a disembodied voice from a small white speaker on the pie-crust table. A moment later, Aunt Beth appeared, carrying a glass of water in one hand and a white capsule cupped in the other.

"Here," she said and handed the pain pill and then the water to her niece. "How are you feeling?"

"I know I just woke up, but I'm still sleepy. How long was I out? Is Detective Morse gone?"

"A couple of hours, and yes, the good detective left not long after you fell asleep. She didn't ask anything else, and we didn't offer up anything, either. And you needed the rest. We left you in here with the baby monitor so you could have some peace and quiet."

"We had an idea about our quilting," Mavis said as she, too, came back into the studio from the kitchen. She was carrying a small plate of triple chocolate cookies and a fresh cup of tea for Harriet. "We were thinking maybe we could change up who was working on what."

"What do you mean" Harriet asked.

"We're getting to crunch time for the auction quilts," Mavis started.

"And I'm going to be running the long arm machine," Beth added.

"You aren't going to be able to sit at your sewing machine for a few days," Mavis continued. "So, we thought I could sew *your* tumbling blocks together on the sewing machine, and if you can, we thought you could work on appliquéing the dog-bone wreath block I'm supposed to do. My block is more than half-done, so it won't take much to finish it."

"You can start on that first thing tomorrow," Aunt Beth interrupted. We're going to stitch a little more, but Aiden brought you a couple of movies and we thought you could watch them upstairs. We moved the television into your bedroom so you could keep your foot up."

"Aiden was here?" Harriet said. "Wait, you moved my TV?"

"Well, you can't watch in your TV room," Mavis explained. "You'd have to prop your foot on the table. You're using your ottoman down here."

"How could I forget? Is there anything else you've done on my behalf I should know about?"

"Well, we did ask Aiden to bring us all burritos from Tico's," Aunt Beth confessed.

"That part's good. About the quilt project, don't forget *I'm* supposed to be appliquéing a dog-bone wreath block, too."

"I think you can hold off till tomorrow and still have time to finish all the appliqué," Aunt Beth said.

Any further argument on the topic ended when the doorbells tinkled and Aiden came in carrying two large white paper bags from Tico's Tacos.

"Jorge sent you your own carton of guacamole and a bag of chips that are still warm from the fryer," he told Harriet. "He also sent some of his special soup that he says is guaranteed to cure your kidney." He set the bags on the big work table and crossed the room to lean down and kiss her. "How are you feeling?"

"I've been better, but the sleep and pain meds are helping."

192

Beth and Mavis picked up the two bags and carried them into the kitchen.

"You need to take it easy for a while," Aiden said. "These should help." He held up two red envelopes Harriet recognized as DVD movie mailers. "Guaranteed to make you cry."

"I take it you're not staying to watch," she said, knowing how much he hated watching chick flicks with her.

"I wish I could, but after dinner I've got to go back to work. A small group of patients are well enough to be neutered, which is one of the hurdles they have to get over to move toward adoption."

"That's so sad," Harriet said. "It seems like all they've known in their lives is pain, and now, in order to help them, you have to cause them more pain."

"I try not to think of it in those terms," Aiden said. "And we *will* provide anesthesia and pain medication."

"I'm sorry—I wasn't trying to be critical. I just feel bad for the dogs."

"Well, I feel sorry for you. You were only trying to help a friend, and someone had to do this to you."

"I just wish I'd learned something that could help DeAnn."

"Well, superwoman, sometimes it has to be good enough that you simply survived to fight another day."

He was holding her hand when Aunt Beth and Mavis came back into the studio. Both carried a tray with the guacamole and chips and Harriet's soup. Mavis followed with a stack of plates, utensils and the foil-wrapped burritos.

✄- - -✄- - -✄

"I can't eat another bite," Harriet announced when she'd finished all of her guacamole, her soup and half of her barbacoa burrito. "Jorge once again outdid himself."

"The man can cook," Mavis said. "I'll give him that. He's nosier than my pappy's old bluetick hound, but he can surely cook."

"Can I quote you?" Aiden asked with a grin.

"Brat."

Aiden looked like he was going to say something, but his cell phone rang, interrupting their banter. He listened, letting his caller do the talking.

"Wow," he said after a moment. "I do remember that."

He gestured toward Aunt Beth, making writing motions in the air. Beth got up quickly and grabbed a pen and pad from Harriet's desk, then put it into his outstretched hand. He lodged the phone between chin and shoulder and scribbled a name and address on the tablet.

"Thank you so much for getting back to me," he said. He talked for another minute, pacing across the room as he asked how his caller was and listened for the reply before saying goodbye and ringing off.

The three women were looking expectantly at him when he turned around and returned to the sitting area.

"Ladies, I think we just got a piece of the puzzle." He sat down and picked up the large cup of cola he'd brought with him from Tico's, taking a drink before continuing. "That was Nabirye Obote. She said she didn't have any half-sisters who could fit the bill, but she did have a cousin who had been adopted as a baby."

"What's the cousin's name?" asked Harriet.

"I'm coming to that. This cousin was adopted in America and…" He exaggerated the *and*. "…she happens to have visited Africa while I was there."

"And her name was Neelie Obote," Harriet interjected.

Aiden looked at her but continued his story at his own pace.

"While she was visiting, I was working in the same village Nabirye was. It was the rainy season, and just before the visitors arrived we had a mudslide that filled the hut I was staying in with slime. I had to temporarily share Nabirye's tent."

"Ah, it all becomes clear," Harriet said.

"No, it doesn't. I wasn't the only one who had to move to the water project tent, but maybe her cousin didn't realize that."

Harriet started to interrupt, but he went on speaking.

"Her cousin's name was—"

"Neelie," Harriet guessed.

"No," he said. "It was Nancy—Nancy Lou, to be exact. I'm sure she picked Neelie because it's an African name, and honestly, would you have believed her story about bringing her sister's child if she'd said her name was Nancy Lou?"

"Good point," Aunt Beth said. "And who knows, maybe her birth name *was* Neelie."

"Did your friend say how old her cousin was?" Mavis asked.

"She said she wasn't sure. She was a child herself when the adoption originally happened. And the aunt who gave Nancy or Neelie up for adoption died from AIDS when Nabirye was a teenager. Given her age now and her memories of the incident, she's guessing Nancy Lou was probably in her late twenties when she visited."

"So, she went back to discover her roots or something," Harriet said. "Then she saw her cousin and a man with distinctive eyes, who she presumed was her cousin's lover, and a plan was born."

"That's about it."

"Wait a minute," Mavis said. "Aren't you forgetting something?"

"A big something," Aunt Beth added.

Harriet looked at them without saying anything.

"Kissa," Mavis said. "I think we've already established they don't hand babies out at the local Walmart. Somehow, that young woman came up with a blue-eyed baby of an appropriate age to be passed off as Aiden's offspring."

"Maybe that's the connection to Rodney," Harriet speculated. "He seems like the kind of resourceful guy who could come up with a baby—his own or otherwise—on short notice."

"Well, we're not going to solve this tonight, and I've got to get back to the clinic and someone here needs to rest." Aiden crumpled his burrito wrapper then stacked the used plates and carried them to the kitchen.

"He's right," Aunt Beth said. "Let's get you upstairs so Mavis and I can come back down and sew."

Chapter 34

The next two days passed in a blur of stitching, movies and sleeping. Aunt Beth and Mavis let the Loose Threads know Harriet wouldn't be receiving visitors until the weekend, and everyone respected that, which was strange given Sarah could almost always be counted on to do the exact opposite of whatever the rest of the group decided on.

"Good morning, Merry Sunshine," Aunt Beth said on Saturday morning when Harriet crutched downstairs.

"What's got you in such a chipper mood this morning?"

"I'm just being my normal cheerful self."

Harriet laughed. "Since when?"

"Okay, maybe I'm a little hysterical with relief that I finished quilting the last quilt this morning."

"You finished our applique quilt?"

Beth made a face. "Oh, please. It's not like it was a California king or anything. Get yourself situated in your chair, and I'll bring you some breakfast."

"You don't have to fix me breakfast on top of all the quilting you've been doing."

"Don't worry, Aiden stopped by with some breakfast burritos Jorge made us. He was on his way to work and said to tell you he'll be back in a couple of hours. He said all the clinic vets were going to have a meeting to decide if any of the hoarding victims could be adopted out in conjunction with the auction. I guess the fundraising committee is really pressuring the clinic. They think the hoarding story will bring in big-dollar donations and having a few survivors at the dinner and auction might help."

"I'd like to be a fly on the wall for that meeting. Aiden told me he feels it would be like abusing the dogs twice, making them go out in public so soon," Harriet said. "I'm just glad we're going to have quilts finished to auction."

A knock sounded on the studio door, ending the discussion. Aunt Beth headed to answer, talking as she went.

"I volunteered to host the Loose Threads meeting here today, since you can't go anywhere yet." She opened the door, letting Jenny, Connie and Carla in along with a crisp gust of wind.

"Oh, honey," Connie said and came to stand by Harriet's chair. "We've been so worried about you."

"As you can see, I'm fine."

"You don't look fine."

"The doctor put me in an over-sized cast to force me to stay off my ankle, but it really is just an ordinary sprain. And my kidney is much better."

"I'm glad to hear that, but you just take it slow for a while anyway."

Carla brought Connie a cup of tea then pushed one of the wheeled chairs from the desk area to the space beside the gray chair and sat down.

Mavis and Lauren arrived together, each carrying a pillowcase that appeared to be holding a quilt. They set their bags on the large cutting table and continued on into the kitchen to prepare their drinks.

Everyone was surprised when DeAnn arrived with Robin. They, too, were carrying bags with quilts in them.

"I take it things are going better with Iloai," Harriet said when DeAnn had pulled a chair into the circle and sat down.

"Quite a bit has happened since..." She nodded at Harriet's foot.

"Since my accident?" Harriet suggested.

"I didn't want to say attack, but it sounds like that's what actually happened."

"True, but it sounds so dramatic, don't you think? So, enough about me, tell us what's happened."

"I think you know that Joseph has gone missing," she started, but was immediately interrupted by Sarah, who had come in while DeAnn was getting her chair and getting situated.

"Joseph's not missing," she said. "I just saw him. I was at the pet store getting some of those green treats for my Rachel, and I saw him there buying insect larvae for his dragon."

"Excuse me?" Harriet said. "He has a dragon?"

"Well, not exactly." Sarah sat down in one of the wingback chairs. "I think it's some kind of lizard. The geeks that keep them call them dragons."

"You seem to know a lot about it," Lauren said.

Sarah pinched her lips together in an apparently successful attempt to stop whatever rude remark she was about to make.

"Ever since my parents decided to let anyone in the community use the all-purpose room at the senior center for meetings if they were willing to let residents sit in on the gatherings, any time more than three weirdoes want to get together, they come there, including the dragon people."

"And Joseph's one of them?" Harriet asked.

"Isn't that what I just said?"

"How long ago did you see him?" DeAnn asked. "We've been trying to reach him for days. He doesn't answer his phone, and Phyllis doesn't know where he is. And she said he took our file home."

"I'm telling you, I stopped at the pet store on my way here."

"Are you sure it was Joseph?" Harriet asked.

"Now you're getting insulting," Sarah said with an affected pout.

"So, what kind of game is he playing?" asked Harriet.

"That's what I'd like to know," DeAnn said.

"He did look a little stressed, but I thought it was because he was grossed out about the larvae. You know how some people don't think ahead when they get exotic pets. He probably just decided how cool it would be to have a frilled lizard, and didn't even think about—"

"Sarah," Aunt Beth said in a firm voice, "exactly how was he acting stressed? Tell us what you saw."

"Well, first of all, he completely ignored me when he came in the store, and I was standing right by the checkout register, looking through the sale bin and—"

"*Joseph*, Sarah—what was *Joseph* doing?" Mavis asked.

"He waited until there was no one in the bug aisle, and then he went to the larvae tray and started picking larvae into a carton. But he kept looking from side to side, like he was watching for someone. And he dropped the carton once and had to start over, and he didn't even pick up the ones he dropped. And—"

"Thank you, Sarah," Aunt Beth said.

"So, he's hiding somewhere," Harriet said.

"He's not hiding," Sarah protested. "I'm telling you, he's at the pet store."

"Okay, we get it, he's at the pet store," Harriet said. "Do you think he's still there?"

"Well, no. I waited until he left, just to see if he'd talk to me after he got his baby bugs."

"Did he?"

"No, he went right by me like I wasn't there—and after I've been so nice to him and his geeky friends. I even touched his lizard."

"I'm not sure I'd mention that in polite company," Harriet said.

Carla chuckled then blushed. Aunt Beth glared but didn't say anything.

"So, DeAnn," Harriet said. "What were you about to say you're doing in the absence of Joseph?"

"We went to Phyllis, of course, but as I said, she told us he had taken our file home and apparently everything else associated with Iloai."

"I wonder if that's usual," Mavis said. "We'll have to check with Phyl."

Aunt Beth excused herself and went into the kitchen. Harriet watched her leave and wondered what she was up to. Everyone had fresh drinks, and Connie had brought a plate of layered bar cookies.

"Go on," Harriet said, giving DeAnn what she hoped was an encouraging look.

"My husband decided we needed to investigate more, so he called a friend of his at the University of Washington, and that guy checked with the campus foreign studies center and found us a translator. The guy is great. He speaks several island dialects, and he has small children himself. He agreed to come to our house yesterday and talk with Iloai."

"And?" Harriet was anxious to hear the punch line.

"She was quite chatty with him, once she got comfortable. Unfortunately, she was chatty at a three-year-old level. The perplexing thing is that she talked about Mama, Dada, Sister and Aunt—in Samoan, of course. She talked about a dog and about fish, and she said her dad fished. She has a whole fantasy world peopled with family members who work a lot and fish a lot."

"That's weird for a child who was raised in an orphanage," Harriet said.

"Maybe it was in a fishing village, and they took the children to the beach," Jenny suggested.

"Children are able to do imaginary play when they're that age," Connie said. "But usually it's simple—they pretend they're their dolls' mother, or other basic games. I'll look in my child-development book when I get home and see what it says, but I think that kind of detail isn't usual. I don't know how being in an orphanage might affect a child's fantasies at that age."

"Lauren's list of words has been a big help, and the professor helped us with proper pronunciation, but it's clear, even though she's not crying all the time, Iloai wants to be somewhere else."

"Oh, honey, I'm sorry this has been so hard on you and your family," Mavis said.

"I just feel for Iloai," DeAnn said. "She's been miserable, and until Lauren brought us the Samoan word list we weren't getting anywhere. Now at least we have somewhere to start trying to figure this thing out.

"And I'm here. Things were calm enough this morning that David and the boys should be able to handle it. I put the binding on one of the quilts last night. I needed to do something that wasn't related to small children for a few hours and to feel like I'd done something toward the auction."

"We're glad you're here," Aunt Beth said as she came back into the studio.

"Speaking of the quilts," Mavis said. "Let's get them out and see what we've got."

Connie and Lauren got up and pulled a quilt out of its pillow-case, then held it up for the group to see. Connie had provided a slate-gray landscape fabric for the doghouse roofs, and Lauren had hand-dyed a pale-blue fabric so it had random streaks of white that looked like clouds. These two features provided a unifying effect among the blocks made by the various Loose Threads members. Mavis had found a print with small doghouses for the outer border, and they had used a dark-brown Moda Marble for the inner one.

"That came out nice," Jenny said.

"It's okay," Lauren said, "but let's be honest—if this is the best we've got, we're in trouble."

Mavis and Beth got up next but kept their quilt folded in half, obscuring the front.

"As you know, we've been working on the snowball blocks. We tried fussy-cutting images for the center, but once we saw the star blocks, we felt ours were too similar," Mavis said.

Aunt Beth took up the story. "Next, we tried using small-scale coordinating prints—bones, paw prints, that sort of thing. They would have made a serviceable quilt, but when we put a couple of rows together, it was too boring."

"We decided it was time to get creative," Mavis said.

"So, when you guys go off the rails it's creativity, but if I do it, I'm not being a team player," Lauren said. "How's that work?"

Mavis ignored the interruption.

"We were doing a computer search for dog pattern fabric when this one came up." On cue, Beth stepped to the side, opening their quilt. "It's dogwood and daffodils."

The main fabric used for the quilt had a mauve background with pink dogwood flowers and cheddar daffodils with brick-red trumpets. They had alternated the snowball blocks with green and dark-salmon-colored nine-patch blocks.

"Who makes that fabric?" Jenny asked.

"It's a Phillip Jacobs print for Rowan," Mavis replied.

"Well, it's cheating, but I have to admit, we might have a chance with that in our arsenal," Lauren grumbled.

Robin stood up and removed the quilt that was folded up in her bag, Carla took one corner and stepped aside, opening it to the group's view.

The quilt was composed of multiple-sized star blocks with a fussy-cut realistic dog for the center and a taupe background. The points of the stars were made from prints that coordinated with the center images.

"That came out real cute," Mavis said.

"How did you find images that were spaced far enough apart to fussy-cut like that?" DeAnn asked, referring to the technique of cutting a quilt piece at any angle or direction that resulted in a particular image being centered in the piece.

"We didn't," Carla said. "If you look close, you can see where we added solid-colored fabric to the edges of the dog fabric."

DeAnn stood and picked up the corner of the quilt, looking closely at one of the blocks.

"Very clever," she said and went back to her seat.

"What about Harriet's quilt?" Sarah asked. "Do you need me to finish it?"

Harriet blanched at the thought of Sarah touching her quilt. Even knowing Aunt Beth and Mavis had already finished it, the idea of Sarah, who never met an instruction she couldn't disregard, even coming close to her design was frightening.

"Thank you, honey," Mavis said, "Beth and I finished the quilt for Harriet when she got hurt."

Beth stood up and went to Harriet's work table to pick up the folded quilt. She handed two corners to Mavis and stepped to the side with the other two, allowing the quilt to unfurl.

"Whoa," DeAnn said when the image was revealed.

Blocks appeared to cascade from the center of the quilt. The three dimensional cubes each appeared to have a dog inside it, due to Harriet's clever instruction to everyone to fussy-cut a diamond-shaped dog image to form one side of each block.

Harriet had chosen deep reds and brown tones that ranged from a light caramel to a brown so dark it was almost black. The overall effect was striking. The pile of blocks were appliquéd onto a black background.

"Wow," said Robin. "You sure couldn't tell how dramatic that was going to come out just from doing a single block."

"I think we have a contender for raffle quilt," Jenny announced then looked around the group, silently daring Lauren or Sarah to challenge her assessment, but they remained silent.

"Let's see the dog-bone quilt," Harriet said.

"We made a change after the last meeting," Jenny said and got up to take the quilt from Aunt Beth's work table. "The original plan was to have a different breed of dog in each bone wreath, but when I drew up the diagrams, it looked too disjointed, so I changed the plan and made each dog face different colors and expressions, but all based on a Yorkshire terrier." She unfolded the result and held it up for the group to see. "Beth just finished it, so of course, it isn't bound yet, but here it is."

The dog faces were appliquéd in tan, white and black with touches of gray. Pink had been used for the dogs' tongues and some of the bows in their topknots. They were set in two rows of three on a medium rose-pink background. Dark-green vines and dark-pink and white flowers twined around the outside of the dog blocks, framing them, and the final border was cut in deep scallops. The scallop area had been quilted in a closely set crosshatch pattern. Jenny explained that the binding would be the same dark green as the flower vines.

"We may be competing against ourselves for the raffle quilt," Robin said. "This one is definitely a contender, too."

Jenny blushed a becoming shade of pink. "I don't know about that, but at least they should be able to sell it at auction."

She picked up Connie's plate of butterscotch chocolate bars and handed them around the group again before sitting back down.

Connie was explaining that grated carrots were the secret ingredient in her bars, but she stopped when someone knocked on the door. Harriet looked around. Most of the people she knew were already in the room, and Aiden was at the vet clinic—and he wouldn't have knocked, in any case. She mentally reviewed her quilting schedule, trying to think of any customer she might have a forgotten.

Aunt Beth went to the door to let Detective Morse in.

"What's she doing here?" Harriet blurted.

"Mind your manners, child," Aunt Beth said. "I called Detective Morse and told her about Sarah's story of seeing Joseph. She wants to question her, and I told her to come on over." She ushered Detective Morse into the center of the circle of chairs.

"Ladies," she said. "I'd like you all to meet Jane Morse. She's a detective, and she's investigating the murders."

She didn't need to say which murders—they all knew. No one moved or said anything.

"She's also a quilter," Beth added.

"What kind of quilts do you make?" Lauren asked.

"Mostly machine piecing," Jane replied. "I'm learning to appliqué, but I'm not very good on inside curves yet."

Carla smiled at the last comment.

"I'd love to look at the quilts you have here, but first I need to ask…" She glanced at a small notebook in her hand. "…Sarah Ness a few questions."

Everyone turned to look at Sarah.

"I'm Sarah. But if you think I'm going to rat out Joseph, you're mistaken. I'm no one's snitch."

"Sarah!" Aunt Beth and Mavis said at the same time.

"This isn't some B-grade gangster movie, Sarah," Harriet said. "People are dead. You could be endangering Joseph by not telling the detective what you know."

"She's right," Lauren seconded. "We're just assuming Joseph killed those two people and attacked Harriet, but it could be his only crime is running."

"Why would he run if he didn't do anything?" Sarah asked.

"Geez, Sarah," Lauren said. "Make up your mind whose side you're on."

"Is there somewhere I can talk to Ms. Ness alone?" Detective Morse asked.

"Sure," Aunt Beth said. "Come on, Sarah," she prompted and led the two women into the kitchen.

The Loose Threads used the half-hour while Detective Morse was questioning Sarah to discuss the details of the pre-auction meeting where the raffle quilt would be selected. The contenders would be judged by a committee made up of local city council members as well as representatives from several animal-related businesses and nonprofit employers. Each guild would present their quilts along with the all-important narrative about the design and construction of each entry.

"Have any of the rest of you seen or talked to Joseph Marston in the last week?" Detective Morse asked when she and Sarah returned to the studio.

"Aiden and I saw him at the Steaming Cup last weekend," Harriet offered.

"Did you talk to him?"

"We did—or at least, we tried to."

"What do you mean?"

"He was acting kind of jittery, and when I asked him a couple of questions, he was sharp with me—he raised his voice. Said things like 'What difference does it make?' Normally, he's kind of quiet and patient, but that night he wasn't."

"Has anyone else heard from him?" Morse looked at DeAnn.

"Not in the last week," DeAnn told her. "We've tried to get hold of him, but he hasn't returned any of our calls."

"Well, thank you, ladies," Morse said. "Beth told me you're making quilts for the pet adoption benefit. Do you mind if I look?"

"You don't belong to the Small Stitches, do you?" Connie asked.

"No, I haven't found a quilt group since I moved to Foggy Point."

Connie glanced at Mavis then Beth and Jenny. Each in turn gave an almost imperceptible affirmative nod.

"Let's start with the doghouses," Mavis said, and Carla and Lauren held that quilt up for the detective. They displayed each of the others then refolded them and piled them on the work table.

"Those are really beautiful," Morse said. "They should bring a lot of money in."

If Detective Morse didn't already have her invitation to join the Loose Threads in the bag, her compliments would get her one for sure, Harriet thought. Seemed like the good detective would be thinking it was a conflict of interest—unless she had another reason to try to plant herself in their midst.

Chapter 35

The meeting broke up at that point. The quilts that needed their binding finished were collected, and the rest were carefully re-folded, put into their cloth bags and set on Harriet's to-do shelf.

"I've got to go get ready for my lunch date," Sarah said. "Ta-ta, ladies." With that, she swept out the door, putting on her raincoat as she went.

Lauren sat in the chair next to Harriet's.

"Did you notice the side of Sarah's face?" she murmured.

"No, she didn't come close enough for me to notice anything about her," Harriet replied as softly. "Why?"

"It looks like she has a bruise along her jaw line, like maybe a handprint. And it's not the first time she's had a noticeable bruise."

"I haven't noticed anything, but I haven't paid that close of attention."

"She does make you want to look anywhere else but at her when she's running her mouth, which admittedly is most of the time, but since I've been spending so much time at the senior center, I've had occasion to…study her, if you will. I hate to think it, but she looks like someone who's being battered."

"Does she do patient care ever?" Harriet asked. "If she works with difficult patients that might account for bruises and scratches."

"I'll have to check that out. All the conclusions I was coming to were not good ones. Have you seen her boyfriend?"

Harriet thought for a moment. "I don't think I have. Why?"

"He's shockingly good-looking. And before you tell me I'm being mean, or talk about sour grapes or whatever, hear me out. You know as well as I do that Sarah is full of herself, annoying and doesn't really have very good taste in most things. I'm telling you—this guy is way too handsome, sophisticated...I know I'm not explaining this well, but believe me, something's not right."

"I don't know what to say."

"I'm not sure why I thought you'd be any help," Lauren complained and started to get up.

"Wait," Harriet said. "Sit down, please. I feel awful that I haven't noticed, but this isn't about me. As soon as I'm able to leave the house alone, I can check up on her."

"I guess I'm feeling guilty, too. She really is annoying, but no one deserves to be abused if that's what's happening."

"I know I have no right to ask, but would you be willing to help me with one little thing?"

"What do you want me to research?" Lauren asked with a sigh.

"Never mind, I'll do it myself."

"Sorry, I didn't think you were that sensitive. Can we skip the drama and go straight to what you want?"

Harriet told herself to relax and take a deep breath.

"I got some more information about Neelie, the woman who died." She related the information Aiden had passed on earlier that morning.

"So, you know her real first name and that she was adopted as a baby or young child."

"And that she'd be in her mid- to late twenties now."

"That's not a lot to go on."

"I'm not sure we can make any assumptions, but she was most recently living in California," Harriet added, referring to Rodney's information that Neelie had been living in "east bay," which meant either Oakland, Berkeley or one of the smaller communities on the east side of San Francisco Bay.

"Well, I can try searching adoption databases on the West Coast. If she waited until she was almost thirty to go searching for her African roots, she may have recently left footprints on some of the bulletin boards that adoptees use. The fact we know where she found her cousins should help, too."

"Anything you find could be helpful, and I understand the usual disclaimers apply."

"You're learning," Lauren said as she turned to go. She stopped at the door and, instead of going out, stepped aside and held the door to let Phyllis Johnson in.

"Hi," Phyllis said and came to where Harriet sat. "I hope I'm not disturbing you." She held a bundle in her arms.

Harriet looked at her aunt and Mavis, but they seemed as confused as she was by this unexpected visit.

"Hey, Phyl," Aunt Beth said. "What brings you here this fine morning?"

"This is a little delicate."

"Well, just spit it out," Mavis said.

"You know I belong to the Small Stitches quilt group," she said and paused. "And I'm sure you've noticed that some of our members are…" She paused again. "Well, they're…"

"Just tell us," Aunt Beth said, "whatever it is."

"I've seen what the Small Stitches are making for the auction, and frankly, it's embarrassing."

"Here, sit down," Mavis said and pointed Phyllis to a chair. "I'm still not sure why you're telling us this."

Phyllis eased herself into the chair, and the energy seemed to go out of her.

"I'm telling you this because I made a quilt for the auction, by myself."

"So the others in your group don't know you're doing this?" Aunt Beth asked.

Phyllis dipped her head. "No, they don't. But I couldn't just stand by and do nothing."

"What do you want from us?" Harriet said. "Did you bring the quilt for me to do the stitching?"

Phyllis had the good grace to blush. "I know you're all busy, especially since Harriet's accident, but I was hoping somehow you could fit it in. I could pay extra for a rush order," she said.

"I don't think that will be necessary," Aunt Beth said. "As you can see, Harriet's not on her feet yet, but I'm all caught up, so if you don't want anything too exotic, I should be able to fit it in."

"I guessed Harriet wouldn't be back to work yet, judging by how she looked in the hospital. Have the police figured out who did this yet?"

"If they have, they haven't told us," Harriet said.

"I hope they don't think Joseph did it," Phyllis said. "I know he's been distracted lately, but I can't believe he'd do anything violent."

"He's not helping his case by running and hiding," Harriet said.

"Hiding?" Phyllis said. "Do you *know* he's hiding? Or *where* he's hiding? Anything about where he is?"

"Sarah claims she saw him this morning at the pet store," Mavis said.

"I can't imagine why Joseph would have killed either of those two people—or anyone else, for that matter."

"Everyone has secrets," Aunt Beth said sagely. "Since we can't figure out what Joseph's are, let's have a look at *your* little secret."

Phyllis had competently constructed a pieced quilt using the traditional block patterns. Harriet thought she recognized Jacob's Ladder, Churn Dash and Goose in the Pond, along with some flying geese and simple pinwheels. Most of the blocks shared common elements—squares and half-square triangles and four patches, all done in only one or two size pairings. Her quilt looked complicated, but had probably been relatively easy to cut out and stitch.

Phyllis had used an impressive variety of dog print fabrics and somehow pulled them into a cohesive whole. It was scrappy, but a very well-organized scrappy.

"If you could do an all-over pattern of stitching—a diagonal grid, maybe, or really, whatever you think would look good and that you could get done in time for me to bind it before the show, that would be fine with me. As I said, I'm willing to pay a premium."

"This looks real nice," Mavis said as she ran her hand over the surface of the quilt top.

Phyllis pulled a piece of sewn flannel from her cloth bag.

"I pieced the back from a couple of large pieces of flannel and did a little appliqué around the spot where the label will go."

She held the backing piece up. She had cut out several of the smaller dog images from some of her fabrics and stitched them in a continuous rectangle so that when the label was in place, they would appear to be running around it, frame style.

"Have any of you spoken to DeAnn lately?" she asked. "With the mess Joseph left us in, I haven't had a chance to follow up with her or her husband. I hope things have settled down."

"I think things are going better for them now," Aunt Beth said with a glance at Harriet that told her to keep her mouth shut.

✂ - - - ✂ - - - ✂

"Why didn't you tell her about DeAnn's daughter not being African?" Harriet asked her aunt when Phyllis was back out in the driveway, getting into her car.

"If Joseph has been playing fast and loose with Phyl's business, she's going to have a stroke, literally. I don't want to get her all wound up until we have a better understanding of what actually happened.

"As we've discussed, it could have been a mix-up on the other end, or a simple mistake, or Joseph may be running a scam of some sort. He's been like a son to her, and it's going to kill her if it turns out he's been embezzling or sabotaging the business or I don't know what else."

"Unfortunately, his disappearing act is making the last choice the more likely one," Mavis said.

"I hate this," sighed Aunt Beth.

"I do, too," Mavis agreed.

"I'm glad Phyllis made her quilt," Harriet said. "I was starting to feel guilty about tricking the Stitches into using Sarah's design. At least this way they'll have one respectable entry."

"I guess that's something," Aunt Beth agreed. She turned to Mavis. "Shall we go see if your car's ready? I need to check out the sale shelf at Pins and Needles for more fabric to use in the functional dog quilts."

"How many of those quilts have you made?" Harriet asked.

"I've only done six of them, and they need so many more. We have to go to town to get Mavis's car anyway. She left it at the garage on her way here to have the oil changed. It won't take that

211

long, and Aiden should be coming back shortly, in any case. Do you need anything before we go?"

"I don't suppose you'd consider letting me come with you."

"Not a chance."

"Come on, I'm not an invalid. I have a sprained ankle and a sore back, and it's been almost five days."

"No way, and don't even think about going out on your own while we're gone."

"We'll call Aiden," Mavis added. "We'll tell him you're here waiting for him."

"You guys are mean."

"Okay," Beth said, ignoring her protest. "You've got your book and your water. You better be right where we left you when we get back."

"I promise, I'll be right here," Harriet said. "Have fun."

Aunt Beth followed Mavis out the door, locking it when they were outside. Harriet listened for the crunch of tires, indicating they had driven away. She waited another minute before struggling to her feet—well, foot—and picking up her crutches. She went to the connecting door and backed through it into the kitchen. Fred meowed as she entered.

"I'll bet Aunt Beth has had you on a diet, too, huh, big boy?" she said.

She reached into the cupboard below the bar where she kept Fred's kitty treats and, balancing on her good foot, set her crutches aside and extracted a small handful. She'd just bent down to put them in his food dish when she heard a noise that sounded like tapping on glass.

She turned and looked toward her studio. She heard the noise again. It definitely sounded like it was coming from the studio. Fred's ears were upright, and he stared at the connecting door.

"Well, cat, let's go see what's going on," she said as she picked up her crutches and worked her way back into the studio.

Joseph Marston stood on her porch, tapping on the etched glass of the studio door. She hesitated for a moment then went to open it.

"Joseph," she said. "There are a lot of people looking for you."

"I know, it's why I waited until everyone was gone before I came to your door. We've probably only got a couple of minutes…"

"Well, come in, then, and let's talk."

"No, I can't come inside. What if someone comes?"

"No one's coming. Come on."

"We're wasting time. We need to talk about what happened."

"Are we talking about what happened at your house? Are you going to tell me why you attacked me?"

"No...I mean, yes...I mean, it's complicated, and I need your help."

"You attacked me, and you want my help? The only help you're getting from me is a nine-one-one call to the police." She reached for her phone in her pocket then remembered she'd left it on the arm of the gray chair.

"I think you'd better leave," she said.

He held his hand out toward her. "Please, you have to understand," he said. Tears glistened in his eyes.

"Is this about the adoptions?" she asked as she looked frantically around for a weapon of any sort.

"You know about the adoptions?"

Before she could answer, they heard the sound of tires at the bottom of her driveway. Joseph turned abruptly and jumped off her porch in one leap, then ran down the opposite end of the driveway as Aiden drove up and parked.

"What are you doing outside?" he called.

"Joseph Marston," she yelled back. "He was here—he just ran down the other side of the driveway." She pointed where Joseph had just gone.

Aiden dropped his phone and keys and the paper bag he was carrying and ran in the direction Harriet was pointing. He was gone for a couple of long minutes before returning, this time at a slow trot.

"There's no sign of him," he said. "He must have gone to the end of the street and into the woods."

Harriet's street terminated at a wooded greenspace that went all the way down the back side of her hill.

"I went down the trail a little way, but he could have gone any direction. If he went off the trail, he could be anywhere. What did he want?"

"I don't know. He said he wanted to talk about what happened at his house, and he said he wanted my help."

"That takes nerve. Why would he think you'd want to help him?"

"No idea. I asked him if it had to do with the adoptions, and he seemed surprised I knew anything about them."

"I'm sure he was. He probably thinks he had a foolproof system going. And for the most part, he did. Whatever scam he's been running has probably been going on for a while—years, maybe." He picked up the things he'd dropped and came up on the porch. "You're freezing," he said and rubbed his hands up and down her arms. He picked up the crutches—she had dropped them and not even realized it. She took them and hobbled back into the studio.

"I brought donuts," he said. "You want some tea or something?"

"I can get it." She started for the kitchen.

"Whoa, you need to sit down. If your aunt sees you up, she'll kill me."

"She won't see me. Besides, it's got to be bad for my circulation or muscle tone or something to be sitting so much."

"It's probably true it won't hurt you to get up a little bit by now. With my patients, if we can keep them down for twenty-four hours, we consider it a success."

"Glad to know I'd make a good dog."

He gently pulled her into his arms. "I would never compare you to a dog," he said, and kissed her softly on her lips. "I've missed you."

"Me, too," she said. "As annoying as you can be, I *have* missed you, and I don't like it that we were fighting."

"I'm sorry about that," he said and looked into her eyes. "I really am."

"You've had a lot going on."

"Yeah, but that's just an excuse. I had no right to bite your head off. I've had a lot of time to think while I've been taking care of the hoarded dogs."

"And?" She wrapped her arms around his neck.

"And...I realized that if I had been you and had seen that woman and that baby, I would've had to at least ask."

She twined her fingers into his silky black hair and pulled his face down to hers for another kiss.

"You're forgiven."

Aiden slid his hands down her back, inadvertently touching the bruised area. She winced.

"Oh, Harriet, I'm sorry," he said and stepped back away from her. "I lost track of your boo-boo."

"It's okay," she said in a tight voice. "And I think this qualifies as slightly more than a boo-boo."

"Let me help you to your chair."

"I'm fine," she insisted, and took a couple of measured breaths. "Just let me get my tea started."

She hobbled into the kitchen and got out a cup and teabag and set them on the counter.

"I guess I could use a little help filling the teakettle," she admitted.

"Would you please sit while I finish this? If your aunt comes home and sees you making tea, she'll kill me."

"Fine," she said, and crutched back to the studio and her gray chair. She had just gotten her pillows arranged the way she liked them when he brought two mugs of tea and the bag of donuts.

"Have you had any more thoughts about Joseph?" he asked as he pulled two maple bars from the white bag.

Harriet groaned as she bit into her bar. The maple was thick and creamy, and the body of the bar was as light as air.

"I don't know what to think. He said he needed my help. Suppose he killed Rodney in self-defense. Maybe he thinks I saw something that could help him prove it."

"He can't possibly imagine you would help him after he whacked you in the back and threw a body on you."

"It makes no sense. He seemed real agitated, so he's probably not thinking clearly."

They each took another bite of their donut.

"I can't believe I'm saying this, but I wonder if I should call the detective who's working on all this."

"I can't believe you're saying it either, but yes. The police are here to protect and serve, and they can't do that very well if you don't tell them when there's been a threat. By the way, I put their numbers in your phone's address book."

Harriet picked up her phone and dialed the non-emergency number for the Foggy Point police. As soon as she was connected to Detective Morse and had told her Joseph had come calling the detective told her to sit tight and she'd be right there.

"I'm not sure where she thought I was going to go, but I told her we'd be waiting here," she said to Aiden when she'd pressed the end-call button.

He pulled one of the rolling chairs next to her and reached over and took her hand in his.

"You did the right thing," he said. He held her hand while they finished their donuts.

Chapter 36

Aunt Beth and Mavis returned just as Harriet was finishing her first run-through of what had transpired while they were in town. Jane Morse listened silently until Harriet had finished her account.

"Very curious," she said. "Why do you think he believes you can help him?"

"I have no idea. I really can't imagine why he would come here."

"I'm going to increase the patrols on your hill for the time being," Morse said.

"I'm going to do better than that," Aunt Beth interrupted. "I'm taking Harriet and Fred to my house out on the strait."

"Who's Fred?" Morse asked.

At the repeated mention of his name, Fred jumped into Harriet's lap, one of his feet landing in her tea cup, splashing tea onto the leg of her jeans. Morse raised her eyebrows in understanding.

"Do I get a say in this?" Harriet asked, dabbing her leg with a napkin. "I think I should stay here in case he comes back."

"That's exactly why you *shouldn't* be here," Beth countered.

"We could try planting a decoy here and see if he tries to make contact."

Harriet looked at Aiden, who was now pacing back and forth across her workroom.

"I think your aunt's right," he said. "If you were at full strength, I might think otherwise, but you'd be a sitting duck if he came back."

"Fine, I'm too tired to argue."

She went through the sequence of events three more times, but she couldn't add anything to her original account of Joseph's visit, so the detective thanked her for calling and left.

"I'll go get your overnight bag," Aunt Beth said.

"Haven't we already done this once?" Harriet asked. "Remember when I went and stayed with Mavis for safekeeping? That didn't work out so well, did it?"

"That was different," Aunt Beth said as she went into the kitchen. Mavis followed her after announcing she would gather Fred's things.

"How is it different from when I went to stay at Mavis's cottage when Aiden's uncle…" She trailed off, not really sure how to continue, since the cause of her having to leave her house in the spring had been Aiden's murderous Uncle Bertie. "I'm sorry," she muttered and reached out for his hand. He came back and sat on the arm of her chair.

"I know your aunt and Mavis are being overprotective," he said, diverting the discussion away from his family. "But what can it hurt? You can't really work until they take the cast off your foot, so why not let them spoil you a little bit? And you can look out over the strait. You might find it calming."

"When did you get so Zen?"

"Maybe when I realized there was no point in fighting my mother, your aunt or Mavis when they had their mind set on something—which, by the way, happened when I was about ten."

"Fine," Harriet said. "Like you said, it's not like I'm getting any work done anyway."

He leaned toward her and put his arm around her shoulders.

✂ - - - ✂ - - - ✂

"Things are completely different this time," Aunt Beth said as she and Harriet picked up their argument again in the car. "I talked to Jane while I was packing your stuff, and she agreed with your idea

218

of having a female officer stay at your house as a decoy to see if Joseph will come back here."

"Well, at least that's something. I guess that's why you insisted on coming around and picking me up in the garage."

"Yes, and that's why I need you to lay your seat back far enough your head isn't visible in the window."

Harriet did as she asked.

"This seems a little silly," she said. "Joseph took off down the hill. I'd be surprised if he came back this soon."

"You're assuming he's working alone. Whatever made him murder Neelie and Rodney could be big. He could have accomplices."

"I suppose anything is possible."

"I brought along some handwork for you," Aunt Beth said, nimbly switching topics. "We need labels sewn on the quilts that are finished. And I have several of the kennel quilts that need their bindings sewn on."

"Can't you just machine-sew the bindings for those."

"If I was willing to give away a functional quilt that had a jagged-looking stitching line around the border, yes, I could just machine the stitching on, but I think even a dog deserves a nice-looking quilt."

"You could use clear nylon thread in the bobbin or do a wide zigzag stitch," Harriet pressed, describing two of the common remedies for the problem everyone had when applying binding to a quilt by machine. When encasing an edge in fabric, only the side of the casing you're looking at as you stitch can be seen, leaving the condition of the bottom, or blind side, up to chance.

"I'm well aware of the methods people use, and if you are that opposed to hand-stitching a few little quilts then I'll just do them myself after I finish Phyl's quilt."

"You aren't going to go to my house and work on Phyllis's quilt, are you? It's not safe."

"It's not safe for *you*, but Joseph didn't hit me and he's not looking for me. Besides, there will be an undercover officer dressed like you and using crutches just in case he shows up."

"I don't understand why Joseph would be after me," Harriet said. "Why wouldn't he be after you, too? I mean, you know everything I do."

"Yes, but I wasn't found snooping in his windows. And I haven't uncovered any murderers this year, either."

"Still, we're missing something. A big something, if you ask me."

At the bottom of the hill, Aunt Beth went straight through the intersection instead of turning left, which would have been the most direct way to approach her house on the strait.

"Where are we going?" Harriet asked.

"Jorge prepared food for your recovery and wanted me to come by and pick it up. I tell you, that man is like a mother hen trying to protect his chicks. He's called me three times a day since you got hurt."

"Did you ever think it's just an excuse to get to talk to you?"

"Not a chance," she said. "And don't you even be thinking like that."

She took her eyes off the road to glare at Harriet, but Harriet looked out the window, her slight smile reflecting off the glass.

"I'm afraid you're going to have to hide again," Aunt Beth said as they got close to town.

✂ - - - ✂ - - - ✂

With only a little more cloak-and-dagger action, Harriet and Beth finally arrived at the little house on the Strait of Juan de Fuca Beth had moved into.

"I figured you could sleep in the TV room," Beth said, referring to the downstairs bedroom she used as an office and which was also furnished with a large television and a convertible sofa sleeper. Her own bedroom was upstairs and had French doors that led to a small balcony overlooking the strait.

"That sounds fine," Harriet said and started for the front door. Her aunt followed her with two shopping bags full of food from Tico's Tacos.

Aunt Beth's phone was ringing as they came into the house, and she answered it, talking to her caller for several minutes.

"That was Detective Morse. She was checking to be sure we arrived without incident. She'll have hourly patrols come by here. She talked to Aiden, and they agreed that when he finishes with his dogs, he'll go to your house," she said after hanging up. "Jane wants him to stay an hour or so, and if all is quiet, he can sneak out the back and into the woods and on down the hill. Carla will give him a ride over here, and I'll take him home after dinner."

"Seems like you guys have thought of everything."

"It's not us guys, it's Jane and her team," Aunt Beth protested. "I hope it's not all for nothing."

"Me, too. I want to go home. I appreciate your hospitality, and so does Fred, but we'd rather be in our own home."

"I know, honey, but Jane is sure Joseph will show up, and sooner rather than later."

"Do you care if I use your computer?"

"You know I don't mind," Beth said. "I have to go back to your house. Jane needs me to spend time there if we're going to pull this off, but I need to get Phyl's quilt on the machine anyway. Don't worry, Mavis is coming to sit with you."

Harriet rolled her eyes but kept her mouth shut.

"You sit down, and I'll go get my laptop."

"Since when do you have a laptop?"

"Those little netbooks went on sale at the Walmart in Port Angeles week before last, and I got one, and don't you be making fun of me."

"I'm not making fun. I just didn't realize you were so tech-savvy."

"I decided to make an inventory of my stash, and I thought it would be easier if I had a little computer to take to the fabric instead of writing it all down and entering it later."

"Sounds smart."

"It was made for searching the internet, so it should be able to do whatever you want."

"Thanks, and you don't have to wait for Mavis to arrive. I'll be fine."

"You'll be a sitting duck is what you'll be," Aunt Beth said. "Mavis will be here any minute. Until then, I'll make you some tea. I got a new herbal. It's called rooibos. It's from Africa."

"Bring it on."

Aunt Beth brought the computer to Harriet along with a cup of the rich red tea.

"You behave yourself while I'm gone," she said. "Don't let her talk you into anything," she told Mavis, who had just arrived and was settling on the opposite end of the sofa.

"*You* be careful," Mavis said. "We'll be just fine."

She dug in her quilting bag and pulled out a needle and a pink silk thread that matched the backing on the snowball quilt. She threaded the needle then pulled out the label she'd made at home and began appliquéing it to the bottom right corner of the back.

"What are you doing?" she asked.

Harriet sat with her aunt's netbook balanced on a pillow across her lap.

"I thought I'd approach Iloai's situation from a different angle. I'm looking around the missing and exploited children bulletin boards to see if anyone has reported a child around her age missing."

"You think she's a kidnap victim?" Mavis sounded shocked.

"We know she's not from Africa like she was supposed to be, and from what the translator is saying, I think there's a good chance she's not the abandoned orphan DeAnn thought they were getting. Joseph is on the run, which tells me he's been doing something he needs to hide from the police. So, I figure we now know the child is Samoan, or at least speaks that language, and she may have a family. It seems logical that, if that's the case, her family might be looking for her."

"How's it going?"

"I just barely started, and I'm not nearly as proficient as Lauren is at this. I'm learning my way around the search terms, but then hopefully, I can do some real digging."

She jumped an hour later when her phone rang. She didn't recognize the phone number, but she knew the area code. The caller was in Oakland, California.

"Hello," she said. She listened to the response then quickly put the call on speaker phone.

Jasmine, she mouthed to Mavis.

"Yes, I did leave you a message asking you to call me back. I was wondering if you could answer a few questions about Neelie Obote."

"You seen Neelie?" the disembodied voice said.

"When did you last see her?" Harriet countered.

"Maybe three weeks, maybe a little longer," Jasmine said. "I went to Vegas. I thought she was stayin' here, but when I got back she was gone. Then Rodney went lookin' for her, and now I can't get hold of him, neither. You know where Neelie is?"

Harriet looked at Mavis, and the older woman nodded.

"I don't know how to tell you this, but Neelie is dead—Rodney, too. I'm so sorry."

An animal-like moan came from the speaker. They heard a loud thump like something had fallen on the floor.

"What happened," she wailed. "Did they crash the car? I tol' Rodney that car was a death trap."

"Jasmine. Can you hear me? I need you to pull it together. I need to know about Neelie's baby."

"Neelie don't have no baby," she gasped between sobs.

"She did when she came here."

"She…don't…have…no…baby." Jasmine repeated emphatically.

"Was Rodney her husband?" Harriet asked.

Jasmine made a noise Harriet thought was supposed to be a laugh.

"Honey, he wasn't nobody's husband. Their daddy, is more like it, and I'm not talking parenthood here."

"Rodney was her pimp?"

"Don't you go talkin' ill of the dead. If it wasn't no crash, did someone kill them? It wasn't one of them murder-suicides, was it? He was sort of sweet on her. More than the other girls, and that girl always did have trouble followin' the rules."

223

"The rules?"

"Yeah, you know, the house rules."

Mavis and Beth raised their eyebrows as they looked at each other, but neither woman said anything.

"Did Neelie go to Africa recently?"

"Why would she go and do that?"

"Why wouldn't she? Wasn't she trying to trace her family?" Harriet guessed.

"She didn't have to trace nobody. She know where she come from. Her momma sold her in Africa when she was a little thing. She found her cousins a long time ago."

"How long are we talking?"

"How am I supposed to know?"

"You must have some idea."

They could hear a sigh

"Must of been a year, year and a half. Something like that. Rodney was real mad. She got her a wad of cash, and then she just took off and went to Africa. Then, when she come back, she told her story to anybody who would listen, tryin' to get sympathy, like. Rodney said she was scarin' the customers off with all her talk of buyin' and sellin' babies."

"So exactly what *was* her story?"

"Who are you? And what's it to you what her story is?"

"Let's just say I'm someone Neelie came to see in Washington."

"Why would she come see somebody in Washington? An' how do I know you're tellin' me the truth? She don't know no one in Washington. No one she wants to see, anyhow."

"What do you mean?" Harriet pressed. "Did she know someone else here? Besides me?" she added, in an attempt to keep her deception going.

"If you know her, than you know who else she knows there. Like I said, she told her story to anybody who'd listen. Who are you, and why are you disrespectin' the dead?"

"Okay, listen. I met Neelie when she came to Foggy Point with a baby she claimed belonged to a friend of mine."

"I told you, she don't have—"

"I heard you," Harriet cut her off. "Now, you listen to me. She came here with a baby and said it belonged to her dead sister in Africa. She said the sister asked her to deliver it to my friend."

"She don't have no sister. Not a real one, anyway. She has a couple cousins in Africa. When she would get a few dollars extra, sometimes she sent it to her cousin for some water project or something."

"I'm trying to find out what happened to her and Rodney. I might be the only one. The local police certainly don't care. Anything you can tell me might help. Let's start with who else she knows in Foggy Point."

"She was living in a foster home there, and she aged out. Let's see, I think she said that woman was Mary Ann Martin or Martins or something like that. She used to say how weird it was that a witch like that had the initials MAM. Kinda like *mom*, only she said the woman was the least motherly person she ever met. The only reason she stayed till she was eighteen was to try to protect the littler foster kids that lived there."

Mavis scribbled the name on a piece of paper she pulled from her quilting bag.

"I don't suppose you have a phone number for Ms. Martin," Harriet asked.

"No, I don't have no number. Why would I? The girl had a cell phone. She kept her own numbers."

"Do you know what Neelie's name was before she took her African name?" Harriet didn't have positive proof Neelie Obote wasn't her original name, but it seemed like a good possibility.

"Oh, yeah, I do know that. She was Nancy Lou Freeman. We always laughed about it. My birth name was Nellie Jean Smith—quite the stage names."

"You're an actress?"

Jasmine snorted. "Yeah, we're actresses, alright. In our dreams. Now we use our actin' skills to get by."

Harriet paused and looked at Mavis to see if she had any questions. Mavis shrugged.

"I gotta go," Jasmine said. "Someone's here."

Harriet rang off after promising to call Jasmine if she found out anything about what had happened to Neelie.

She and Mavis sat speechless for a moment.

"Wow," said Mavis at last.

"Wow is an understatement," Harriet agreed. "So Nancy Ann-slash-Neelie really was a local girl? And none of the Loose Threads recognized her?"

"Sounds like she left when she was eighteen, and that it was probably eight or ten years ago. She could have been in school with one of my two younger boys, but I didn't really know a lot of the girls' mothers. I wouldn't have known her unless she'd been in an activity with one of the boys, and she wasn't. I had my hands full with them and work and all."

"I can email the Threads with her real name and see if it rings a bell with anyone, but we need to talk to her last foster mother. She should be able to tell us something about her."

"I know what you're thinking, and your aunt will kill me."

"*Will* kill you, as in, after we get back?" Harriet said as she set the computer on the sofa and struggled to her feet.

"This is against my better judgment, but I can't see how we could get in trouble if we stick to just talking."

A quick scan of the Foggy Point phone book revealed that Mary Ann and Robert Martin lived in a neighborhood at the base of Miller Hill. The Martin house was a tidy bungalow at the end of a wooded cul-de-sac. The yard to the right side of the house was surrounded by cyclone fencing that enclosed several play structures on a base of cedar bark dust.

Mavis guided her car onto the gravel parking pad in front of the house then helped Harriet get out and on her crutches and organized.

The front walk was lined with purple, yellow and white winter-flowering pansies. A large ceramic pot with ornamental kale sat on the front porch. Harriet balanced on one crutch and rapped on the door with the other one.

"Hello," the trim forty-year-old woman who answered said. "May I help you?" Her gaze went to Harriet's cast and then back up to her face again.

Harriet introduced herself and Mavis.

"We were hoping you could answer a few questions about a young woman who died recently."

"I'd like to help you, but I don't know anyone who died recently."

"Her name is Neelie Obote," Mavis said.

"I think I read about that in the paper," Mary Ann said. "But I still don't understand why you're asking me. I don't, or didn't, know anyone named Neelie."

"We think you knew her by another name," Harriet said and wobbled a little as she took the weight off her sprained ankle.

Mary Ann looked at her then stepped back and held the door open.

"Would you like to come in?"

Harriet looked at Mavis. Mavis gave a slight nod, and they followed Mary Ann into a comfortable living room. The two women sat on the edge of a blue upholstered sofa, and Mary Ann sat on one of two coordinating side chairs.

When everyone was settled, she said, "Now, who is this Neelie, and how could I possibly help?"

"We think her real name was Nancy Lou Freeman," Harriet said.

The color drained from Mary Ann's face.

"Nancy is dead?" she said in a whisper. "How? Why?"

"That's what we were hoping you could help us with," Harriet said.

"We were hoping we could tell you what we know, and then you could maybe fill in some blanks," Mavis added.

Harriet explained the sequence of events, starting with Neelie/Nancy showing up at the quilt store with a baby and ending with her dead in the bushes outside Aiden's house.

Mary covered her mouth with her hand.

"This is a lot to take in," she said. "A baby? Nancy had a baby?"

"We're pretty sure it wasn't her baby," Harriet said.

"We don't know *where* the baby came from," Mavis told her. "We verified it wasn't her sister's baby, and that her sister, who in fact was actually her cousin, we think, isn't dead."

227

"She doesn't have a sister," Mary said. "At least, she didn't when she lived here."

"We were hoping you could tell us about when she lived here," Harriet said.

"I don't mean to be rude, but you're not police, right?"

"No, we're not," Harriet admitted. "It's complicated, but someone attacked me a few nights ago, and we think it's related to what happened to Neelie. Her…friend Rodney was also murdered, and someone attacked me, and well, they threw his body on me, and frankly, that's left me wanting a few answers the police aren't giving me."

"Wow," Mary said. She sat back in her chair. "I'm not sure what I can tell you that would be helpful. Nancy lived here for two years. She came to us when she was sixteen. She'd been in the foster care system most of her life.

"When a child reaches that age and is still in the foster care system, the chance of them being adopted is pretty slim. We try to help them prepare for life on their own. When we have older teenagers, we help them get signed up for college or trade school programs and teach them how to manage their money and cook and do their own laundry—you know, basic life skills."

"And you did that with Neelie?" Mavis asked.

"I'm not sure you could say that. She was a special case. She already knew how to take care of a household, except for the money management part. She had been involved in a bad situation when she was younger. I don't know the details, because her records from that time have been sealed, and due to a plea bargain arrangement, no one is allowed to talk about it.

"Nancy didn't want to talk about it, so we don't really know the whole story, but we think she was involved in an adoption where the parents' purpose was to acquire live-in help. She wasn't sent to school or allowed to have contact with the natural children. Her job was to clean, cook, iron—you name it."

"How old was she when that happened?" Harriet asked.

"She would have been in grade school," Mary replied. "I don't know where she lived or how she lived before that. I know she was with those people until she was around twelve and ran away repeatedly. Eventually, social services caught up with her and took over her care.

"We were her sixth foster family, and she lasted here longer than she had anywhere else, but she was a handful. She'd sneak out at night and meet with kids who were up to no good. When we had younger teens here, she'd help them sneak out.

"She had a special education tutor, so her school hours were different from the other children we had here, and she would get them to skip school to keep her company. She was caught shoplifting, and pretty much, you name it, she did it. I think we were starting to make progress just before she turned eighteen, but..." She spread her hands, palm up.

"She aged out of the system?" Harriet guessed.

"No," Mary said. "Well, yes, but we told her she could stay here even after she turned eighteen. We told her she didn't have to pay us anything. We just wanted her to complete her education and learn to take care of herself, but she couldn't get out of Foggy Point fast enough."

"Where did she live when she was younger?" Harriet asked. "When she was enslaved?"

"As far as I know, she's lived in Foggy Point her whole life—after Africa, of course."

"That's really sad," Harriet said.

"It is," Mary said. "I have to say, though, my husband and I always feared the day someone would give us this news. It was never a question of if, just when and how."

The front door opened, and a small Asian girl with long black braids and thick-lensed glasses came in, followed by a chubby blond-haired boy who looked like he was similar in age to the girl.

"Hi, Trin, Hi, Niko. Put your backpacks in your cubbies. There are cookies on the kitchen table, and I'll pour you some milk in just a minute." She stood up. "I need to get them their snack," she said. "Let me know if I can help with anything else."

"You've been very helpful," Harriet said, as she stood and arranged her crutches.

"Do you know if anyone is making funeral arrangements for Nancy?" Mary asked.

"I'm sorry, I don't."

They left, confident Mary would rectify that situation.

"Not quite the snake pit I expected," Mavis noted.

"Yeah," Harriet said. "I was expecting a dirty, overcrowded hovel. Mary seems like the mother every child dreams of. Those two kids were well-dressed, clean and seemed sort of well-adjusted."

"They looked well-fed, too."

"The business about Neelie being a slave was sort of interesting," Harriet said. "Given how normal we just decided Mary is, it makes me think she might be telling us the truth."

"It would go a long way toward explaining why Neelie was so troubled."

"If she lived in Foggy Point most of her life, I wonder if she was adopted here, too."

"Phyllis would know," Mavis said. "She always held classes for prospective parents that were open to all adoptive parents regardless of who was handling their transaction. That way, she could keep an eye on the competition."

Mavis looked at her watch.

"I don't know how long your aunt plans on quilting before she stops for dinner, but you better hope we get home before she does."

"She'll probably stay at my house as long as she can in hopes she'll be there if Joseph comes calling."

"Let's just hope he comes to his senses and turns himself in before anything else happens."

Harriet's cell phone rang as they pulled into the parking area in front of Aunt Beth's house.

"It's Aunt Beth," she said to Mavis. She pushed the answer button. "Hi, I'm going to put you on speaker phone so Mavis can hear."

"I was just calling to let you know I'll be working late on Phyl's quilt tonight. Aiden is going to go pick up a pizza and eat here with me to keep up the pretense. You two can go ahead and eat without me. If you're not too hungry, Aiden says he can pick up another pizza and come by with it. He said you can call and let him know what you decide."

230

"How's the quilt coming?" Harriet asked.

"It's coming. Of course, I keep stopping and looking out the window, but otherwise I'm moving along."

"I wish we could help," Mavis said.

"You are helping—keeping Harriet safe."

Harriet and Mavis shared a guilty smile then said their good-byes to Aunt Beth.

"How about we let you rest a while and then decide about dinner," Mavis suggested.

"I hate to admit it, but I think I could use a little rest."

Chapter 37

Mavis was asleep in the padded rocker in Aunt Beth's living room, her feet up on a tapestry-covered hassock, when Harriet shifted slightly and the edge of a cushion poked her sore kidney. She'd been napping on the sofa but awoke with a start at the sudden pain. She scooted carefully into a sitting position and reached for her aunt's netbook.

A few keystrokes woke the computer and returned her to the search she'd been working on. She quietly worked while her friend napped.

"Oh, my gosh," she said out loud. Mavis woke with a start. "I'm sorry," Harriet said when she realized she'd awakened her.

"What happened?" Mavis asked then noticed the computer.

"I think I've found something about Iloai. I've been looking at missing children listings and websites related to the South Pacific. I found something on a missing person bulletin board. The timeline works, and the description could be Iloai."

"Let me see," Mavis said. She shook her pant legs straight and shifted her weight back and forth, restoring the circulation to her feet, then moved over next to Harriet.

The computer screen showed a grainy family photo; two adults and five children were grouped in front of a palm tree. One of the children looked to be around the right age, but the photo was too blurry to tell if it could be Iloai.

Harriet shifted to the next screen. It was a bulletin board posting asking for any information on a three-year-old girl who had disappeared from an early childhood education program in American Samoa.

"Well, you're right. It could be her. Or not, unfortunately," Mavis said thoughtfully.

"I think I'll call Lauren."

"Good idea—and see if she's eaten yet. Maybe she'd like to eat with us."

Harriet called, and with only a few pithy remarks, Lauren agreed to come have a look at what they'd found and to stay for dinner.

"If it's okay with you, I think I'll go look over what Beth has in her freezer and see if I can put together a home cooked meal for us," Mavis said. "I like Jorge's food as well as the next person, but I always eat more than I should. I can put his goodies in the freezer, and you and Beth could have them tomorrow."

She got up and went to the small but efficient kitchen. She returned a few minutes later.

"I called Beth, and she has a meat loaf in the freezer and I can make mashed potatoes and gravy, but that will take an hour to bake, or I can thaw some chicken in the microwave and then sauté it with some vegetables and we can put it on rice."

"Since my aunt undoubtedly has a selection of those precut, pre-cleaned veggie bags, the chicken would probably be the easiest. She has an electric rice cooker, too, doesn't she?"

"She does, indeed," Mavis replied. "Do you need anything else before I get started?"

She brought Harriet a glass of water then went back to the kitchen to prepare their meal. Lauren arrived a few minutes later.

"Door's open," Harriet called at the knock on the front door.

"Show me what you've got," she said without preamble.

Harriet refreshed the screen and turned it toward her, and she read in silence for a few moments.

"I don't know, Harriet. The dates do fit, but this picture could be anyone."

"But you agree it could be Iloai?"

"It could. Let me see if I can sharpen this up a little." She e-mailed the picture to herself then pulled her own full-sized laptop from her shoulder bag. She turned it on and booted it up.

"Do you know the password to your aunt's wireless?" she asked Harriet.

"Quiltbag," Mavis called out from the kitchen.

Harriet and Lauren were silent for a moment, and then both burst out laughing as Lauren keyed in the code. Her fingers flew over the keys then stopped. She stared at the screen and chewed on her bottom lip. She tapped a few more keys then turned her computer toward Harriet.

"This is as good as I can get it without additional software that I don't have on my laptop. I don't think we'll need to do that, though."

Harriet looked. Lauren was right. The sharper image showed a child that could be a twin to Iloai.

"Wow," she said. "This definitely complicates things."

"Makes you wonder exactly what Joseph's been up to all these years, doesn't it?" Lauren said.

"It makes me wonder how we're going to break the news to DeAnn and her family."

"Easy," Lauren said. "We're not going to break anything to anybody. That's not our job."

"We can't just sit on this," Harriet argued.

"It must be a real burden running the whole world," Lauren said.

"Are you suggesting we ignore this?"

"Of course not, I'm not heartless. I just have my ego in check."

"So?"

"So, we show this to the detective. Someone needs to verify it, and then someone needs to arrest our buddy Joseph."

"It's so hard to believe Joseph could do that to DeAnn and then come around asking the Loose Threads to make quilts for him a week later."

"Hello! It's the baby he did something to. DeAnn's known the kid for…what? A week? The poor kid got ripped from what looks like a large loving family, and who knows when that actually happened."

"I thought we agreed the dates matched between the family's missing child report and DeAnn's adoption."

"Those dates match, but according to the internet, these child theft scams usually involve some sort of school or healthcare deception. The family thinks their child is going to a larger clinic for some bogus health problem, or going for special evaluation or schooling in a larger city. They have every expectation their child will return in a few days or a few weeks, if not months. By the time the family realizes their child is actually missing, a lot of time has passed and the trail is cold."

"Are you ladies ready for an appetizer?" Mavis asked from the kitchen, and before Harriet or Lauren could answer, she brought a plate that held small slices of smoked Gouda cheese, water crackers and a small bunch of grapes.

"This should hold you until dinner's ready, which shouldn't be too much longer. If Aiden calls, tell him I've got enough for him, too."

Aiden did call just as they were sitting down to eat. He assured Harriet he could be there before they had their napkins unfolded. Mavis dished up a plate for him and put it in the oven to keep warm, but he arrived before the women were half through with their meal.

"Things are pretty calm over at your place," he said to Harriet when he was seated at the table. "Your aunt was going to leave a half-hour after I did. The police figure Joseph will wait until he thinks 'Harriet' is alone."

"Is this where the party is?" Aunt Beth asked as she let herself in the front door a short while later. "I was booted off the quilting machine for the night by Harriet's clone."

"I told them the police are trying to sweeten the trap for Joseph," Aiden said. "If he's bought the clone act, he needs to think she's alone."

"The real action's been over here, anyway," Lauren said. She proceeded to explain what she and Harriet had uncovered about DeAnn's new daughter.

235

"That's bizarre," Aunt Beth said when Lauren had finished the story.

Aiden pulled Aunt Beth's step stool from its place in her broom closet and unfolded it next to Harriet's chair.

"Slide around here and put your bad foot up on this. If we're going to sit out here, you need to keep your ankle elevated."

"Does anyone else think it's weird that we have two baby dramas going on at the same time in one small town?" Harriet asked when she was settled. "Frankly, the odds of having two murders and two baby situations at the same time have to be astronomical."

"You've been a one-woman crime wave since you moved back to Foggy Point," Lauren offered. Mavis glared at her until she looked away. "You can't tell me it hasn't crossed anyone else's mind," she muttered without looking up.

"Beth and I had the same conversation the day before yesterday," Mavis said referring to Harriet's comment. "You're right—the chances of adoption fraud, a baby con and two murders happening at the same time and not being connected are pretty small. The problem is, no matter how we rearranged what we knew, we couldn't get the dots to connect."

"There has to be a connection between Neelie, Rodney and Joseph, but what it is—or was—is anyone's guess," Harriet said. "I heard her arguing on the phone with someone when she was staying at Aiden's, but after I met Rodney, I assumed it was him. I suppose it could have been Joseph."

"I can look him up on the internet and see what I can find out about him," Lauren offered. "It'll take a little while, though."

"If Neelie was in foster care here, I suppose it's possible she and Joseph knew each other before she turned eighteen," Harriet said.

"She would have been underage when they had whatever relationship they had," Aiden pointed out.

"That's creepy," Harriet said.

"Anyone want tea or coffee?" Aunt Beth asked.

Everyone stated their preference and retreated to the living room except Mavis, who was clearing the table and loading the dishwasher while Beth made coffee and the beverages.

"So, Iloai really was stolen?" Aiden said when he finished looking at Lauren's sharpened photo. "Wow."

Harriet's phone rang, and she struggled to twist around and reach it off the end table. Aiden picked it up and held it out to her.

"Hello," she said after she'd keyed it on. She listened in silence. "Okay, thanks," she said. "Sure, we'll be up." She ended the call and looked at her assembled friends.

"They caught Joseph," she said.

"What?" Aunt Beth said. "Who was that?"

"It was Detective Morse. She didn't have time to talk, but she wanted us to know Joseph is in custody and it's safe to return to my house. As they expected, he approached the studio a short while after you all left, and they apparently grabbed him without incident."

"What a relief," Mavis said. "Now we can concentrate on getting our quilts done."

"Did he say anything?" Aiden asked.

"If he did, she didn't tell me. She said she'd call back in a couple of hours if we were still going to be up. I told her we would be."

"I'm going back over to the studio, then," Beth said. "Phyl's quilt isn't difficult, but time is getting short. I can get another hour or two in while we wait for Jane to call."

"I'm coming, too," Harriet said.

"No, you're not," chorused Mavis, Beth and Aiden.

"You still have to rest," Aunt Beth said. "You don't need to be moving home in the middle of the night."

"Eight o'clock. That's the middle of the night?"

Aunt Beth picked up her bag and left, ending Harriet's protests.

"I better get going, too." Lauren said, and stood up. "By the way, I didn't get anywhere with Neelie Obote."

"Oh, I almost forgot," Harriet said. "I have a better name for her."

"Oh, great—and you were going to tell me when?"

"Hey, we just found out this afternoon."

"Things like that I need to know right away. That could have saved me hours of searching."

"I'm sorry. Do you want to know her name or not?"

"Fine," Lauren said then listened in relative silence as Mavis and Harriet related the information they'd learned about Nancy Lou Freeman.

"Let me see what I can do with this," she said. "Thanks for dinner."

"How are the dogs doing?" Harriet asked Aiden when they were alone in the living room.

"I think we're finally turning the corner on most of them—physically, anyway. Now we begin the process of trying to figure out who is mentally well enough to be adopted and who will need socialization."

He was describing the process he went through trying to decide if a rescue dog was ready to be adopted when the doorbell sounded. Aiden got up and opened the door, letting Detective Jane Morse in.

"I hope you don't mind my coming by," she said. "I know I said I would call, but I had to come right by here on my way home, so I thought I'd stop."

"Would you care for some tea or coffee?" Mavis asked from the kitchen door.

"Tea sounds good," said Detective Morse. Her medium-length brown hair was swept back from her face and probably had covered her ears at the start of her day. Now, one ear poked out between drooping strands, dark smudges shadowed her eyes and her lipstick had worn off. It was clear she had put in a long, hard day.

Aiden's cell phone rang. He spoke in low tones for a moment then ended the call.

"I'm sorry, but I have to go. That was one of the techs at the clinic. One of my patients chewed her stitches out. I need to go sew her back up."

"Harriet will be going to bed early," Mavis said as she brought a plate of ginger cookies from the kitchen and set them in front of the detective.

Aiden looked at Harriet, and they both smiled.

"I'll pick you up tomorrow around ten," he said.

Mavis raised her eyebrows at Harriet as Aiden turned and left.

"I know you and my aunt think my sprained ankle and bruised kidney rendered me mentally incompetent, and I do appreciate everything you're doing for me, but I made arrangements to go to breakfast with Aiden in the morning."

"No one said you couldn't," Mavis said and returned to the kitchen.

"I don't mean to sound like a broken record," Morse said, "but can you think of any reason why Joseph Marston would be so determined to talk to you?"

"I'm sorry," Harriet said. "I've given it a lot of thought, and I keep coming up empty. I barely know the man. I did go to his house, but I didn't see anything, I didn't hear anything. I'd never been there before the night I was attacked."

"Maybe you saw something and don't realize it," she suggested.

"I can't imagine what it could be."

"Anything could be significant," Morse said, "even if it doesn't seem like it right now."

"What did Joseph say when he was arrested?" Harriet asked.

Jane Morse paused while Mavis brought her a cup of tea on a saucer that held two sugar cubes and a teaspoon as well as the cup.

"Joseph isn't saying anything," she said.

"That says something in itself, doesn't it?" Mavis asked.

"No, I mean he isn't saying *anything*—not asking for a lawyer, not proclaiming his innocence, not asking to use the bathroom. He's being evaluated, but I think he's had some sort of breakdown."

"Is there any chance we have it backwards?" Harriet asked.

"What do you mean?" Morse asked.

"What if *Rodney* is the bad guy here? Maybe he came to collect Neelie, and she didn't want to go, so he killed her. Neelie might have turned to Joseph for help when she realized Rodney had followed her to town. Rodney saw her talking to Joseph and decided he had to eliminate him, too. Maybe he went to Joseph's to kill him, and Joseph somehow got the upper hand and killed Rodney instead. Then he freaked out and ran."

"That's a nice theory, but do you have real evidence to support it?" Morse asked.

"A week ago Friday, we had a shower for our friend DeAnn. Neelie was staying at Aiden's house at that point. She left during the shower, supposedly to buy baby formula. I later learned she was seen during that time having lunch with a guy who matched Joseph's description. I don't know what they were talking about, but it proves they knew each other."

"We also know Rodney was probably Neelie's pimp," Mavis added.

"You ladies have certainly been busy," Detective Morse said. "What else have you learned about the players in this case that you haven't told me?"

Harriet and Mavis gave her a quick rundown of the call from Jasmine and their visit with Neelie's foster mother.

"Even if Neelie and Joseph knew each other, it's still a big leap to him trying to help her escape Rodney Miller and killing him in the process."

"In any case, it should be safe for me to go back to my house, shouldn't it?" Harriet asked.

"I wish I could say an unqualified yes, but until we can interview Marston, I'm afraid we just don't know. I'd feel better if we knew why he was so desperate to talk to you."

"We may never know that, though, right?" Harriet persisted.

"Unfortunately, that is a real possibility, given the state of things. With Neelie Obote and Rodney Miller both dead and Joseph Marston unwilling or unable to speak, we don't have a lot to go on. Of course, we'll question everyone who knew them again and see if we can uncover anything new, but for now we wait to see if Joseph comes back from wherever he's gone."

"Can we do anything to help?" Mavis asked.

"I can't think of anything," Morse said. "We don't know why Marston would have attacked Harriet, but we don't have any evidence that anyone else was involved, and with him in custody, it would seem the immediate threat is over."

"Hopefully, life can return to normal around here," Mavis said. "We have a dog adoption fundraiser to put on."

"I heard about that. Do you have any more of the quilts here?"

"The ones we have are at my studio," Harriet said. "You're welcome to drop by and see them if you want. I should have them all by Monday afternoon. We have to hang them at the community center so the judges can decide which one will be chosen to be the raffle quilt. We'll sell tickets on that one for the next six months or so, but the rest will be auctioned next Saturday at the benefit dinner."

"I'll try to get over there," Morse said. "And thanks for cooperating." She drained the remains of her tea and stood up.

"Here, I'll take your cup." Mavis did so then escorted her to the front door. "So, you were playing nice," she said to Harriet when the detective was gone.

"I'm always nice. Especially when I want to be sure we get the latest information from the police."

"I'll take you to the doctor Monday morning for your follow-up," Mavis said. "Beth wanted to be sure she had the extra time for Phyl's quilt if she needs it."

"You guys make me feel like I'm twelve when you arrange my affairs without asking me." It wasn't the first time Harriet had mentioned this, but her heart wasn't really in the argument this time, since she wouldn't able to drive herself until the cast was off, and she had to admit all the pampering had been sort of pleasant.

"What are we going to do about Iloai?" she asked. "I know Lauren thinks we should let the detectives handle it, but I think we owe it to DeAnn and her family to warn them what's about to happen. And I'm not sure it's an issue for the local police. I'm wondering if we should talk it over with Phyllis before we do anything else, too. I mean, Joseph is her employee, and if he's been involved with stealing children, she could be liable. At the very least, she'd know how to handle it."

"We don't even know for sure Joseph was involved," Mavis pointed out. "The orphanage on the other end might have pulled the switch. We need to talk it over with your aunt in the morning, but I agree we need to tell DeAnn before anything else happens."

"Are we having a Threads meeting on Monday, or are people just dropping off quilts?"

"I think people want to meet. Jenny and Robin both left me messages with reasons we needed to get together as a group, but I think they just want to know what's going on."

"I'd like to see Connie and find out what, if anything, is happening with Kissa."

"I'm curious about that myself—I haven't spoken to her today. Do you feel like watching a show?" Mavis asked, ending their discussion of quilts, The Loose Threads and the recent troubles.

Chapter 38

D o you think any of the Threads would be willing to volunteer to hold dogs?" Aiden asked the next day when he and Harriet were on their way to breakfast.

"What do you mean?"

"It's just a theory at this point, but I think these hoarded dogs would heal faster if we began the process of socialization. I want to try having volunteers come sit with the them, one on one, and pet them and hold them and generally give them attention. None of them are so big they couldn't sit in a lap."

"I'm sure they would. Well, Sarah won't, and Lauren will com plain first, but I think everyone else would be happy to do it. Where will you be doing this?"

"Dr. Johnson said we could set up one of the storerooms with rocking chairs and a television and DVD player."

"Sounds nice, actually."

Aiden drove down to the waterfront in Smuggler's Cove and parked in front of a small storefront restaurant with a view of the dock. They both had eggs cooked in a cup-shaped slice of organic Black Forest ham. Cinnamon toast and sliced fruit completed the meal. Aiden drank coffee while Harriet sipped tea. For once, they met no one they knew and were able to enjoy a relaxing meal.

"Want to play hooky and go for a drive?" Aiden asked. "Dr. Johnson told everyone they couldn't call me unless it was a dire emergency, which didn't include simple re-stitching jobs."

Harriet agreed, and he did take her for a drive—to Port Angeles. They went to a double feature movie then drove to Port Townsend and had sushi at Ichikawa.

"I can see why Ichikawa keeps winning the best Japanese food in Jefferson County award," Harriet said as he paid the bill and they made their way to the front of the downtown eatery. He kept his hand lightly against her back as they strolled down the sidewalk.

"I'm glad they caught Joseph," he said.

"Me, too. I just wish I knew why he attacked me."

"Besides the fact you were trespassing and being a peeping Tom or Tomasina or whatever girl voyeurs are called?"

"Do you think he could get off because of that?"

"I'd be more worried about you getting arrested than him getting off. I haven't heard anyone say yet that they actually have any evidence against Joseph in the murder of either Rodney or Neelie. Given what you've dug up on them, it's quite possible someone connected to them followed them here and murdered them."

"If that's true, we've ruined Joseph's career and maybe his life by helping make him a suspect."

"That's what I was thinking," Aiden said. "Almost makes you hope he's guilty."

"If he isn't guilty, he's acting pretty weird. You saw how stressed he was at the coffee shop and then he no-showed at work and disappeared when I was attacked and Rodney was killed."

"He could just be scared. Wouldn't you be, if everyone in town thought you were a murderer?"

"I don't know what to think," Harriet said with a sigh. "I wish Neelie Obote never came to our town with her pretend baby and claims about her nonexistent dead sister."

"If what you learned from her foster mother is correct, it's her town, too. She was coming home."

"I know I'm not being generous but I don't care if this was home. She should have stayed away."

"With Joseph in jail and my dogs all on the mend, maybe we can leave the drama behind and get on with our mad, passionate love affair."

"Don't even think the word *affair* around my aunt or Mavis," Harriet warned as he stopped and pulled her into his arms for a slow kiss, ending all discussion.

✂ - - ✂ - - - ✂

"Where have you been?" Aunt Beth asked from the porch as Harriet hobbled up the path toward the front door.

"We went to breakfast," Harriet replied with a smile.

"For eight hours?"

"It was a long breakfast."

She made her way into Aunt Beth's living room and sat down on the sofa.

"I'd like to go home," she said.

"Honey, I know you were jerked around by your parents, and I know that left you feeling helpless. I also know that you compensate by being stubborn about your independence. Ordinarily, I'd try real hard to respect that, but tonight, I'm just too pooped to peep.

"As long as you're on crutches, you need help, whether you think so or not. Mavis or I would have to go to your house, and after running the long arm machine all day, I just want to sit in my chair and watch one of my programs and then go to bed. Tomorrow, when you get your walking cast, I'll move you back home."

Harriet held out her hand, and her aunt came to sit beside her on the couch.

"I'm sorry. I'm being selfish. I do appreciate how much work it is for you when I'm out of commission. Not only have you taken good care of me and Fred, but you've had to do all my quilting. Meanwhile, I'm acting like a spoiled brat."

"Oh, honey. You're allowed to be out of sorts when you're hurting."

"I'll just take myself off to bed and you can rest."

Aunt Beth offered and Harriet declined both dinner and a snack. She and Aiden had gotten ice cream cones for the trip home, and she was pretty sure she'd never be hungry again.

"I think I'll go upstairs and read," she said. "I enjoyed my day out, but I am pretty tired, and tomorrow is a big day," she said and wiggled her encased foot.

"See you in the morning," Aunt Beth said with a yawn.

Chapter 39

Don't stress out if it takes longer than an hour at the doctor," Aunt Beth said as she picked up her purse and coat the next morning. "I've got a little more to go on Phyl's quilt, so I'll be at your house when the Threads arrive. I can entertain them until you get done."

"I thought you said Phyl's quilt was going to be simple," Harriet said. She balanced on her good foot as she reached into the coat closet and pulled out her gray hoodie and put it on. She was wearing jeans that had the side seam split open to the knee to accommodate the soon-to-be-removed cast.

"It could have been, but I'm doing a dense stippling pattern in the cream-colored background areas. It looks real nice, but it's taking me a little time."

"Anyone waiting for a taxi?" Mavis asked with a smile as she came through the door without knocking.

"I promise, I'll make this up to you two," Harriet said. "I'll drive you everywhere when you're not allowed to drive anymore."

"Honey, I plan on going to my grave with the keys to my Town Car in my hand," Mavis said and laughed.

"I'll see you ladies at Harriet's," Beth said as they all went outside.

Harriet wasn't sure how it was that you could have the first appointment of the day at the clinic and still be made to wait for twenty minutes before they called you in. She spent another twenty minutes getting the heavy cast removed before she was able to finally move into the doctor's examination room.

The wait turned out to be worth it when Dr. Eisner came in and proclaimed her healing process to be better than average and offered her a lighter, removable air cast if she would promise to continue to mostly use her crutches for another week. She agreed, and after a few probing touches to her still-tender kidney, she was released back into Mavis's care.

"Well, what did he say?" Mavis asked when they were back in the car.

"He said I was healing nicely. He said if I use my crutches most of the time, I can wear this removable air cast."

"We should be only fashionably late to the Threads meeting," Mavis said. "What did he say about your kidney?"

Harriet gave her a full report as they drove back to her house, where they found the driveway full of Loose Threads cars.

"Harriet," Lauren said as she came through the door to the studio, "I was just telling DeAnn you'd found some really interesting information on your computer."

"Lauren," Harriet said in exasperation, "what happened to not running the world and letting the detective deal with things?"

"Oh, so if you meddle it's a virtue, but if I open my mouth I'm a troublemaker?" Lauren grabbed her long blond hair and swept it off her shoulders to her back.

"What are you two talking about?" DeAnn asked.

Harriet glared at Lauren, who merely shrugged and turned to talk to Jenny, who was sitting on her left. She looked for Mavis or her aunt, but neither woman was in the studio. They were probably in the kitchen getting refreshments.

"If you know something, spill it," Robin urged. She was dressed in the fall version of her usual yoga outfit, the seasonal difference being that her black stretchy pants were full-length and she'd added a fitted pastel hoodie to her costume. Her clothing might have been casual, but she was using her best courtroom voice, and Harriet found it very compelling.

"This is more of a show than a tell," Harriet said, and crossed to her computer desk. She turned the machine on and pulled up the website with the picture of the Samoan family. She'd also e-mailed herself a copy of Lauren's cleaned-up version of the picture, and she displayed that, too.

DeAnn was silent. A minute passed, then two. Without saying anything, she pulled out her cell phone and dialed the tollfree number listed on the screen under the picture. She listened, and then said, "English."

Harriet returned to the sitting area, giving DeAnn privacy to deal with what had to be a very painful conversation. Robin joined her.

"That's really tough," Harriet said.

"I'm sure DeAnn's thinking it's nothing compared to what that family has to have been going through, thinking they might have lost their daughter forever."

"So, what's the next step?"

"I'm going to recommend to DeAnn they have a DNA test done, just to be certain, but I imagine they could learn all they need to know by showing the picture to the little girl."

"Should we call Phyllis?"

"She'll have to be told, so she can figure out where the break-down in her system occurred. It could be Joseph, or it could be they were dealing with a corrupt person on the other end who produced good quality forgeries for the required documents," Robin explained. "I don't think she needs to be involved right now. This…" She pointed to DeAnn. "…will be between two families and be about doing what's right. The blame game can come after that."

"I need to go home," DeAnn said when she'd finished her phone call. "The quilt is in my bag. Can you deal with it?" she asked Robin.

Robin assured her her family should take precedence and of-fered to drive her home, but DeAnn insisted she was okay to drive.

"It's really for the best, don't you think?" Lauren said when DeAnn was gone.

"Actually, yes," Harriet snapped. "I do. My problem is with you. We agreed to one thing, and then you did the exact opposite.

If we're going to work together on projects, it isn't going to work for me if you always do the opposite of what we agree on."

"That's a two-way street, you know," Lauren fired back.

"Shall we look at the quilts, ladies?" Connie stood, speaking in her best schoolteacher tone, silencing them both.

A knock sounded on the door, and Carla came in with Wendy balanced on one hip and a canvas quilting bag on the opposite shoulder.

"I hope it's okay that I brought Wendy with me," she said. "We're going to Toddler Time at the library when we're done."

Connie took the little girl from her.

"Wendy's always welcome," she said and tickled the child's tummy, causing her to shriek in delight.

Carla sat on one of the folding chairs Aunt Beth had set up in a circle around Harriet's gray easy chair.

"I'll start," Jenny said, and unfolded the dog-bone appliqué wall hanging. She turned it around so the chocolate-brown back showed, revealing the label and sleeve, both sewn into their proper place with almost invisible stitches.

"That came out really nice," Harriet said. "The dog faces capture the essence of small dogs everywhere."

"I love the way the flower stems intertwine with the bones to form the wreaths," Robin said.

"Kind of makes you feel sorry for the Small Stitches and the bone blocks they're copying," Lauren said.

"Why is that?" Sarah asked. "If they do a decent job of copying my design, they should be great blocks."

"I'm sure they won't copy them with anywhere near the skill you made the original with," Lauren said with a wicked smile. "It's really too bad we couldn't use them, but after they copied them it was out of the question."

Harriet whacked her on the arm.

"Behave yourself," she muttered, but she couldn't stop herself from smiling.

The group revealed the rest of the quilts one by one, oohing and ahhing over the finishing work and the overall result. Mavis's and Beth's snowball quilt had come out beautifully, and Harriet's tumbling block design with its three-dimensional effect was striking. The star block quilt had perfect points and charming fussy-cut dog images. Connie and Lauren's doghouse quilt was raised from nice to exceptional thanks to their skilled choices of color. They declared themselves as done as they were going to get, and Aunt Beth retreated to the kitchen to fetch a plate of brownies Jenny had brought.

"Have you had any news about Kissa?" Robin asked Connie.

"Absolutely nothing," Connie replied. "I've taken her for her well baby exams, and other than being a little underweight for her age, she's healthy. She's meeting all her developmental milestones, too."

"Do they have any idea where she came from?" Lauren asked.

"She seems to be African, but that's guesswork on our part. So far, no missing person reports match her. They did a simple blood-type matching between her and Neelie Obote and Rodney Miller and she doesn't match either of them, but that only rules them out as potential parents as a couple. One of them could still be her parent if you assume she got her blood type from the unknown parent."

"So, what will happen to her?" Jenny asked.

"Officially, she's in foster care. If they find no one to claim her, I imagine she'll become a ward of the state and eventually be eligible for adoption—hopefully by someone younger than Rodrigo and me."

"Has anyone heard any more about who killed Rodney Miller or Neelie Obote?" Carla asked.

"All I know is they have Joseph Marston in custody and he's not speaking," Harriet said. "Aiden was pointing out that, given the fact we now think Rodney was Neelie's pimp, there's a good chance someone followed them here and all of it had nothing to do with Foggy Point or anyone who lives here."

"Rodney was a pimp?" Sarah said, the excitement clear in her voice.

"Coffee or tea, anyone," Aunt Beth asked, before she could get started.

The Threads ate brownies, sipped coffee or tea and congratulated themselves on a job well done. They were divided whether they thought Harriet's tumbling block design, Jenny's dog-bone wreaths or the doghouse quilt would be chosen for the raffle quilt. They agreed that while Beth's and Connie's quilt was quite lovely, the fact they had used dog*wood* fabric instead of actual dog fabric would go against it in the judging.

"Can everyone come help hang the quilts this morning?" Aunt Beth asked. "The judging is supposed to start at two."

Sarah assured everyone the senior center would grind to a halt if she didn't rush back and put things right. This, of course, was not unexpected, as this was the excuse she always used when there was work to be done. Carla had to take Wendy to story time, and the group assured her Wendy's library time was more important than hanging quilts. She apologized profusely then left, baby once more on her hip.

The phone rang, and Aunt Beth answered, speaking in low tones to her caller. When she'd finished, she turned to Harriet.

"That was Phyl. I told her I'd finished her quilt, and I hope I didn't speak out of turn, but I said that if she'd bring her binding over and machine stitch it to her quilt, you wouldn't mind doing the hand-stitching part, since you have to sit in your chair with your foot up while we go hang quilts."

"That's fine with me," Harriet said, "At least then I'll feel like I'm contributing something, even if it is for the other team."

"Now, honey," Mavis said. "You know all the quilts go for the same good cause. It doesn't matter who makes the raffle quilt as long as it brings in a lot of money for the shelter."

"Yeah, and if you believe that, I've got a bridge I'd like to sell you," Lauren said.

"You ladies can go on ahead to the community center whenever you're ready," Aunt Beth said. "I'm going to wait for Phyl to get here, in case she needs help setting up to sew her binding on."

Everyone knew Phyl could thread any sewing machine with her eyes closed and one hand tied behind her back. They also knew Beth wasn't ready to leave Harriet alone, even if Joseph *was* in custody.

"We'll see you over there," Jenny said as she buttoned her cardigan and picked up her quilt bag and purse. The rest of the group followed, in twos and threes, until only Aunt Beth and Harriet remained.

"You know, you can't make guarding me your life's work," Harriet said.

"I don't plan on it. But it doesn't hurt to be careful." Aunt Beth put on her purple hip-length jacket and picked up her bags but didn't make a move toward the door.

"We both know Phyllis doesn't need help getting set up to sew the binding on her quilt. You already threaded the machine and turned it on. What?" Harriet said when her aunt still didn't leave.

"I might as well tell you—Jorge will be bringing you lunch in an hour or so." She gave Harriet a half-smile and scooted out the door before her niece could react.

Phyllis Johnson came in through the studio door moments later.

"I hope you don't mind my not knocking," she said. "I didn't want you to have to get up."

"No problem," Harriet said. "No one seems to knock these days."

"How's your ankle doing?" Phyllis patted a stray curl back into the cotton candy fluff that was her hair.

"It's better. Have you had any word about Joseph?"

"No, but then, there's no reason I would. I know I'm his employer, and he *is* like a son to me, but in the eyes of the law, I have no claim on him.

"I called the police station, of course, but they were tightlipped. I used to have friends on the force," she said with a sigh. "Everyone's retired now, and these young folks are so serious. They don't seem to understand how things work in a small town."

"I have a question for you," Harriet said. "Do you know a woman named Mary Ann Martin?"

Phyllis bit her lower lip.

"I don't believe I do. Should I?"

Aunt Beth had left two sewing machines in the studio when she gave it to Harriet. They were sturdy workhorse models, strong enough to stitch through the multiple layers of fabric and batting one had to deal with when they were sewing a binding on a quilt. In addition, Harriet had brought her own embroidery sewing machine as well as her smaller travel unit when she'd moved in. Phyl sat down at the studio machine Aunt Beth had set up for her and began sewing on her binding.

"Mary Ann and her husband are foster parents in Foggy Point. I thought they might have taken one of your classes."

"Honey, in thirty years, a lot of people have taken my classes."

"Did you do an adoption for an African girl named Nancy Lou Freeman?"

Phyllis deftly turned the corner on her quilt binding.

"Not that I recall. Why?"

"I just found out Nancy Lou was Neelie Obote's name when she was adopted in Foggy Point. This would have been, maybe, twenty years ago."

"Neelie Obote? The girl that was killed at Aiden's? Are you thinking I knew who that woman was and didn't tell the police?" She shifted the bulk of the quilt as she completed the second corner.

"No, I just thought it was a little strange that Neelie had been adopted here and then was involved in adoption abuse and put back into foster care but that you hadn't at least heard about it."

"I keep trying to tell you—I've processed hundreds of adoptions over the years, I'd like to think I could remember them all, but the fact is, without a file in front of me, I simply can't."

Phyllis turned the third corner on the quilt binding.

"I suppose my aunt told you about DeAnn's little girl."

"Everyone has told me about the problems they're having, and I keep trying to tell all of you that Joseph handled that match. We do our best to match children with adoptive families, but sometimes, in spite of all our hard work, the relationship is incompatible."

Harriet was silent for a minute, thinking. Phyllis rounded the fourth corner of her quilt and approached the point where she'd started. She clipped the thread then cut the excess binding fabric, leaving two tails Harriet would stitch together by hand, closing the gap between the start and finish.

"Did you hear the latest?" she asked carefully, watching Phyllis for her reaction. "It appears DeAnn's child isn't from Africa at all. She's from American Samoa. Or at least, that's the language she speaks."

"I told you, I don't know what Joseph was or wasn't doing on his cases." Phyllis stood up. "I have a spool of thread that matches the binding here somewhere," she said, and dug in her bag.

Harriet kept watching her.

"Phyllis, I have to tell you, I'm having a little trouble believing you didn't know what Joseph was doing. I mean, we saw you grabbing files and stepping in for your other employee when she was covering for Joseph. I've tried real hard to figure out how, in an office with four employees, Joseph could have run an elaborate adoption scam without raising any red flags with you or Jennifer or your secretary. I mean, he had to have been arranging passports, and airfare, and I don't know what else, and they would all be for places that didn't match the country the child was supposed to have come from."

"Are you accusing me of something?" Phyllis stepped closer to Harriet's chair in a sudden move.

"I'm not accusing anyone of anything," Harriet said, her eyes on Phyllis's hands, which were concealed under the quilt, which was draped over her arm. "I'm just trying to figure out what's going on.

"I mean, on one hand, two people are dead. One of those two was adopted in Foggy Point. On the other hand, we have a child who is not from Africa like she was supposed to be, and in fact seems to have a family in American Samoa who are trying real hard to find her. Can you see the connection here?"

"I don't know what you're talking about." Color was creeping up Phyl's neck and into her face.

"I'm thinking both of these situations are connected by adoption—international adoption, at that. And we both know there is only one adoption agency doing international work in Foggy Point—Little Lamb."

Phyllis sighed and sank onto the ottoman. Her hands were still out of view.

"You aren't going to let this go, are you?"

"No, I'm not," Harriet said defiantly. "Not until I find out who killed Neelie and who took Iloai from her family. Since DeAnn has already contacted the people looking for her, that should become clear any time now."

Phyl's shoulders slumped. "Your aunt always did brag about how smart you were. Too smart for your own good, I'm thinking."

She pulled her hands out from under her quilt. One was holding a slender syringe Harriet recognized as the kind used for insulin. She flipped her quilt across Harriet's legs, pinning them to the ottoman.

The older woman was surprisingly strong. Harriet squirmed as Phyllis bore down toward her with the needle. She wished she hadn't taken her air cast off when she'd sat down.

"If you're going to kill me anyway, can you at least satisfy my curiosity?" she pleaded.

Phyllis glanced at her watch, and Harriet hoped the older woman hadn't seen the same crime shows she had, where they told you that in a hostage situation the best course of action was to keep your attacker talking.

"I suppose your aunt isn't coming back until the judging is over," Phyllis said, obviously gauging the time. "Okay, it's simple, really. Nancy Lou was one of my adoptions. There are women in Africa and other places who have jobs that put them at high risk of pregnancy and for whom an unwanted baby would be an...inconvenience. We in American have an endless supply of parents looking for infants to adopt."

"So, prostitutes are cranking out babies and selling them?" Harriet asked, her outrage causing her to temporarily forget the syringe poised over her leg.

"I wouldn't put it so crudely, but yes, that is, in fact, the situation. I didn't realize this when I first got into the international adoption business. The people on the other end handle that. I just pay a fee, which I pass on to the adoptive parents. By the time I realized what was going on, I was in too deep to stop."

"So, why steal a baby in American Samoa?"

"Two reasons, really. First, a lot of the prostitutes in Africa have HIV, which means they don't have healthy babies. Second, the authorities are always shutting my overseas contact down in one place or another, and he's forced to move on to another part of the world. Unfortunately, he became a little aggressive in his methods for procuring children in the South Pacific."

"That's one way to put it. It seems like he was stealing children from their rightful parents."

"Parents who were willing to send their child away to school at an improbable age, don't forget. And do you really believe DeAnn's child was better off with subsistence farmers or fishermen or whatever it was her birth parents did? She'll have a much nicer life here in Foggy Point."

"Like Nancy Lou did?"

"That was unfortunate. I didn't know those people were adopting a child just to be a domestic. And, well, when I discovered the problem, I couldn't risk an investigation for fear my situation would be uncovered. Surely you can understand that."

"So, you knew Neelie was being sold into slavery and could have saved her from it?"

"I didn't know before I sent her, but yes, I did figure it out when I made a home visit. It's unfortunate, but she really was a troubled child to start with."

"Did she recognize you? Is that why you killed her?" Harriet tried to worm herself into a more upright position.

"She saw me at the shower, and then came to see me. As you might expect with someone of her class, she wanted money, an impossibly high sum. What could I do? She said if I didn't give her two hundred thousand dollars, she would go to the authorities. I had no choice."

"So you injected her with an overdose of insulin?"

"That's pretty obvious," Phyllis said and held the syringe a little higher. "I didn't know she'd told all to her pimp. That horrible man." She shivered at the memory. "He came to me with the same demand. I had him meet me at Joseph's—I couldn't have him come to the office, after all, and Joseph's house had the perfect ambush spot.

"He's converted one of the basement rooms into a home gym. I have a key from when I watered his plants when he went to visit his mother, and there's a below-grade basement entry at the back of the house that goes into that room.

"Joseph does seem like the sort who would do something like this. He's always skulking about looking guilty. I've never known what about, though.

"Anyway," she said, returning to her narration, "I had that creature Rodney meet me there. I hid behind the first door, and when he started down to the interior door I whacked him with a weight from Joseph's gym. I know what you're thinking—how can an old fat lady like me hope to overpower a young man. I haven't always been this size. I used to play women's professional softball. It's how I hurt my hip." She patted her ample midriff. "More of this is muscle than you probably think, and you know it doesn't really take a heavyweight to knock someone out if you hit them just so."

"And then *he* got an insulin overdose?"

"Well, yes," Phyllis said. "One has to be sure they've done the job. And you know, they never look for insulin. It's real hard to detect. I put it in that big vein in his arm. I made a couple of extra holes so it would look more like he was a drug user. Fortunately, you've had so many injections from the hospital, one more will go unnoticed."

Harriet rubbed her thigh on the leg that had the sprained ankle as if she had a sudden cramp.

"Don't worry, honey, in a few minutes you won't feel that cramp or anything else."

Harriet knew she had to time her move perfectly. She was frantically looking for a distraction when Fred started scratching on the kitchen side of the connecting door. Phyllis looked briefly toward the door, and Harriet made her move. She grabbed the edge of the folded quilt and unfurled it, throwing it over Phyllis's head.

Phyllis made muffled sounds as Harriet sprang up from her chair and onto the quilt-wrapped woman, knocking her over.

"What's going on?" Jorge yelled as he rushed inside, throwing his bags of food to the floor and coming over to the women tangled in the quilt on the floor.

"She's trying to kill me," Harriet yelled. "She's got a syringe."

Jorge grabbed the edge of the quilt and pulled it back, revealing Phyllis's angry face. Without hesitation and with a swing worthy of an Olympic boxer, he landed a punch square in her face, knocking her out and breaking her nose in the process. He flipped the quilt further back and kicked the syringe out of the unconscious woman's hand, crushing it under his boot.

"Are you okay?" he asked Harriet.

"I am now."

Chapter 40

Harriet was sitting between Lauren and Mavis in a wooden rocking chair in the back room of the vet clinic when Aiden entered, a small dog cradled in each arm. He set a tan Chihuahua-dachshund mix in Lauren's lap then handed a curly-haired black-and-white poodle-terrier mix to Mavis.

"Be right back with Harry," he said and disappeared the way he'd come.

He returned moments later with a mostly bald dog of unknown heritage. He carefully placed the injured dog onto the special fiber blanket draped across Harriet's lap. Harry had lost much of his skin as a result of being in the bottom cage at the dog hoarder's, deluged with waste from the cages above. He'd received skin grafts, some from a pig and some synthetic, which were beginning to peel as his own skin began to grow and heal. The result made him look like some sort of extraterrestrial creature.

The Loose Threads were into their second week of dog socializing, and so far the project was going well. Mavis's lap was draped with a lap-sized dog-bone quilt that, along with several other similar ones, had not sold at the benefit auction.

Lauren lifted the corner of the quilt.

"I can't believe the Small Stitches fell for the decoy quilt pattern," she said.

259

"Well, it serves them right," Mavis said. "What's really silly is that they're good quilters. They don't need to be copying other people's work."

"Why do they do it, then?" Harriet asked between licks as Harry attempted to wash her face.

"Lack of confidence, I guess," Mavis replied.

Robin came through the door, followed by Aiden and a coal-black dog with a white cast on its front leg.

"Sorry I'm late," she said. "I had to file some papers with the court." She took off her pink-hooded yoga jacket and slipped a green apron over her head, tying the strings behind her. "Okay," she said, and Aiden gently set the black dog in her lap.

"I really appreciate the work you ladies are doing here," he said to the group. "The dogs are adjusting better than we hoped. I'm feeling a lot better about their adoption possibilities."

"I have a feeling you're going to have a jump-start on the adoptions," Harriet said and looked over at Lauren, who was talking baby talk to her dog, Carter.

"Speaking of jump-starting adoptions, I don't think DeAnn would mind me telling you all that Iloai is now back with her parents and seems to be settling back in without lingering effects," Robin said.

"That's real nice," Mavis said.

Connie came into the crowded storeroom, whisking off her peach-colored nylon jacket and slipping into her apron. Aiden immediately appeared with yet another small dog, this one another Chihuahua mix of some sort. She petted the little dog, who nestled into her lap while Aiden retreated back into the clinic.

"Did you tell them the news?" she asked Robin.

"I was just getting to that." She turned to the rest of the group. "Connie here suggested that, since the authorities have had no luck so far in finding any record of Kissa's birth, family or anything else, and since DeAnn and her husband have already been qualified as adoptive parents once, perhaps they could be fast-tracked to become foster parents, and then eventually, when the waiting period is over, they could adopt Kissa."

"That's just wonderful," Mavis said.

"It just seemed natural," Connie said. "Rodrigo and I have been having a lot of fun with Kissa, but we're too old to have such a bundle of energy on a fulltime basis. We'll be happy to just be grandparents again. And who knows—maybe we'll adopt *this* little girl to fill our empty nest." She patted the head of her little charge, and the dog wagged her skinny tail.

"Did everyone hear how much Harriet's quilt brought in at the auction?" Aiden asked when he came back a few minutes later to check on them.

"They were there," Harriet said with an embarrassed smile. "Besides, Jenny is the one who should get the credit for maintaining the reputation of our quilt group, since her design was chosen to be the raffle quilt, and who knows how much it will eventually bring in money-wise."

"They were all a group effort," Jenny said modestly. The little dog in her lap barked his agreement, which then set off a chain of yips and yaps, requiring the Threads to concentrate on their task.

✂- - - ✂- - - ✂

Aiden came back into the storeroom-turned-dog socializing area when he'd put the last of his charges back in its kennel and the last Loose Thread had left the clinic. He gently pulled Harriet, who had waited for him, into an embrace. He looked down at her ankle, which was once again in a heavy cast.

"Are things ever going to be back to normal?" he asked.

"You mean normal like when I used to live alone? Before my aunt and Mavis decided I couldn't fend for myself?"

"I do understand their urge to protect you," he said and kissed her. "You do have a way of finding trouble."

"Lots of people who live alone sprain their ankles."

"Not a lot of them have a three hundred-pound woman fall on their sprained ankle while she's trying to kill them, though."

"Whose side are you on?"

"You're right. I feel like a teenager again with those two hanging around, forced to try to sneak a kiss when they turn their backs. And we both know if we went to my house, they'd just follow us. And what's up with Jorge delivering take-out to your house?"

"We just need to let things settle down a little. When more time has passed, things will go back to normal."

"Is that a promise or a threat?"

Harriet balanced her weight on her good foot and pulled him into a serious embrace, running her hands up his back as she kissed him, ending all possibility of further discussion.

END

ACKNOWLEDGMENTS

I'd like to express thanks to the many family members and friends who support the various aspects of the writing and promoting of my mystery novels. First, the family—Jack, Donna, Karen and Malakai, Annie, Alex and Amelia; David, Ken, Nikki, Kellen and Lucas, and Bob and Brenda—thank-you, all. Also thanks to nephews Brett, Nathan, Jason and Chad, who always marvel about my books when I see them.

Special recognition goes to my sister-in-law and brother-in-law, Beth and Hank, who not only support the idea of my writing, but also let me stay at their house when I'm promoting in their state, drive me around, and tell me the cool medical stuff that helps me kill people more accurately on paper. Beth, along with her friends Sally and Kay, also gets special acknowledgement for helping make the dogwood quilt for this book.

Thanks again to my talented knitting students who put up with my promotion schedule when it takes me away from class. They also graciously read my stories even though I haven't put any knitting in...yet.

Thank you, Vern and Betty Swearingen at StoryQuilts. Your continuing help in marketing my books is invaluable. Thanks also to Geri at the Pine Needle in Lake Oswego for including me in her in-store events and shows, and also to Ruth for sharing booth space with me at many events in Oregon and Washington—it's always fun.

As always, my gratitude goes to Susan and Susan for all the conversation, adventure and coffee/hot chocolate breaks.

Without the pressure of weekly critique sessions with Katy, I'd never keep up my writing pace, so thanks, Katy. I'd also like to acknowledge Sisters In Crime, both the national organization and Portland's Harriet Vane Chapter. National provides lots of good information about writing and the marketing of same. Our local chapter provides knowledgeable and interesting forensic folks on a monthly basis to educate and inspire us all.

Most importantly, thanks to Liz and Zumaya Publications for making all this possible.

ABOUT THE AUTHOR

Attempted murder, theft, drug rings, battered women, death threats and more sordid affairs than she could count were the more exciting experiences from ARLENE SACHITANO'S nearly thirty years in the high-tech industry.

Prior to writing her first novel, *Chip and Die*, Arlene wrote the story half of the popular Block of the Month quilting patterns "Seams Like Murder," "Seams Like Halloween" and "Nothing's What it Seams" for Storyquilts.com, Inc. *Quilt by Association* is the fourth book in the bestselling Harriet Truman/ Loose Threads quilting mystery series. Arlene also has written a sequel to *Chip and Die* in the Harley Spring mystery series, *The Widowmaker*, and a scintillating proprietary tome on electronics assembly.

ABOUT THE ARTIST

APRIL MARTINEZ was born in the Philippines and raised in San Diego, California, daughter to a US Navy chef and a US postal worker, sibling to one younger sister. From as far back as she can remember, she has always doodled and loved art.

For years, she went from job to job, dissatisfied that she couldn't make use of her creative tendencies, until she started working as an imaging specialist for a big book and magazine publishing house and began learning the trade of graphic design.

April Martinez now lives with her cat in Orange County, California, as a full-time freelance artist/illustrator and graphic designer.